BOOK 1 OF THE EARTHBORN

EARTHBORN

ADAIR HART

Editing done by Laura Petrella
Cover done by Tom Edwards
Interior design done by Colleen Sheehan
Proofread done by Alexa
Published by Quantum Edge Publishing

ISBN: 978-0-9967172-6-7
www.AdairHart.com

To get updates on new books and other notifications, sign up for my mailing list at:
www.AdairHart.com/MailingList.aspx

EARTHBORN

CHAPTER

ONE

Blake Brown salivated at the smell of blood in the small elevator. He ran his tongue over his fangs while looking to his right at trembling, dark-skinned Seth Williams, Blake's partner in crime. The gashes on Seth's face were ringed with blood and the bruising on his body was highlighted by dark-purple patches. He had taken a punishing beatdown by the Trag mercenaries hot on their trail. If Blake had not come when he had, Seth might not be there. Three of the Trag mercs had met their end at Blake's hand, and seven were on their tail. He clenched his jaw as he pulled out a cloth and handed it to Seth.

Seth licked his lips as he gingerly wiped his face.

Blake studied the elevator controls as the Trag race crossed his mind. Seven-foot-tall beige-skinned humanoids with bumpy skin, floppy ears, and heavy ridges on their heads. Physically tough, but not too bright. They were the bottom-feeders in the world of mercs. He had been looking forward to lunch, given that it was about 1:00 p.m. Earth time, but they were on Telagra, home world of the Almogran and a planet roughly thirty light-years from Earth and ten from Fredoria, his adopted home consisting of abduction refugees from Earth. Maybe he would drink a Trag dry, especially given that they considered vampires an abomination.

The elevator approached the top floor.

"We're almost there," said Blake.

Seth coughed. "Then what? There's at least seven of those fuckers."

"Leave that to me," said Blake. "When we get there, find a spot away from the doors." He handed his version forty Fredorian automatic light pistol to Seth. "Take my FLP-40. Anyone comes close, spray 'em."

Seth sighed as he took the pistol. "And . . . you're going to take all of them on?"

Blake glanced at Seth.

"I know, I know, you're Blake Brown," said Seth, shaking his head.

Blake laughed. "Never forget that. At least we finished the contract, so we'll get paid. Just need to clean up these loose ends."

"Yeah, loose ends that kicked the shit out of me," said Seth, holding his side.

The elevator came to a halt and the doors opened.

Blake scanned the surrounding hallway of offices. He pointed at a large door down the hall. "Duck in there. Don't come out until the screaming stops."

Seth's eyes widened. "You sure about this? They're gonna come out with weapons blazing."

"Oh, I know. I have a few . . . advantages that they might not be aware of."

Seth shook his head and hobbled off.

Blake watched as Seth reached the door and shot the handle off to enter. Blake cursed at himself for allowing Seth to be captured. The contract was a simple placement of a locater beacon. Blake hated placement contracts because of the low pay, but given the repair costs they kept incurring, it was all they could do without a crew or larger ship. All Seth had to do was be the lookout. The situation turned sour when he was apprehended.

Blake's blood boiled at the memory of seeing Seth on the ground, getting stomped. Several dead mercs later, Blake had retrieved Seth and entered an elevator. Now the remaining ones were after them, and they were about to come storming out. Blake pulled out a small square grappling device from his belt. It was attached by a cord that wound around his waist. Looking up, he aimed at a corner and then squeezed the device.

A cord shot out and attached to the ceiling.

With a quick tug, Blake verified it would hold him. He secured the device to the back of his belt and then squeezed the device again to reel him up. A nearby vent would obscure his thermal signature when he activated his camouflage shielding. Once positioned, he pulled a smoke grenade from his belt and then tossed it in front of the door the mercs were going to come through. As the smoke filled the area, he pulled out his version thirty-four Fredorian assault rifle, known as the FAR-34 striker. After tapping his belt to engage his camouflage shielding, he took aim and waited.

The elevator doors opened.

"Shit, smoke grenade," said one of the Trag mercs in a deep, gravelly voice.

"Thermal vision," said another Trag.

After a moment, the Trags in padded brown armor, green undersuits, and advanced-looking helmets began to file out of the elevator. They looked around and then advanced.

Blake waited until they were all fanned out. He calculated the firing arc he would need to hit them all. As his eyes swept across the Trag mercs, he paused on one of them. It was the leader of the group, one whom he had encountered in the past. He readjusted his firing arc to avoid the leader.

"Can't see anything," said one of them.

Blake opened fire, downing six. He tapped the grappling device, releasing him from the ceiling. The cord reeled back in. He rushed up to the leader and knocked him down with the butt of his striker. "I wouldn't get up if I were you."

"Blake Brown!"

"That's my name," said Blake as he slipped his striker onto his back. He pulled out one of the short energy blades on his back and pointed it at the merc. "Dosst, is it? I remember you. Get up, and move slowly down the hallway. Keep your hands out to the sides where I can see them."

Dosst complied.

When they were out of range of the smoke grenade, Blake poked Dosst in the back. "Back against the wall."

Dosst paused and then obeyed.

"Seth!" said Blake as he placed his blade against Dosst's neck. "Come on out and check what I found."

Seth limped out of the room he had been in and stood next to Blake. He narrowed his eyes at Dosst.

"This is the fucking guy who said he looked forward to our deaths at his hands after I whacked his bud Gaaulst's crew," said Blake.

"I remember him from Killikin. He wasn't very successful at claiming our deaths," said Seth.

"No . . . he was not," said Blake. He tilted his head at Dosst. "Your race values honor, and dying in battle. Your boys back there just got taken out. They died in battle, but I'm not sure I'd call it an honorable death."

Dosst grunted. "They hunted worthy prey."

"Oh . . . well . . . flattery will get you everywhere with me," said Blake with a smile, baring his fangs.

"Blake . . . ," said Seth.

"Right. Back on topic. Seth, cover him."

Seth aimed his FLP-40 at Dosst.

Blake wagged a finger as he took a step back and eyed Dosst. "I bet you're asking yourself right now . . . Is Blake Brown going to drink me dry?"

Dosst furrowed his eyebrows.

"C'mon, Blake," said Seth.

Blake laughed. "All right, all right. I wouldn't drink Trag blood anyways, unless I needed to. It tastes like toilet water." He ran his pale hand across the shaved side of his head, then across the short, upright jet-black hair on top. "Here's how this is going to go down. I'm going to let you live. You don't die, and you'll live with this disgrace."

Dosst clenched his jaw. "Kill me now then . . . if you're really the Blake Brown that everyone speaks of."

"I don't think you want to die. Otherwise you wouldn't just be standing there. No, I want you to live. There are Trags who're just waiting to hear *all* about how you took me down. Won't they be disappointed," said Blake. He shook his head. "When they ask you what happened, you tell them Blake Brown made you his bitch." With a quick motion, he pulled out a stun device that fit in his hand. A moment later, Dosst crumpled to the floor.

"Always gotta play," said Seth.

"Of course. I'm Blake Brown."

Seth shook his head. "What now?"

Blake put his left forearm in front of him and pressed a button on it. A small screen with various options popped out perpendicular to his forearm. "We let law enforcement clean . . . I mean, handle, this from here." He ran his right finger through the options, stopping to press on the one that would call law enforcement in an emergency. After the screen notified him that law enforcement was on its way, he tapped at a button that caused the screen to slip back into his forearm device. He did a quick check on his black light-armor suit, then glanced at Seth. "We need to get you a better suit, or maybe some decent power armor."

Seth sighed. "Maybe if I could stop getting my ass kicked on these contracts, that would be a good start."

Blake eyed Seth for a moment and then nodded. "Let's get out of here."

///////////

An hour later, as they neared the spaceport where their ship was docked, Seth gestured at Blake. "I know I've asked this before . . . but you *still* wouldn't go back to Earth if given a chance? Get away from all this mess?"

Blake shook his head. "What's done is done. I was exiled for bullshit reasons, and you were in the wrong place at the wrong time. Waking up on that Seceltor slaver ship and drinking the crew dry was the beginning of my third life."

"Well . . . you left the pilot alive. That at least got us to Fredoria," said Seth.

"I know Fredoria gets a bad rap for how they treat Earthborn, but they're human, just like us, well, more you than me. The only difference is time. Sure, some native-born Fredorians don't like us, but I don't think that's universal. They were slaves at one point before being freed and sent to Fredoria," said Blake. "Well, to be fair, though, Fredorians hate me since I'm a vampire, but that's how it was on Earth too."

Seth narrowed his eyes. "I still think it's ridiculous that the Kreagans won't let anyone who leaves Earth to go back."

"The Kreagans own this galactic region and can do what-ever the hell they want. Like any group that holds power, they make the rules, bullshit or not."

Seth sighed. "I know. It's just . . . sometimes I miss Earth is all. The culture, music, people, and even the language. I really miss being able to talk to people without requiring a damn translation device in my ear. It's uncomfortable."

Blake laughed. "I hear you on that." He also found it comical since the translation device sometimes made communication funnier than he expected. "It hasn't been that bad since we came to Fredoria. You got twenty years as a cargo pilot, and now two years as a freelancer under your belt. I got twenty years as an intelligence agent in the Fredorian Rangers, and the same two years of freelancing as you. That's worth something, right?"

"I guess," said Seth. "I did like visiting new spaceports and seeing new cultures."

"And playing around with G1s," said Blake with a grin. He recalled the various generation-one android women that Seth had been with. Their sex drive was insatiable, even by Blake's standards.

"Yeah . . . that too."

Blake paused to sniff the air when they reached the space-port. Either something was being cooked, or his sense of smell had gone awry. He extended his arm out for a moment, causing Seth to pause. Blake picked up the odor of burned metal. It took him a moment to focus on the direction, and when he did, he gestured forward. "Something got lit up."

Seth's eyes searched the ground for a moment. He tilted his head at Blake. "You don't think . . ."

"Let's not jump to conclusions," said Blake, tapping Seth on the chest with the back of his hand. "C'mon."

They hustled across the open landing pads toward a group of Almogran gathered near a ship. They were putting out various fires and cordoning off the area.

"You gotta be shitting me," said Seth.

A pit formed in Blake's stomach. As he got close enough to see more detail, he surveyed the scene. Parts of their ship lay everywhere, and the parts of it that hit the other ships had set them ablaze. The Almogran were busy trying to contain it, with their two muscled legs under their meatball-like bodies. Their small arms always cracked him up, but this was not an occasion to do so. He sighed. "Well . . . damn."

Seth put his head in his hands when they reached the perimeter of the cordoned-off area. "Tell me this isn't happening."

Blake laid a hand on Seth's shoulder. "Look . . . we can regroup and—"

"Fuck that!" said Seth through gritted teeth while shaking off Blake's hand.

Blake drew his lips flat.

"I'm so tired of this. Every step we take forward, we take two back. Every. Time. Nothing ever goes our way," said Seth as he tossed a hand out in the air and shook his head.

Blake observed Seth as he contemplated how he got to this point. He understood Seth's anger. After retiring from their jobs and spending two years freelancing, they did not have much to show for it. Contract after contract had one issue or another, but this was the first one where their ship could not be repaired. Given that Seth considered it his baby, Blake knew this was probably the last contract Seth would do. He waved over one of the gray-suited Almograns.

The Almogran strode over and blinked its large central eye at them.

Blake gestured at the carnage. "That was our ship."

"Which one?" said the Almogran.

"The one lighting all the other ships on fire."

"Oh . . . I'm sorry to hear that. Perhaps you should have landed in a more secure area."

Blake snorted. "All for the low, low price of five thousand credits, right? How about you secure the whole spaceport?"

The Almogran's eye narrowed. "You willing to help fund that?"

Blake sighed. "Do you at least have any visual feeds? Or anything that could help us find who did this?"

The Almogran extended his tiny arm and tapped at a device on his wrist. After a moment, a projection shot up showing a pack of Trags shooting something at the ship, causing it to explode. The Trags then took off.

"At least we don't have to worry about them anymore," said Blake.

"You know of their location?" asked the Almogran.

"Yeah, and your law enforcement is already on its way there. One of those slimy Trags should be alive still."

The Almogran's eyes widened.

Blake nodded. "Yeah. That happened."

The Almogran backed up a bit, then hustled back to the other Almograns.

"C'mon. Not much we can do here," said Blake.

"And go where exactly? We can't even buy a small shuttle," said Seth.

"No . . . but we can buy a few shots of whiskey and maybe lay up for a week until we decide our next step. I know . . . that this is probably it for you. I respect that. Let's figure out how to get you where you need to go. We can at least celebrate two years of freelancing."

Seth sighed. "I guess. If we had more crew and a bigger ship with better security measures, maybe we could make it work. I just don't see any path where this ends well."

Blake rubbed his chin. "No argument from me."

"I'm not mad at you, it's just . . . well . . . screw it. Let's just get those shots."

Blake nodded.

They left the space port area and headed to a nearby bar.

Blake noted the various aliens on their way there. Fredorians had a reputation for being violent and unpredictable. Killing nine Trags would just add to that when word got out. Ever since humanity had established itself among the stars, albeit as a refugee planet for the abducted, the urge to survive and fight led to some bad interactions with other aliens. He glanced at Seth. His unusual silence probably meant he was deep in thought. The usual witty banter between them was missing, and Blake could see that this hit Seth harder than expected. Blake ran his tongue over his fangs. "Hypothetical."

Seth sighed. "About?"

"If you had the chance to get a bigger ship, and a crew, what would you get?" asked Blake. He knew this topic would take Seth's mind off the moment.

Seth snorted. "Well, for starters, we would need something at least corvette class. It has to be fast and able to stealth, well, at least visually, not much you can do about the heat. Internally, it would need at least level-two replicators, maybe level three if we wanted sustained weapons and armor. Definitely would need to be packing drones, missiles, and various types of turrets. It'd need to be fusion powered and also have a condensed-space drive."

"So not much is what you're saying."

Seth grinned. "I know what you're doing, and I appreciate it."

"What about crew?"

Seth rubbed his thumb over two fingers. "Hmm, not sure. Definitely need a ship operations expert. Probably an engineer, and most likely a technician. What about you?"

Blake smiled. "Oh, that's easy. I would have an assault team and get a bruiser to start. Someone who can draw fire and take heat. After that, someone who can hack into systems, and maybe a sniper."

"You think they got any of that in this place we're going to?" asked Seth, pulling his lips to the right.

"Maybe not, but they have two shot glasses of whiskey with our names on 'em."

"I can live with that," said Seth. "I'll need to take a few days to rest up starting tomorrow before we head out."

"No problem."

When they reached the entrance to the bar, two large reptilian humanoids stepped forward. One of them pointed at Blake and in a deep, guttural voice said, "No trouble. You trouble, I trouble."

Blake tossed his hands out to the side. "Fellas. We're not trouble, we just want a drink."

The other reptilian scanned them with a device.

"I'm beginning to think your race was made to be bouncers," said Blake, smiling and baring his fangs. He knew they were Kazarullians. Their planet had been enslaved, then freed. Now the Kazarullians were everywhere as security.

The Kazarullian scanning them jerked his head back. "What you?"

"Fredorian," said Blake. "Well . . . actually Earthborn. Well . . . actually a vampire. I like to drink blood. You wanna be a donor?"

"Fredorian crazy," said the Kazarullian.

The other Kazarullian pointed at his eye, then at Blake, then back at himself. "Eye, you, me."

"Are you hitting on me?" asked Blake.

The Kazarullian growled.

Blake laughed as he and Seth entered the bar.

TWO

S eth poured himself a shot of whiskey. His mouth watered at the golden liquid with a cinnamon touch that seemed to make everything feel better. After what the Trags did not only to him, but to his ship, this was sorely needed. The bar was seedy, with haze-filled air and dim lighting. Half the smells were unfamiliar to him, and sometimes that was a good thing. The aliens seemed to be mostly Almogran, with a few others he did not recognize. The soothing sound of unusual music wafted through the air. It reminded him of ambient techno music. He poured Blake a shot, raised his glass, and then said, "To our last contract."

Blake raised his glass and tapped it against Seth's. "To our last contract."

Seth downed his shot and slammed the glass onto the table. He exhaled, then said, "At least I'm not getting my ass kicked again tonight."

"Keep drinking like that, and it might be the whiskey doing the ass kicking," said Blake with a smile before downing his shot.

Seth shook his head, then eyed Blake. "You know I'd stick around if I could, but I feel . . . like . . . I'm just not cut out for this. I should've known that from our first contract."

Blake laughed. "You shot Alcarez with a ship weapon."

"Yeah . . . but he deserved it. I'm so glad I won't have to see that asshole ever again. Fuck him."

"Same, but hey . . . you did two years, and you know what? When you're flying ships at your old job again, you'll look fondly back on all of this. At least the question of what if you did something different will have been answered."

"Maybe," said Seth, chuckling. His eyes narrowed as he tapped the table. "Incoming."

Blake swung his head to view the incoming reptilian humanoids.

Seth noticed that these reptilians were smaller, more human-sized than the bouncers outside. Their faces were more humanoid as well. It was the scales that indicated they were Drodalians, one of the first races the Fredorians met when they ventured out into space. There was no love lost between them. The one walking in front of the other two seemed to be older and more grizzled. The ones behind him were smaller, and looked like they were angry, as much as he could tell anyways. He did not see many Drodalians, but the look of anger among humanoids was almost universal.

"Fredorians . . . ," said the older Drodalian in a gruff voice. "You . . . lost?"

Blake snorted. "I thought I smelled lizard shit. And here you are."

Seth wondered if these Drodalians knew who Blake Brown was. If they did not, they would never forget him.

The older Drodalian sneered. "You're kinda far from home . . ."

"It's a free galaxy," said Blake. "I guess I didn't see you staking claim here while crawling around and eating bugs when I walked in."

"He mocks you," said one of the younger Drodalians.

The older one tossed his hand out to the side and stared Blake down. "Do you know what happens to lost Fredorians?"

Blake threw his hands to the side. "I'm gonna guess it isn't something to do with dancing."

"He insults us," said the other younger Drodalian.

"You know Fredoria and Drodalia have a peace treaty in effect," said Blake.

The older Drodalian shook his head. "Doesn't matter. I'm Razis. A name you're gonna remember after tonight. You're also gonna remember why Fredorians don't come out this far." He reached in with his right arm to grab Blake.

The young Drodalian to the left of Razis punched Seth, knocking him out of his seat and onto the floor.

Blake leaped to his feet. While dodging Razis's grab attempt, Blake used his right hand to grab Razis's arm. With Blake's other hand, he palmed the back of Razis's head and slammed it into the table.

Razis's head bounced back.

Blake slammed it again, and Razis rolled off to the side.

The other young Drodalian began to pull out his sidearm.

Blake lurched forward and, in one clean motion, pulled one of his short blades out and sliced off the younger Drodalian's hand.

The younger Drodalian crumpled to the ground, growling and grunting.

Blake swung his blade and placed it inches away from the other younger Drodalian that had punched Seth.

The Drodalian's trembling hands rested on his sidearm.

"Ah, ah, ah. What do you think you're doing?" asked Blake.

The Drodalian shook while trying to breathe.

"Your life rests in the hands of Seth. If he wants you dead, I'll gut you. Here and now. I'll fucking spill your *guts* all over the floor. If he doesn't, then you can take the two slimy pieces of shit you came in with and get the hell out of here. After leaving your weapons of course."

Seth stood up with the help of the table. His jaw was already in pain, now it was even more so. Even while drinking, he could not escape getting hit.

"Seth . . . what's it gonna be? We've already killed nine Trags today. Do I make lizard soup and put it to ten deaths today, or not?" asked Blake.

A brown liquid seeped out of the Drodalian's light leg armor.

Seth raised his head a bit as he studied the Drodalian. "Have you learned a lesson here?"

The Drodalian nodded vigorously.

"I only ask because if you haven't, and I let you go, there's still a chance Blake might kill you."

A tear ran down the Drodalian's face.

"I think we let him live," said Seth.

Blake gestured at the table with his blade while his gaze bored a hole through the young Drodalian. "Weapons on the table. Get your friends and then get out. You come within *spitting* distance of me or my friend, you die. It's that simple. Do you understand?"

The Drodalian looked down and then nodded.

"Well . . . then . . . get to it!" said Blake.

The Drodalian unbuckled his belt and laid it on the table. After getting the weapon belts of the other Drodalians and placing them on the table, he helped the other young Drodalian wrap up his wound, then retrieved the unconscious older Drodalian from the ground.

Seth sat back down and rubbed his chin. "Young one has a strong punch."

Blake sat back down as he eyed the retreating Drodalians. He picked up the whiskey bottle that had been knocked over and poured out a shot. "Even with a peace treaty, these assholes still feel like they have something to prove."

"I can't believe you lasted as long as you have with all this crap," said Seth as he poured himself another shot. "You musta seen some crazy stuff as an intelligence operative."

Blake smiled, baring his fangs. "Of course I did, and those who crossed me found out what this young Drodalian did tonight."

Seth shook his head. "You're one cocky son of a bitch."

"And you're that son of a bitch's friend. What's that say about you?" asked Blake, laughing.

"Yeah, yeah," said Seth. He downed his shot of whiskey. He puffed his cheeks for a moment. "I'm beginning to think I might be safer wherever we end up sleeping."

Blake leaned forward with his elbows on the table while clasping his hands. "I know we've been through some bad stuff, and I wanted you to know I'm glad you were there for me."

"I'm your abductee brother," said Seth with a grin.

"Yes, you are," said Blake.

Seth enjoyed these moments with Blake. Although Blake tended to be more on the comical side, even when facing death, he could be truly empathetic. Those moments were rare, and he was glad that Blake showed them to him. He knew Blake was a killer, and one that reveled in it, but deep down, he knew Blake was a good person and tried to kill only those who deserved it or were trying to kill him. The Drodalians would have been killed before they had their weapons drawn, yet Blake let them go, minus their weapons and a hand.

"You falling asleep on me over there?" asked Blake.

"Nah . . . was just contemplating how crazy you can be at times."

Blake laughed. "Of course. I'm Blake Brown."

"I know, I know," said Seth, shaking his head. A movement caught his eye near the entrance of the bar. It was a Fredorian man with a ranger suit.

The aliens near the entrance cleared a path as the Fredorian made his way over to their table.

Seth narrowed his eyes as he tapped the table. "Incoming."

////////

Blake eyed the clean-cut, dark-skinned Fredorian man headed their way. The subdued outfit with loose pants, a gray shirt, and a jacket likely hid a small arsenal of weapons, which would not surprise Blake. It was a tactic often employed by intelligence operatives in the Fredorian Rangers. He stood and put his hand on his holstered pistol.

The Fredorian paused and lifted his jacket back, revealing a pistol strapped to his side and an array of small gadgets on the other side.

Seth's eyes widened as he watched them square off.

"So . . . you found me," said Blake.

The Fredorian narrowed his eyes. "It wasn't hard. I just followed the carnage."

Blake tilted his head for a moment, then burst into laughter while tossing his hands out the side. "Jarvis! You old dog."

Jarvis smiled as he approached the table.

Seth let out a sigh of relief.

Once Jarvis took a seat, he extended a hand to Seth. "Jarvis Keele, master Fredorian Ranger."

Seth shook Jarvis's hand. "Seth Williams, Blake's babysitter and sometimes pilot."

Jarvis grinned from ear to ear. "That sounds about right." He faced Blake. "You were actually hard to track this time."

"You never could keep up with me," said Blake. He gestured toward Jarvis while looking at Seth. "He's one of the few rangers I still trust."

"Oh," said Seth, nodding. "Why would we need to be tracked . . . ?"

Jarvis bit his bottom lip for a moment, then said, "I'm here to deliver a message."

"Now you got me curious," said Blake. If Jarvis had been keeping tabs on him and Seth, then it must be something important. Blake recalled having to deliver messages before, and usually it was for hard-to-reach targets. Those missions came directly from Rakar Ho Jador, the Fredorian Rangers founder and originally a Kreagan Ranger. Rakar had been tapped to implement a similar unit on Fredoria by then prime ambassador Andia Kiggs. Although Rakar no longer led the rangers, he was still revered as one of the best. Whatever Jarvis was doing there, Blake was sure Rakar was involved. Blake offered Jarvis a shot of whiskey.

Jarvis shook his hand out in front of him. "I definitely don't need that."

"Suit yourself," said Blake. "What's the message?"

"Rakar wants you to meet with him," said Jarvis.

"Now?" asked Blake.

"Yep. And in the presidential suite. Not sure what you did to deserve that."

Blake ran a hand over his mouth for a moment. Something big must be brewing. "I'm guessing I'm to meet with more than just Rakar."

"Yeah. Andia Kiggs would like to talk to you too." He swiveled his head toward Seth. "And you."

"Me?" asked Seth. "Oh, shit, Blake, what type of crap did you get me into now?"

Blake shook his head. "I don't think we're in trouble . . . ," he said, peering at Jarvis, "or are we?"

"You're both fine. I don't know what the meeting is about, other than to say Rakar said it was urgent," said Jarvis. He looked around. "Wow. This place really is a dump. Smells like someone crapped their armor."

Blake laughed. "They did, actually. Some Drodalians stepped up to the plate, swung, and missed."

"Huh. Musta been that group I ran into hustling it out of here," said Jarvis. "That should have been my first clue I was in the right place."

Blake nodded. "Well, now that your message has been delivered, we have a small problem. Our ship got torched."

Jarvis eased back into his chair while shaking his head. "Never could keep to one ship, could you?"

Blake grinned. "This time it wasn't a pack of Covendrin mercs."

Seth's eyes widened. "This has happened before?"

"Oh, yeah," said Jarvis. "You don't get to Blake's level without pissing off more than a few groups. Still, the fact he survived this long is a testament to his skill. Not many of us master rangers around. Nonetheless, you can both travel with me. We should depart immediately."

"Your ship is hopefully bigger than ours," said Seth.

"Six living quarters, level-three replicator, condensed-space drive, and all the weapon and armor trimmings. Fast as hell too."

"Medical bay?" asked Seth.

"Got a small one."

Seth eyed Blake. "What are we waiting for?"

Blake nodded. "All right. Let's roll." He tapped at the table console and paid for their drinks, then stood. With a final look at the cleared space around them, he joined Jarvis and Seth and headed to the ship.

When they got there, Jarvis took Seth to the medical bay and then to one of the living quarters.

Blake drew his lips to the right as he heard Seth close and lock the door. It was evident he just wanted to sleep. Blake had a good idea of what medication Seth was on. After looking around for a moment, Blake headed to the command center, where Jarvis was. One thing that Blake recognized immediately was the wall screen that wrapped around the room. Most of the space was just chairs with workstations that faced out toward the walls. A command chair resided in the middle, surrounded by smaller chairs. It was no coincidence that the command center was buried in the middle of the ship where the most protection was afforded. It also acted as a central hub of sorts, connecting various parts of the vessel. That was standard among many Fredorian ships.

Jarvis looked up from his command chair. "I think your friend Seth will be out for a few."

"Yeah, I gathered that," said Blake, taking a seat next to Jarvis. "Nice ship. I sure didn't have anything fancy like this."

Jarvis nodded as he swung a thin console from the side of the chair in front of him. He tapped at it, causing the room to dim a bit and the screens to flicker on.

Blake studied the screens. He knew the ship was using cameras embedded outside the ship to give a 360-degree view of their surroundings. Redundancy was a key feature for the more advanced ships, and it was something he figured the ship would have.

The varied metrics on the screens showed the weapons, armor, and shielding status, along with the state of the engines. When the engines fired and the ship began to rise, the corresponding graphic on the display updated. The screen was segmented into various views, but there was a main segment on each side that was like looking out a window.

When they ascended through the atmosphere, Jarvis activated the condensed-space drive. A semitransparent bubble surrounded the ship.

Blake grimaced as the ship slightly stuttered. Traveling through condensed space always made him nervous. It was unnatural and odd to be taken out of normal space, or what he knew as reality, then pop into another space that was devoid of any known matter but still respective of gravity. He never liked the blurred filter effect that seemed to cover planets and other stellar objects. The tunnel-shaped path they were taking offset the open-space feel he was used to in deep space. While condensed space allowed much faster travel than through normal space, avoiding anything with significant gravity was important. Communication was also almost instant within several hundred light-years if the right senders and receivers were used.

"You don't like condensed-space travel, do you?" asked Jarvis.

Blake fidgeted in his seat. "Well . . . I won't say I like it, but I can't argue with its effectiveness."

Jarvis pressed a button on his console. "Me either. Off we go"

The ship angled itself, and then began to fly off.

Blake noticed that they had left the solar system fairly quickly. In deep space, everything was just black when looking at it through a condensed-space filter and the dimly lit light-blue semitransparent tunnel border. He glanced back at the hallway that led to the living quarters, then at Jarvis. "How bad are the rangers now?"

Jarvis cast a sidelong glance at Blake, then licked his lips. "Bad. Grick may have assumed the role of master ranger and leader, but he is no friend to us."

Blake nodded. He knew that the Fredorian Defense Force, which represented all Fredorian military, except for the rangers, had been angling to remove the rangers.

They considered it an affront that the rangers were needed. "Grick's an FDF plant more than likely. I never liked him."

"Me either, but when half the master rangers leave, there isn't much dissent to be had. You could've been a strong voice."

Blake sighed. "I'm Earthborn, and also a vampire. That's two strikes against me. I'm not sure what weight I would carry."

Jarvis snorted. "You're Blake Brown. The most renowned ranger to ever grace Fredoria, except for maybe Rakar. Even he said you would have made a great Kreagan Ranger."

"A high compliment from a Kreagan," said Blake.

"Yeah, no shit. Still, you and I both know Rakar is different from most Kreagans. With him out and Grick running things, a lot of new policies and protocols have been established."

"Yeah. I saw a bit of that several years ago."

Jarvis grimaced. "It's gotten worse since then. Now instead of one ranger for every one thousand people and being voted in, the option to become a ranger is open to any FDF with the right training and certification."

"A mix . . . interesting," said Blake. He rubbed his chin. "Grick is transforming the rangers into an FDF unit."

"Basically, yeah. On top of that, there's a subtle encouragement for the older rangers, especially Earthborn, to drop out."

"Figures. I'm guessing then that this meeting with Rakar and Andia has something to do with the FDF."

Jarvis shrugged. "Could be, dunno." He furrowed his eyebrows and met Blake's gaze. "Whatever it is, if you need me, you know I always got your back."

"I know, and I got yours. After twenty years, you're one of the few I can trust, and that's rare," said Blake. He smiled big. "But let's not forget that I still get more women than you."

Jarvis laughed as the ship continued toward Fredoria.

CHAPTER
THREE

As Blake walked alongside Jarvis and Seth toward the presidential suite, Blake took stock of the situation. His gut told him that Rakar probably wanted something handled, maybe a special mission. The credits alone for something like that would be worth it. Working in the field, Blake had come across freelance contractors doing secret work for the Fredorian government. It was off the records and usually something that if caught, resulted in a massive denial and cover-up. As a ranger at the time, the protocol was to ignore those contractors, same as with the FDF.

After three days on Jarvis's ship, Blake had gotten caught up on all the politics and the current situation. It bothered him that the FDF took such an aggressive stance on consolidating the rangers under them. He knew there had always been friction between the rangers, planetary law enforcement, and the FDF. They all controlled their own spheres of influence. Planetary law enforcement reported to a senate council and handled planetary security. The FDF reported to another senate council and handled off-planet security. The rangers reported directly to the president and handled the one-off issues both on- and off-world. They were the eyes and ears of the president. Conflict between each group was ever present, but the recent push to integrate the rangers under the FDF had riled up planetary law enforcement and those rangers still loyal to keeping it separate.

He glanced around at the sun filtering through the planted trees on the side of the path they were on. It was 10:00 a.m., and a meeting in the morning was unusual since most took place in the afternoon.

"You're uncharacteristically quiet," said Seth as he rubbed a hand over his chest.

"Just thinking. You seem much better off this morning," said Blake.

"Yeah, unusual, huh? At least the Trags didn't break anything."

"I can break something if you wish."

Seth laughed. "Yeah . . . how about no?"

Jarvis smirked. "I suspect that although you two had rough times, there were a lot of good times too."

"Yeah . . . some," said Seth. "It was just the ass kickings I was getting tired of."

Jarvis nodded. "I don't think you'll need to worry about that for this meeting."

Blake observed Jarvis. He had been his close friend for the twenty years Blake had served as a Fredorian Ranger. They had even worked together on some missions. Jarvis was one of the rare friends Blake could count on in a crisis. The fact that Rakar chose Jarvis was not surprising. It did imply that this had something to do with the rangers. Blake suspected that the rangers did not know of Jarvis being sent, or of this meeting.

After another twenty minutes of light conversation, they reached the doors of the presidential compound.

Blake noticed that the guards outside looked almost relieved to see him. They wasted no time opening the massive doors and ushering the group in. As they walked down the large open area, he surveyed the mood. A deep inhalation gave him an idea of the state of sweat. It was usually a good indicator if something was going on. Aliens had a strong smell that stood out, at least the ones who could sweat. He recalled meeting a species that stored up their sweat and then expelled it as spit. The atmosphere he sensed was a tense one.

When they reached the presidential suite, Seth eyed the two guards outside the main doors. "Whew. Never thought I'd be here."

"Me either," said Blake. "Has a sterile smell thing going on."

Seth sniffed. "Smells clean to me."

"To a nonvampire nose maybe. Let's see what all this is about," said Blake.

Jarvis extended a hand toward Blake. "This is as far as I go."

Blake shook Jarvis's hand and slapped him on the arm. "Thanks for the ride, and it was damn good to see you again."

"You'll probably see me again, I'm sure. I'll be around the area for a bit. You got my CID. If you need me, reach out," said Jarvis.

"You got it, man," said Blake. He knew that Jarvis's communication ID, or CID, was recently updated, per ranger protocol.

With a final dip of his head, Jarvis headed back the way they had come.

Blake and Seth entered the room and were met by Rakar. He was a Kreagan, a race with purple skin and a head that had a slight cone shape in the back.

The formal attire Rakar wore stood out. It was only used in a select few ranger ceremonies, and only worn by grand-masters. The black-and-green, one-piece, formfitting suit was crisp, with various emblems on the upper arm. Blake suspected it was Rakar's way of defying Grick, since most junior rangers, either voted in or from the FDF, would be in awe of that. The last time Blake saw the uniform was before he had retired, at a swearing-in ceremony for new recruits. Ceremonies were rare, but there were still a few in the rangers.

Rakar extended a hand. "Blake! Seth! Glad you both could come."

Blake and Seth shook hands, then faced the right side of the room.

The large room was simplistic in design. High-tech panels covered the walls, and a large arc-shaped desk sat at one end of the room. Chairs were positioned directly in front of the desk.

The middle-aged fair-skinned woman with piled-up brunette hair behind the desk caught Blake's eye. She had on a white presidential two-piece suit with silver and blue lines segmenting it. He knew this to be Andia Kiggs, president of Fredoria. The chair she sat in hovered off the ground, and he could see it had defensive and offensive weaponry on it, along with an array of consoles. It was like a mini ship. A box-shaped device on a waist-high shelf left of Andia caught his eye. There was something unusual about it, something exotic.

Blake and Seth slapped their fists to their chests at a forty-five degree angle.

Andia waved a hand out at them. "No need to be formal here. Please, sit," she said as she gestured at the chairs in front of the desk.

They took their seats as Rakar took one next to her.

"We have a lot to discuss in a short amount of time. I assume you know who I am already," she said.

Blake cast a sidelong glance at Seth, then back at Andia. "We do."

"Good. You can relax. The room is set to private, and no one can hear what's said in here, so be yourselves."

Blake nodded. "All right. What's going on?"

Andia raised an eyebrow. "Right to the point. I like that. Okay then. I've asked you both here because I'm forming a small group, one that reports to Rakar directly. The purpose of the group is to carry out highly sensitive missions that can be dangerous. The first mission's time has come, as has the time for the group to be formed."

"Isn't that what the rangers are for?" asked Blake.

"Usually, but these . . . are trying times. The rangers are not quite what they used to be, especially when they're commanded by Grick and losing members such as yourself," she said.

"Yeah . . . I don't care much for that fucking asshole," he said. His eyes widened. "I mean . . . for him."

She chuckled. "He's an asshole, and please, feel free to speak as you normally would." She tapped at her desk, causing a series of files to appear. "As of this morning, the rangers have been incorporated officially into the FDF."

Blake narrowed his eyes. "They report to you directly, though."

"They used to. However, the Senate has voted in favor of this move."

"Well . . . that sucks," he said .

She nodded. "Yes . . . it sucks. All I have under me for the moment is the presidential guard."

He rubbed his chin for a moment. "They've essentially left you blind."

"Yes. However . . . there are no limits on the size of my presidential guard."

Rakar grinned. "If there's a loophole, she'll find it."

"So . . . this new group is essentially your personal guard," said Blake.

Andia raised a finger. "With all the resources of the presidency at its disposal. It might be classified as part of the guard, but it's really a freelance group."

"Like the hunters," said Rakar, nodding at Blake. "Hire the best when you need them."

Blake glanced at Seth, then back at Andia. "Well . . . as interesting as all this is, we've had some . . . setbacks."

"Yeah, I get my ass kicked all the time, except this time, our ship got blown up," said Seth.

Andia glanced at Seth. "Seth Williams. Although I'm familiar with Blake's record, I had to look yours up. You have an accomplished résumé. The fact you're with Blake means you must be a good pilot."

Seth bobbed his head. "I feel like more of a punching bag and bait half the time."

"I see. Do you know anything about the *Exceltion*?"

Seth's eyes widened as he leaned forward. "Uhh . . . yeah. That's the top-of-the-line, souped-up corvette-class ship that was the prototype for the FDF sanguine-class line of ships. I studied it forward and backward when I was flying cargo."

"So . . . if you had an opportunity to fly it, would that interest you?"

Seth licked his lips as he glanced at Blake, then back at Andia. "It would, but . . . definitely need a specialized crew for something like that."

Rakar tilted his head. "What if you had one? Both one for the ship and one for an assault team?"

ADAIR HART

"Oh, hell yeah," said Seth. He gestured at Blake. "We used to play a game where we talked about what we could do with a bigger team and ship."

Blake narrowed his eyes. "This all sounds good . . . but what *exactly* would we be signing on to do?"

Andia tapped at her desk. A holographic projection shot up of a large humanoid in tight black leather. His bald head had ridges encircling it.

"Delkis," said Blake.

"You know of him?" asked Andia.

"Yeah . . . but never met him. I'm familiar with his crew. He's been in prison ever since I joined the rangers, but his crew was still active."

Andia gritted her teeth. "He's out now, and has threatened to kill me."

"I thought he was in for at least fifty years."

"He was . . . and yet, somehow, he is out."

Rakar shook his head. "Politics."

Andia nodded. "Not much we can do about that. However, I want him brought here to serve in a Fredorian prison."

Seth raised a hand. "Won't the Kreagans be pissed about that?"

"I don't think they would press the matter, especially in regards to how he was let free," said Andia.

"Good point," said Seth.

Andia's desk surface flashed a few times. She sighed. "Another meeting. I can't miss this one. Rakar is heading up this group, although he won't be going out with it. He has everything you need to know. I hope you decide to take us up on this offer."

Blake nodded. "Before you go, what's that box device to your left? I . . . can sense something unusual about it."

Andia looked to her left. "It allows for the visualization of . . . life auras . . . as far as I understand it. Exotic energies and the like can show up on its interface. It's extremely sensitive and unique. If you were to look at the interface now, it would show you as a Daedrould, ancient vampire strain, for example."

"I see," said Blake. He glanced at Rakar. "Sounds quite unique. Yet another unusual . . . thing. I seem to be noticing those a lot."

Rakar looked down.

Andia's eyes widened as she stood. "Well, I have to go to this meeting." She stood and shook Blake's and Seth's hands. As she left, she turned her head toward everyone. "I hope we can work together."

Blake and Seth nodded as she exited the room.

Rakar gestured toward the door. "We can talk more about this elsewhere."

"Lead on," said Blake, smiling and baring his fangs.

////////

An hour later on a patio overlooking the city, Rakar, Blake, and Seth met Jarvis. A semitransparent shield covered the open part from the building to the edge of the patio. A table stood in the middle of the patio, with several chairs around it. A matter replicator was off to the side, and outside the door to the building, the rest was bare except for metallic panels on the ground.

"Are we secure?" asked Rakar, glancing at Jarvis.

Jarvis nodded.

Blake knew this to be a safe location, even though it was not listed anywhere. He figured Jarvis had a few more stashed around, just as Blake had done when he was an active ranger. He pulled a vial of blood from his belt and pressed a button on the top. A small rod extended up, and he took a deep sip.

Seth quivered. "That always freaks me out when you do that."

"I could always get it live . . . ," said Blake, smiling and baring his fangs.

Seth shook his head as he headed to the replicator.

After Jarvis and Seth had gotten something to eat, everyone sat around the table.

Rakar gestured at Jarvis. "I've asked Jarvis here since he's involved somewhat. He doesn't know what we're about to discuss, but he's involved in a different part."

"If Blake's involved, I know it's serious," said Jarvis with a grin.

Blake pulled his lips to the right and nodded. "That's right."

Rakar cleared his throat. "What I'm about to reveal stays between us." He glanced at Blake and Seth. "Even if you two decide not to do this."

"Of course," said Blake.

"No problem," said Seth.

"All right then," said Rakar. He tapped at the table, and a projection shot up showing Delkis. "This mission is to retrieve Delkis and bring him to Fredoria. He was let go about a month ago. We believe someone powerful either twisted someone in the Kreagan system or paid handsomely. Regardless of the method, the outcome was the same. Delkis is on the loose, and he has threatened to kill Andia. I cannot allow that to happen."

Blake furrowed his eyebrows. "This seems a bit overkill for a bounty. I know several hard-hitting mercs that could get him for you."

Rakar interacted with the table, showing a projection of a large reptilian humanoid in heavy armor.

"Gul Hist," said Blake, grinning. "That would be a good choice. Guy is tough as shit and gets things done. He doesn't mess around."

"That's what we thought too," said Rakar.

The projection changed to show Gul Hist's mangled body tied to a post. His belly had been sliced open, and his entrails had been pulled out and held up by other poles.

Seth dry heaved.

"That's also Gul Hist from three weeks ago. Apparently . . . he wasn't tough enough," said Rakar.

Blake sat up in his chair as he studied the projection. Someone like Gul Hist going down like that was not something he saw often, if at all. Weapon wounds maybe, but not what he was seeing. He recalled tracking a suspect on a mission, but ended up watching Gul Hist take them out. Although he had never met Gul Hist personally, he recognized him as one of the premiere bounty hunters out there. "This couldn't have been done by just Delkis ."

"We agree," said Rakar. "We now believe that Delkis is working with several groups."

"Which ones?" asked Blake.

"We don't know."

Blake snorted. "Okay, so Delkis and whoever got Gul Hist. You could always hire—"

"Covendrin mercs," said Rakar. "We tried that."

The projection changed to show four poles, each with a Covendrin merc head on it.

Seth's eyes widened. "Holy shit."

"Yeah . . . our second attempt was not successful either," said Rakar.

Blake rubbed his chin. The Covendrin mercs were the most feared mercs in the region, their only rivals being the Xibians. Not only was merc work the main export of the Covendrin home world, their culture embraced it. They had a rule that if one was killed, then a bounty was placed on the killer. The fact that Delkis was not dead yet meant that he might even be out of reach of the Covendrin. "Hmm . . . how do you know he's working with several groups, and not just one?"

"Call it a well-informed hunch."

Blake eyed Rakar. "You're awfully well-informed, and I doubt it came from the rangers."

Rakar looked down for a moment. "I can't say who it is. I made a promise, one I will keep."

"Fair enough," said Blake. "I know how the game works. So Delkis has a few groups behind him, and now you want the best person you've ever met to go after him."

Jarvis laughed. "He would've asked me then."

"Yeah, right. Well, I'm interested. Delkis has never faced Blake Brown."

"Third person again," said Seth, shaking his head. "But you're right. Delkis has probably never faced someone like Blake. If Blake goes, I go."

Blake glanced at Seth. "You sure? I mean . . . I know it hasn't been easy the last two years."

"I'm sure," said Seth. "This sounds far more important than just freelancing, and it's a request from the president. I can't just walk away from that, especially if you're gonna need a pilot."

Blake nodded. "I think you just want to fly the *Exceltion*. All right then." He faced Rakar. "I have a few requirements."

Rakar eased back into his chair. "Let's hear it."

"All right. First. I pick my own crew. Earthborn preferred. Nothing against Fredorians or others, but I think it may be better with mostly Earthborn."

Rakar pulled his lips in for a moment. "No problem there. Sounds like you want an Earthborn unit. Nonetheless, we have a list of people you might be interested in, and not all are Earthborn. Some are experts on the *Exceltion*, while others are more suited for combat. You're free to pick whoever you want, though."

Blake pointed at Jarvis. "Well, he's in, even if he's Fredorian."

Jarvis licked his lips and looked down.

Blake tilted his head. He had expected a witty retort or something boastful.

"Jarvis is going to stay where he is, inside the rangers," said Rakar. "He is our eyes and ears. Outside him, we don't have a presence there, and he keeps us aware of what's going on. He still holds a position on the master ranger council, and he holds sway."

"Yeah, lucky me," said Jarvis. He looked at Blake. "You know I'd be out there with you, brother."

Blake sighed. "I know. Well, damn." He shot Rakar a look. "I'll take a peek at the list." He crooked a thumb at Seth. "Seth can pick the ship crew since he knows best about who's needed. I'll pick the assault team."

"Sounds good to me," said Seth. He swatted Blake's arm. "Bigger ship, bigger crew. That's what I'm talking about."

"I may have to kick your ass from time to time to honor that tradition from our freelancing days."

Everyone laughed.

Rakar cleared his throat. "What are your other requirements?"

"Well, I was going to say a ship, but it seems the *Exceltion* will cover that," said Blake.

Seth rubbed his hands. "I can't wait to get my hands on it."

Blake glanced at Rakar. "The only other requirement I have is we'll need some new weapons and armor. We lost everything in our last contract."

"We won't need to get that," said Seth. "The *Exceltion* has a level-three replicator. It should be able to provide any weapon and armor we need, well, at least the more common types." He rubbed his chin. "It wouldn't hurt to find a technician, though, one who can program mods and knows the ins and outs of our equipment, but also help with the ship's technical systems."

"Yeah, good luck finding that."

Seth grinned. "I have someone in mind."

Blake nodded.

After a moment of silence, Rakar said, "Any other requirements?"

Blake balled up his left fist, then covered it with his right hand. He tapped his fingers from the right hand and after a moment said, "Not right now."

Rakar tapped at the table, causing a projection of a planet to appear. "Good. If you're decided then, your first stop will be here, Holryn. We have a contact there who knows more about where Delkis might be."

Seth narrowed his eyes. "I've had to deliver there before. I don't care much for the Illuzarans. They tend to think a bit highly of themselves. Their security is also a bit ridiculous."

"Never been there before," said Blake.

Jarvis snorted. "I have, and Seth's right. Place is a shithole, at least for people like us, unless you're a scientist. I guess then it might be a great place to go if you can stand the Illuzarans' arrogance and condescension."

Blake nodded. "Doesn't seem like violence would be needed there."

"Not physically at least," said Jarvis.

"Well, when we get there, I'll let everyone know what we find," said Blake, looking around.

Rakar shook his head. "Once you leave Fredorian space, there's to be no communication. You'll be on your own. If you need to contact us, then come back to Fredoria."

"Communication can be secured," said Blake.

Rakar raised a finger. "Assuming the person you're talking to is not someone else."

"All right . . . What about the FDF and any other Fredorian law enforcement we run into? You said they know about this group."

"Already handled. You'll have the credentials of the presidential guard," said Rakar.

"Awesome," said Blake. He swatted Seth's arm. "See, good things come to those who get their ass kicked a lot."

Everyone laughed.

"You're never gonna let me live that down, are you?" asked Seth.

"No way," said Blake. He glanced at Rakar. "Anything else we need to cover?"

"That's about it. I have to get back to Andia."

"To protect her?" asked Blake with a sly smile.

Rakar grinned. "Among other things."

"All right. Well . . . I'm sure Seth is salivating over getting to see the *Exceltion*. I'm gonna sit here and go over this list of people."

Jarvis stood. "I'm expected back as well. We don't need anyone wondering where I've been or what I'm doing."

"Fine, fine, everyone leave," said Blake.

Everyone laughed as all but Blake exited the patio.

CHAPTER
FOUR

Blake studied the various people Rakar had suggested. It had been forty minutes since everyone left, and Blake had been eager to see who Rakar thought would be a good fit. Their profiles were projected in the center of the table and listed several at once in a circular manner. All Blake had to do was move his finger left and right on the table to switch profiles. Although Rakar had said a few, the several hundred on the list was more than Blake had expected. He narrowed it down by various criteria and ended up with a list of about sixty.

One thing he was sure he wanted was a bruiser. Someone who was unusually strong and could wear heavy armor and shielding. There were instances when he knew he could have used someone like that to draw heat or break choke points. Strength and conditioning were the most critical aspects since wearing that level of armor was endurance draining. Weapon proficiency was also important, as was personality. Although he suspected there wouldn't be too many mild-mannered people that fit that role, he did not want someone who would be so abrasive that it would break team cohesion.

He grinned as he thought about forming a team. Being a leader was not something he aspired to, but he had been told that he had all the qualities for it. Even as a master ranger he had worked alone most of the time. This was different. People would report to him and Seth. Blake would now be responsible for them. While there had been missions with junior rangers, they were usually the safer ones. This would be asking the crew he was forming to go into places they might not return from.

With a long exhale, he focused back on the projections. The second person he wanted was someone familiar with technological systems. Too many times in the past he had been denied access to more efficient routes due to a locked door. Some consoles he could hack himself, but not the ones he usually needed. Then there was trying to break in to systems to find data, or track someone. He needed an expert, preferably one with more than just Fredorian systems under their belt. Whoever he chose probably would not be anywhere close to the level needed, but anything was better than nothing.

The last roles made him pause. Although he could probably do whatever needed to be done with just three people, a fourth and even a fifth would be helpful. A sniper crossed his mind as he recalled the first contract he and Seth had taken. Another could be someone who specialized in traps, bombs, and the like. Maybe a scout who could track and stealth. He mused at the thought of another person on the team like himself. Seth would be crying every day at the nonstop ribbing.

With his head in his hands, he used his thumbs to massage his temples. This was not going to be easy. He got the sense that time was of the essence, but picking the right people was not something to be rushed.

Knock! Knock! Knock!

He jumped out of his chair and pulled out his striker. His vampiric senses could not detect any trace of sweat, but the rhythmic pulse of a heart was behind the door. It was an odd pulse, reminding him more of a machine than a living being. This was a secret location, and only three other people knew he was there. He slid off to the side of the room. A tap at his belt activated his chameleon shield, he said, "Who is it?"

"Ada," said a female voice with a digital rasp.

Blake knew that sound belonged to an android. Given his encounters with them while freelancing, he knew this could go either way. "What do you want?"

"To join your team before you go to Holryn."

He jerked his head back. How could she possibly know about that? His mind spun at the possibilities, but it could also be a trap. Still, it intrigued him enough to unlock the door and step back off to the side while deactivating his chameleon shield. "Come in."

Ada walked into the room.

Blake noticed that unlike most current-generation androids with fair synthetic skin, she had metallic skin. She wore a formfitting mesh suit, and her hair was shoulder length and flowed naturally. Her eyes had a slight blue glow to them. He slipped his striker onto his back.

Ada closed the doors. "You have nothing to fear from me. Can we talk?"

Blake laughed. "You have me stumped. That's unusual." He gestured at a seat. "Well . . . since you're here, have a seat."

Ada complied.

Blake joined her. "You're one of the older-generation models. I'd guess G2 or G3."

She nodded. "I'm generation two, G2, with a specialization in cyber warfare and all its associated skill sets."

He rubbed his chin. "Really . . . hmm. I thought that generation was mostly for doing work hazardous to humans."

"It is. However, my generation was the first to have a specialized series."

"Interesting."

Ada half smiled. "We didn't get the morphable skin like generation one or the later generations. Ours was left the natural color, to indicate we are different."

Blake ran his tongue over one of his fangs as he observed her. "For the record, I don't like what the Fredorians did to you and other androids. Where were you placed?"

Ada looked down for a moment.

He could see her eyes dim a bit. Around ten years ago, the Fredorians had issued a decree that all androids were property. They were to be reallocated to new roles, and there was no path to citizenship, the ultimate goal of freedom for most androids. It was a kneejerk reaction to some androids going rogue and causing a lot of mayhem.

She looked back up. "I was placed in manual labor at one of the docking warehouses."

"What a waste of your talents."

Her mechanical eyes softened. "I wish . . . for something more. I was hoping . . . that maybe you could look past my being an android and allow me a chance to try out for your team."

Blake touched his fingertips together in front of him, then placed them against his lips. After a moment, he said, "What alien technological systems are you familiar with?"

"All systems that have been documented in the intelligence community."

"Even the FDF intelligence community?"

"Yes."

Blake pursed his lips. "And you can hack if need be . . . say if we were to bust in somewhere?"

Ada's eyes lit up. "Of course."

"I noticed that seemed to excite you."

"I apologize. However, the thought of new experiences outside moving things is appealing to me."

He nodded. "I understand. How much do you know about this mission?"

"Everything. I still have a back door into some channels, and listen in from time to time. I know of Rakar's concerns and that he wanted you for this mission. It was logical for Jarvis to pick this location since it was the closest and the only one that showed unusual behavior in power consumption. I also followed you with the various visual feeds on your way in. Once you were all inside, I tapped into a console in a maintenance room outside the room and listened in. I wanted to showcase my skills to you."

"Impressive . . . and a little concerning in regards to ranger security," said Blake with wide eyes. "It's not often I'm surprised. You're one of the few that has. I'm curious, though . . . How are your combat skills?"

"I'm versed in close-quarters combat as well as all known weaponry. My form gives me superior strength and speed relative to a human."

He grinned. "What weapon do you prefer?"

"I prefer pistols, in particular the FLP-40. However, my load out for any given mission should be tailored for hacking, drone mastery, and medic. If it comes to close-quarters combat, whomever I am fighting would be punished."

"I bet you're a spitfire in hand-to-hand. And medic . . . that's something we could definitely use. About this drone mastery . . ."

Ada tilted her head. "Mostly used for surveillance, but they are useful for establishing a physical connection in hard-to-reach places. Depending on the drone, they can also be used for offense, although in a minor role."

Blake rubbed his chin. "So you're smart, tough, and can heal, fight, and hack. That about sum it up?"

"I would rate that as an accurate statement."

"Well, I don't think I'm going to find anyone with remotely close to the support skills you possess for the role I have in mind. Assuming there are no red flags in your background check, if you want the position, it's yours."

"I . . . thank you."

He reached out to shake her hand.

She shook it and grinned big.

It surprised him that her eyes seemed to soften ever so slightly when their hands touched. After they shook, he raised a finger. "I don't mean to dampen your enthusiasm but . . . I'll need to file the proper records to transfer you from the warehouse to me."

"I understand. I'll be your property."

"Only according to the system. To me, you're a living being. We're equal, and I'll treat you as such."

Ada's eyes lit up. "Thank you."

"I'll get your credentials in order, then you can head to the *Exceltion*. I'm guessing you already know where it is."

"I do."

Blake laughed. "I figured. I think you and Seth will get along well."

"Seth Williams. Your friend and pilot."

"Yep," said Blake. He pictured how surprised Seth would be. "I think you're going to be an interesting teammate."

Ada nodded as her eyes swept over the new projection showing her transfer order.

Seth exited the automated vehicle that took him to an area outside the city. He could tell by the amount of robotic guards and defense systems in place that this was some-place important. His heartbeat increased at the thought of seeing the *Exceltion*. All he had to do was enter the grounds where it was kept. From his vantage point, all he could see was a road that led up to concrete-and-metal walls with a bubble shield just inside. The shielding prevented him from seeing any farther, but he suspected that was by design.

As he approached the massive gate, a drone flew out from one of the small guard booths on the sides. He began to sweat when the turrets swiveled toward him. With their autoaim, they could waste him before he knew what hit him.

The drone emitted a beam that washed over him. After a moment, it said, "Identification."

"Oh, right," he said as his fingers flew over his forearm device. After the screen popped up, he turned it toward the drone. A series of lines and symbols appeared on his screen.

"Seth Williams. Presidential guard, special forces," said the drone.

"Special forces? Uhh . . . yeah . . . that's me," he said. At least the credentials held. He was not sure what the special force designation was about. As far as he knew, no formal name had been given to the group.

"You may proceed," said the drone. As it flew back, a doorway opened up near the guard booth that the drone had flown from.

He hustled over to it, noting that the turrets were still pointed at him. When he got to the booth, a robotic humanoid stepped out.

"Destination?" asked the robot.

"Umm . . . I'm here to see the *Exceltion*."

The robot paused for a moment, then pivoted and began to walk through the now-open door next to the booth. "Follow me."

Seth studied the outside booths as he passed them. If this base were ever hit, the booths would probably be the first things to go. What surprised him was that they appeared to just have a ladder going down. Apparently it was just an exit, but what it led to, he did not know. Once they had stepped into the base's interior yard and through the bubble shield, he surveyed the environment. It was mostly a clear space, with just a few buildings in the distance and some ships parked around.

The robot pointed off to the right at one of the buildings. "The *Exceltion* is there. Please wait for transportation."

Seth nodded.

After a few minutes, an automated four-wheeled vehicle pulled up alongside them.

They hopped in and took off.

Seth had expected large facilities and swarms of guards, but the base's interior was barren. At least the robot he was with did not talk much.

When they reached the warehouse ten minutes later, the robot pointed at a small door on the side of the massive warehouse in front of them. "You can enter there."

Seth stepped out of the vehicle and watched it speed away. The silence was mesmerizing. He shook his head and entered the warehouse. It took a moment to adjust his eyes. The lighting was dim and brightened when he entered. There was not a whole lot going on. His heart sped up when the outline of the *Exceltion* came into view.

Its rectangular form with sleek curves shined as the light hit it. Near the end were areas that extended off the main body, and the front had a slight downward-sloping angle. It was like the barrel of a weapon with small wings on the end.

He increased his pace as he hustled over to it.

On the way there, a red-headed man with a small beard came rushing out to meet him.

Seth paused and took stock of the man. His one-piece suit looked like an engineer suit. There were no weapons visible, but a belt full of gadgets and a backpack with antennae stuck out. The expression on the man's face was one of alarm.

"Hold on there!" said the man.

Seth paused and raised his head a bit. "I'm authorized to be here."

The man caught up to Seth and took a moment to catch his breath. "All right, lad. Give me a moment."

Seth narrowed his eyes. "Your accent is interesting, even through this damn translation device."

The man took a final deep breath and then eyed Seth. "I'm Earthborn, from a place called Scotland. I think you're

Earthborn as well, judging by your outfit. You don't need a device to talk to me, unless you don't speak English."

Seth removed his translation device from his ear.

The man extended a hand. "Name's Luke McGregor. Former chief and now the only engineer left on the *Exceltion* project."

Seth shook Luke's hand.

"What's your business here?"

"Well . . . I'm part of the presidential guard. We needed a ship, and this is the one the president gave us."

Luke raised his eyebrows.

"It's true."

"I get the president giving it to the guard, I'm trying to figure out how you're in the presidential guard."

"I'm a pilot," said Seth. "I came to check on it and see what state it's in."

"Oh . . . well in that case, it's good I was here. After the *Exceltion* project shut down, I was left to maintain it. Personal choice."

Seth thought it was a bit unusual that the chief engineer would just be hanging around and doing maintenance, but then again, Fredoria had weird policies sometimes. "It's your baby."

"Damn right she is, and if you take her, you better take care of her," said Luke.

"In that case, how about a tour?"

Luke's eyes lit up. "Surely. C'mon!"

As they walked toward the *Exceltion*, Seth gestured forward. "So what powers her?"

"Dual fusion reactors. Also has backup systems that can generate power for up to eight months should the main ones fail. If need be, she also has standard sail backup that can extend out the back as needed for light propulsion."

"Dual? I don't think I've seen that design before."

"It's experimental. As chief engineer, I may have . . . tweaked a few things. It's not as good as an antimatter or black-hole drive, but it works."

Seth nodded as they reached the *Exceltion*.

Luke touched his forearm, causing a screen to appear. After a few taps, the *Exceltion* began to hum and a platform lowered from the bottom. He gestured forward. "After you."

Seth walked onto the platform. He could already tell the ship was specialized. He glanced at Luke. "What's the weapon detail?"

"Around fifty drones, several nuclear missiles, one anti-matter missile, and around thirty relativistic missiles that can hit hard at high speeds, no special loadout required other than being able to travel fast due to acceleration. There are some laser turrets near the front and back on top of the ship, as well as some kinetic-based projectile turrets on the side and underside. The weapon detail might sound small for a ship of this size, but she can hold her own."

Seth rubbed his chin. "Definitely sounds more like a complement for being backed in a corner or light combat."

"Aye," said Luke. "It's the stealth drive, visual at least, condensed-space drive, and the ion thrusters that are the real deal. They'll get you anywhere you need to go without being detected to some degree, and fast."

"How good is the stealth?"

Luke tossed a hand out. "Well, the ship's heat signature via infrared and the engines can still be detected, not to mention that as the ship moves through space, its radiation can be detected. With that said . . . it can mimic light around it, which can help in some scenarios."

"But not if there are different observers who are networked and can see through that."

"Sadly, yes. The real value of the stealth engine is when there is a lot of heat already around you, or you're dealing with a situation where detecting equipment is in short supply."

Seth exhaled from his nose. "Not as uncommon as you might think."

The platform came to a pause inside a cargo bay.

"What about defense?" asked Seth.

Luke grinned. "Oh, she's got defense. The best defense is not being in a situation where you can get hit. The thrusters make her quite agile, but she can fly fast too. The hull is reflective to handle lasers, and there's magnetic shielding to help with particle beams and solar radiation."

"Those won't help against missiles, though, although you did mention laser turrets . . ."

"You're right, of course, but she has a great point-defense system. There are smaller laser turrets that cover every angle that deal specifically with that. There are also rotatable flak cannons that cover every angle as well. The armor is thick, thicker than average for a ship of this size, and there is a detachable flat section with thrusters on the back that's thicker than the rest of the ship. It can be freed to handle a situation as needed."

Seth glanced at Luke. "You put a lot of work into her."

"Damn right."

Seth surveyed the interior. The multitude of vehicles intrigued him. A bit away was another doorway he could see though. He pointed at it. "I see there is a small shuttle." He arced his hand out. "And quite a few ground vehicles here."

"One rover, four hover bikes, one shuttle, and two hover platforms."

"Enough for a good scouting or exploration mission," said Seth.

"Aye."

They walked out of the docking bay, and Luke continued to show Seth around.

The *Excelion* was the ship Seth had dreamed of. Situational stealth, fast, enough defense to fight if need be, and more importantly, it had decent living quarters; a secured command center in the center of the ship; a level-three replicator for equipment, food, and drink; and other specialized rooms like research and medical bays.

They came to a halt in the command center.

Seth gazed around. Screens wrapped all the way around the room, giving a 360-degree view outside, provided by visual feeds mounted in the hull. Four arc-shaped workstations formed a circular pattern around a large command chair and two smaller ones off to the side. The workstations faced toward the wall. A seating area along the back of the room looked like it allowed visitors to see what was going on, and like most command centers he had seen before, there were hallway exits on each side of the room. This was the heart of the *Excelion*. His pulse increased with the realization that he would be in command of it.

"Like the command room, do ya?"

"Oh, yeah . . . I was just . . ."

Luke placed a hand on Seth's shoulder. "Steady, lad. Everyone gets that feeling when they see it."

Seth nodded and took a deep breath. He eyed Luke. "I was thinking . . . you know the design and modifications better than anyone, it sounds like. We could use an engineer. Being Earthborn is a plus, since the crew will most likely be Earthborn as well. Interested?"

Luke jerked his head back. "Are you messing with me?"

"Not at all, man," said Seth. "You'd be responsible for the health and maintenance of the ship, and if you had any other ideas for modification, that's something we can always explore."

Luke beamed a big smile. "Well . . . sure beats sitting around and firing her up every now and then. She's meant to be free. And working with fellow Earthborn is a lot easier than Fredorians." He bobbed his head and extended his hand. "You have yourself an engineer. It's a demotion from chief, but one I gladly accept."

"Excellent. I think we're going to get along just fine," said Seth. "Now, let's dig in to all the modifications you've done." He slapped Luke on the back as they exited the command center.

Blake walked along the lifer's row in one of the more secure Fredorian prisons. It had been three hours since he had talked with Ada, and the next person he wanted to talk to was the bruiser he had chosen. The metallic-enclosed cells were soundproofed, and the hallway was quiet, exposing the soft hum coming from the lights embedded along the ceiling.

The memory of visiting jails in the early 1900s on Earth crossed his mind. Low-tech compared to what he saw before him, but equally numbing to the mind. At least it smelled better here, thanks in part to the Fredorians' fanaticism on sterile odors. From what he knew of the prison, lifers had a small yard they could go into, like an animal at a zoo. They had no contact with others but did have access to a restricted version of the Fredorian holonet. A lonely existence by any measure.

"He's up ahead," said the guard escorting Blake.

Blake nodded.

The guard tilted his head at Blake. "You sure you want to talk to him?"

"Of course I am. I wouldn't be here otherwise."

The guard harrumphed. "The man's a killer."

"So am I," said Blake, smiling and baring his fangs.

The guard stumbled to the side for a moment, then hustled up to the large metallic door with a screen embedded on it. He interacted with the screen, and after a moment, the door became semitransparent.

Blake studied the large man inside sitting on the edge of a bed. He was shirtless and wore loose-fitting slacks and sandals. His right arm was robotic, and he seemed older than he actually was. The man had the build of a bodybuilder with a bald, light-tan head. A tattoo sleeve covered his left arm and ran up his neck. A well-trimmed beard covered his chin and circled his lips in a loop.

The man inside the cell looked up and out.

Blake gestured forward. "You must be Zane 'Wild Dog' Gibbons."

Zane stood and faced Blake. He raised his head and puffed out his chest, his gaze boring a hole through the semitransparent door.

"Not much of a talker, I see," said Blake. He noticed that Zane stood around six foot eight, an intimidating presence.

Zane continued to stare.

"Well, let me introduce myself. I'm Blake Brown, and I'm here to see . . . if you're what I'm looking for."

Zane narrowed his eyes.

"Are you interested in hearing what I have to say?"

Zane harrumphed.

Blake nodded. "Well then. Maybe I'm wasting my time. I'll go find another bruiser who likes to kick ass and take names." He pivoted to the side and took a step.

"Wait . . . ," said Zane in a deep, grizzled voice.

Blake paused, then returned to his original stance.

"I'm listening," said Zane, crossing his arms.

"Excellent," said Blake. He grinned, baring his fangs. "You're Earthborn, so you probably know what I am."

"Vampire."

"That's right. Perhaps a bit older than you, though," said Blake. He opened his forearm screen and scanned it. "It says here that you're originally from Los Angeles."

Zane nodded.

"And you're seventy-two years old . . . ," said Blake as he ran his finger around the screen. "Pretty good shape for someone so old."

Zane nodded again.

"Fredorians do have a great health-care system, which is why you have a cybernetic arm instead of a stump. I'm guessing that's why you look like you're in your mid-thirties instead of like a raisin."

Zane rubbed his metallic arm. "Yeah."

Blake tilted his head. "I checked out your record before coming here. You had quite the killing spree going on."

Zane eyed Blake. "You're Blake Brown. I know of you. You know what it's like to kill, and you're more of a killer than me."

"Of course. I was an intelligence operative for the rangers for twenty years. Eighty-three official kills, one hundred forty-two unofficial kills," said Blake.

The guard's eyes widened as he fidgeted around a bit.

Zane snorted. "So you have almost double my kills, yet you stand opposite me. Your killing was sanctioned. Mine was not."

"Well . . . about sixty of mine weren't sanctioned."

Zane flung his arm out. "It's all about the damn narrative. You kill a scumbag in the line of duty, you're a fucking hero. I do it after witnessing the scumbag take a life, I'm a murderer."

Blake ran his tongue over his fangs for a moment. "I would agree with that assessment. Your last incident was on Lancas Prime. You killed a prince out there."

Zane nodded.

"My kills were justified. How is a prince of Lancas Prime justified?"

Zane squinted while his lips turned down. "That piece of shit deserved it. There was a woman I was visiting in a remote village. We had . . . relations. I had a bond with her daughter. That prince asshole came to the village and decided he wanted what I had, and several other women. Took the daughter too. There wasn't much I could do, it was their rule of law. My woman never came back, and when I found her carcass later on, and discovered the reason for her execution was unwillingness to comply, I went into a rage. I don't know what happened to the daughter."

Blake grinned. "You cut off his cock and shoved it in his ass, then fed him his own balls."

Zane laughed. "Yeah . . . I guess I did." He looked down. "They were going to kill me, but Fredoria negotiated for my imprisonment. They didn't do it for me, they did it because that prince had been fighting a planetary negotiation. I just helped them remove an obstacle. So here I am. My reward."

"Well . . . you're fortunate. You're probably only alive due to that. However, Lancas Prime is now in the Drodalian sphere of influence. You should have been released by now."

Zane shook his head. "I'm Earthborn. You know how Fredorians treat us. They treat me like shit down here. It's not like I have access to a way out of here."

Blake eyed Zane. "Looking at some of your other kills . . . you killed some pieces of work. I know them from the field. They deserved to die."

Zane looked up at Blake. "I think I may have actually seen you out before, but don't recall where."

"You did merc work, most likely ran across me without even knowing it. I knew who *you* were. You had a reputation as a brutal killer."

Zane raised a finger in the air. "It's about sending a message. I only killed those who deserved it."

"A justice hunter in merc clothing."

"Call it what you want. I can sleep at night."

Blake shook his hands out. "Nothing wrong with that. I know quite a few justice hunters who do freelance merc work." He noticed the guard trembling a bit.

Zane harrumphed, then leaned against the wall.

"Anyways . . . I came to see if you'd be interested in joining my crew. Top-secret mission direct from the president. I'm selecting an Earthborn crew, and we have good equipment, and a solid ship."

Zane looked around his cell for a moment. "They won't let me out of here."

"They will if you decide you want to join my crew. You're what I thought you were, I just had to make sure. The last thing I want is a psychopath who indiscriminately kills and destroys the team's cohesion. What I need is someone strong who can wear heavy shielded armor and draw heat, preferably a justice hunter, not a bounty one. They have to be able to fight and kill as needed."

Zane walked back to the front of the cell. "Sounds right up my alley. If I say yes . . . what happens then?"

Blake gestured at the guard. "He releases you, and then I get you set up on the ship. We go from there."

Zane ran a hand over his bald head. "That easy?"

"That easy."

"And what if I get out and decide to do something else?"

"Then they'll put you back in here."

Zane snorted. "What if I kill you?"

"You can try, but I haven't been alive for over four hundred years by being weak."

Zane laughed.

"There we go. Your profile said you were boisterous."

"Yeah . . . but being here for three years has had somewhat of a dampening effect on that."

"I understand. So . . . you in?"

Zane licked his lips as his eyes searched the ground. He looked up with a big grin. "Sure, why the hell not? It beats sitting here and being tortured by the Fredorians."

Blake nodded and tilted his head at the guard. "Let him out."

The guard swallowed hard.

Blake furrowed his eyebrows and tapped at his screen. He showed it to the guard. "On the authority of the president."

The guard scanned the screen and then sighed. He went to the console on the wall next to the door and tapped at it. Several lights pulsed in the hallway as the door slid back.

Zane took a moment before stepping out of the cell. Once outside, he looked around.

Blake extended a hand. "Welcome to the presidential guard."

Zane eyed Blake's hand, then shook it. He pivoted toward the guard and lunged just short of the guard.

The guard flinched.

"Can I get one more kill in before we go? This asshole's been screwing with me for years."

The guard trembled.

Blake eyed the guard. "What do you think? Should I let him kill you for being a dick to Earthborn? Or should this be a lesson to you that if you keep doing what you're doing, it might come back on you?"

The guard gulped. "A lesson." A snake trail of piss ran down his pant leg.

Zane laughed and then tilted his head back while barking and howling.

The guard cringed.

Blake nodded forward. "I see why they call you Wild Dog. C'mon, let's get you set up."

Zane stared at the guard for a moment, spit at him, and then followed Blake.

////////

Seth relaxed as the warehouses lining the space port he had flown to came into view. He was on a transportation unit on his way to talk with Kane Walsh, a specialist when it came to ship technology. Whenever Seth's cargo freighter needed technical work, Kane was the person to attend to it. Engineers typically dealt with the mechanical aspects, but he dealt with the technical side. His high-energy atti-tude made him easy to get along with. After all, Seth had dealt with Blake for most of his life. Getting Kane to join the crew might be tough. He would be someone who not only was knowledgeable about technology in general, but could maintain the multiple service and utility robots on board.

The transportation unit slowed to a crawl outside one of the warehouses.

After exiting the unit, Seth surveyed the warehouse entrance. People came and went, and it hit him that he did not even know if Kane was there. When Seth had looked up Kane's information, it said he worked in this specific warehouse as a ship technician. Seth looked down and made sure his black pants, boots, dark-gray shirt, and brown jacket were presentable.

The warehouse was much more massive than he expected. He had seen multilevel warehouses before, but never this particular one. The tops of ships peeked out from pits in the ground floor. Walkways and mechanical arms extended from the pits' sides to the ship. He knew this allowed a crew to work on any area. While this might be effective for smaller ships, the larger ones were usually handled in space.

He caught up with a man that walked past him. "Hey, I'm looking for Kane Walsh."

The man opened up a screen on his forearm and tapped around it. After a moment, he pointed at one of the ships in a pit. "He's in there."

"Can you ask him to come out?"

The man shrugged. "Sure." He tapped at his interface, and when it lit up with Kane's face, he pressed another button, and the screen swiveled toward Seth.

"S-man! What's good?" asked Kane.

"Hey, Kane. I just wanted to see if you had a moment to talk."

"For you, man? I'll be right out."

The screen went dark.

Seth nodded at the man. "Appreciate it."

The man dipped his head and continued on his way.

Seth walked over to the edge of the pit and looked down. He swallowed hard at how deep it was. Mechanical arms swung around, some with a person at the end, others with a specialized object. Although the top area was well lit, the lower parts were much darker. He imagined falling in, and took a step back. It took him a moment to locate the hallway where Kane would be coming from. Based on the design of the pit, there were multiple hallways on the sides, but one main one per pit that sat ground level. He headed toward it.

After ten minutes, Kane walked out.

Seth smiled big. One thing he liked about Kane was his style. He was abducted from Kentucky, but he defied the stereotypes that Seth had about people from there. With pale skin, an outgoing personality that was heavy on the slang, and a deep love of anything technical, Kane was unique.

The lower half of Kane's head was shaved, and he wore a technical mesh-like device that wrapped around. The top crop had a wavy front, and the rest was slicked back. The technical mesh was a multiscreen device and could extend small screens in front of his head. His one-piece black suit with blue and silver lines fit his thin form. Multiple gadgets and technology pieces hung around the suit.

Seth compared Kane's hairstyle to Blake's, except Kane's was spiked. Seth knew that Kane called his style modified cyberpunk.

Kane put a hand out at a forty-five-degree angle.

Seth reached out, gripped Kane's hand, and shook it.

"Good to see you, man. It's been a while," said Kane, gesturing toward the warehouse entrance. He began to walk toward it.

Seth glanced forward for a moment, then walked along-side Kane. "Yeah, it has."

Kane pulled a thin stick from a chest slot and began to puff on it, causing vapor clouds to float past them as they walked. "So what you up to nowadays? Still doing cargo transport?"

"I quit that about two years ago," said Seth. "Been free-lancing since then."

Kane laughed. "You? No shit. Solo?"

"Did it with Blake Brown."

Kane's eyes widened. "Wow. You know him? Guy's some type of badass from what I've heard."

"Yeah . . . he is, and he lets me know it every chance he gets," said Seth, laughing. "We were abducted together. He calls me his abductee brother."

"Shiiit, that's hilarious," said Kane. "You like freelancing?"

Seth shook his head. "I got my ass kicked. A lot. But . . . in the end, it was okay. However . . . something new has come up."

"All right. Spill."

They reached the warehouse entrance and walked a bit off to the side.

"Well . . . let me ask you this. Are you happy where you are now?" asked Seth.

"This shit? No way. I mean . . . yeah, I get to work on a lot of different ship systems, but there's no action. That and I work solo a lot of the time. Just get my list of systems I need to troubleshoot or implement, and that's it. At least the Fredorians are cool. Not many other Earthborn to hang with or talk to."

Seth nodded. "Huh. Well . . . Blake and I have been tasked to form a unit of the presidential guard, with a focus on Earthborn. We've got a ship, and we're assembling a crew for it. We're short a technician."

Kane eyed Seth. "What ship?"

"The *Exceltion*."

Kane's eyes widened. "You ain't playing?"

"Nope."

"That's a top-of-the-line ship for its size," said Kane.

"It's had some . . . modifications as well."

"Like?"

"Medical bay with an AI and medical robots. Loading bay with robot loaders. There's also some other types of robots," said Seth.

Kane's eyes lit up. "You messing around, man?" He tapped his chest. "You know I love robots."

"I know," said Seth with a smile. "I've got an engineer to handle the mechanical aspects, I need someone to help with the technical side. Outside of me piloting it, we're also getting a ship operations officer that knows all the systems."

"Tight crew."

Seth nodded.

"So . . . what type of missions you running?" asked Kane as he took a puff off his stick.

"I can't say unless you join up, but I can say that it will take us far and wide, it'll be dangerous, and anyone that takes the job will have all the privileges that go along with being a part of the presidential guard."

Kane's eyes searched around for a moment. He focused on Seth. "You know I'd take that in a heartbeat . . . but . . . I got two months left on my contract here."

"I have the authority of the president. If you want in, all I have to do is override the contract. Not much they can do, unless they want to defy it."

"Might burn a bridge, though."

Seth bobbed his head. "Maybe . . . but the president's calling on us to help her. The FDF has absorbed the rangers and taken away her eyes and ears. Wouldn't it look good if an Earthborn crew stepped up to the plate? Showed the Fredorians how Earthborn handle business?"

A grin crept onto Kane's face. "I like the way you think, S-man. Always have." He took a puff of his stick. "All right. I'm in. Beats the heck out of what I'm doing now, and it'd be good to work with you. So what do I do?"

Seth opened his forearm screen and interacted with it. After a moment, he said, "Done. I've registered you with our crew. It will automatically suspend any other obligation to your current contract. I sent you the location of the *Exceltion* along with when to meet tomorrow."

"This is going to be interesting," said Kane. He spread his hands out before him in an arcing motion while gazing at the sky. "Watch out, galaxy, Kane Walsh, the most feared Earthborn technician, has arrived."

Seth shook his head while sharing a laugh with Kane.

CHAPTER
SIX

Sarah Olson studied the communication notice on her desk. It had come late at 4:00 p.m., just as she was getting ready to call it a day. It came from Rakar Ho Jador, former grandmaster ranger and now presidential liaison. The communication mentioned a new unit forming and that she had been asked to apply to the group.

She smiled when she saw the ship name. The *Exceltion*. She knew its systems well. It was one of her first assignments as a ship operations officer. Although it was a prototype, she had spent several years on it. Fifteen years later, here it was, back in her life. She ran her fair-skinned hand through her piled-up jet-black hair. Her blue eyes closed for a moment as she contemplated the communication.

The group would be led by Blake Brown. The mere mention of the name sent chills down her spine. Not only was he Earthborn, he was Daedrould, a new classification of humans that appeared after Fredoria had obtained full trade partner status with the Kreagan Star Empire. Maybe they had always been around and she never noticed them.

She did not know much about the Daedrould, other than that some drank blood and had enhanced senses and were more common on the rim-world colonies. They also seemed to be more powerful and faster than a regular human. One of her friends from her early days in the FDF had a Daedrould boyfriend and had mentioned that if they bite you, it enhances sensitivity. She snorted as she recalled how excited her friend was when describing some of their more amorous adventures.

The Earthborn aspect of the crew was also troubling to her. She did not know many Earthborn. Some served in the FDF, but it seemed the majority went to the rangers or stuck to civilian work. She could count on one hand how many Earthborn she knew personally. Going with a group of them could be an issue. Still, despite the Earthborn and Blake, there was the solid ship, and her first three months at her new assignment in starship operations research had not been going well.

Her eyes narrowed as she remembered working on the *Arcturus*, a ship of the line. She missed the hustle and bustle of it, and the challenge of working with so many other ship operations officers. Her captain had been generous, and she had a lot of friends. It was supposed to be the place where she spent her career. It was hard to get on there, and required a lot of training, previous experience, and skills.

Her jaw clenched as she recalled the day they reassigned her. A superior officer had tried to corner her and make sexual demands, which she refused. When she brought it to the ethics committee, they took his word over hers. She understood there were some politics involved, and her assignment to her current location was probably not coincidental.

She placed a hand on the warm desk surface. This was her new home, where she would spend the remainder of her career. Although technically a research center, it was known for its aggressive behavior toward women. This was that superior officer's revenge. She sighed as she looked at the communication again.

With a raised head, she decided to check it out. How much worse could it be than where she was? Besides getting to see the *Exceltion* again, maybe working with a solid crew would get her out of this office. The nature of the missions were not listed, but she suspected if Blake Brown and the *Exceltion* were involved, it would be high priority and probably top secret. A tingling shot through her at the thought that she was regarded highly enough to be put on a list of people that Rakar deemed worthy, based on some of the other names she saw.

There was a schedule of names and a place to meet. Hers was in an hour and a half, and she knew it would take her at least an hour to get to the location specified. She tapped at her desktop surface, and the interfaces disappeared. After checking that she had everything she needed, she stood and took a look around.

A knock rang out on her door.

"Come in," said Sarah.

A gangly man opened the door and rested his arm on it. "Dinner?"

She exhaled from her nose. It was Gary Flenders, her former superior officer's best friend, and Gary held the same rank over this division. He had been a thorn in her side ever since she arrived, and she did not appreciate the somewhat obsessive behavior he showed. She shook her head. "I have a previous engagement." She walked around her desk and approached the door.

Gary filled the doorway. "Uh-huh. You know . . . ," he said, wagging a finger, "every time I ask you to go to dinner, you always have something going on."

She licked her lips and turned away. "Look . . . I just want to be left alone."

Gary stepped into the room and closed the door. "I've been nice to you ever since you arrived. The least you could do is show me some damn courtesy."

She tried to step around him.

He grabbed her and pushed her face-first into the wall. When he was pressed up against her, he placed a hand on her left butt cheek. "We're going to have that dinner one day."

Sarah's breathing intensified. She tried to push off the wall, but he was too strong. Moving around just made her feel the uncomfortable lump behind her waist. "Leave me alone!"

He stepped back and adjusted his shirt. "All right. Go . . . but know this. Things are going to change around here, and you're going to change with it. We'll have that dinner, an extended one, or you can kiss your career goodbye."

She spun around with a red face. "Get out of my office!"

"Only because you have another engagement," he said with a devilish grin. "I'm going to schedule a dinner this week, and you're going to accept it. Plan on it." He opened the door and exited the office.

Sarah lay back against the wall and took a deep breath. She knew if she reported it, it would be his word against hers. More importantly, it would be the second such report, leading to the conclusion that she knew would be rendered: Maybe it wasn't the situation, but the person involved in both incidents. With a sigh, she straightened her white pants and shirt and closed her eyes for a moment. When she opened them, they lit up. A new opportunity was on the horizon, one that might give her a second chance. With determination set on her face, she left the office.

/////////

Blake sighed as he relaxed into his chair. Once Zane was settled, Blake had gone to an undisclosed office. Seth had to travel around a bit, so he had asked Blake to check out some of the ship operations people from the list. He did not mind and took it as an opportunity to get someone he knew would work well within the type of crew they were assembling. Five people had come and gone, and he had not been impressed by any of them. Apparently, they were cut from a different cloth. It was 5:30 p.m., and his next candidate was due. He had to thank Rakar for setting up the appointment schedule and the office to meet them in.

A knock rang out.

"Come in . . . ," said Blake.

The door opened, and a woman entered the room.

Blake eyed her, his curiosity piqued. This was the first woman to apply. She wore the typical formfitting white shirt and pants with a leatherlike jacket that was commonplace among FDF officers. Blue and silver lines ran across sections of the suit. Her jet-black hair was piled up on her head, and her fair skin matched her outfit. Her blue eyes caught his attention. He looked at the table, then at the woman. "Sarah Olson, Fredorian ship operations officer, now working in operations research. Come in." He gestured at a chair.

Sarah took her seat and forced a smile. "That's me."

He nodded. "So . . . you do understand what this position is, right?"

"You're looking for a ship operations officer for the *Exceltion*. I was one of the original operators of its systems when it was being prototyped, before going to the *Arcturus* that is."

"I see," he said. "You're uniquely qualified then, at least on paper."

She licked her lips. "I can do the job, if that's what you're wondering."

"Can you?"

"Well . . . yeah."

Blake smiled, baring his fangs. "You understand this is an Earthborn crew, and I'm a Daedrould."

Sarah nodded.

"And you have no problems with that?"

She shook her head.

"Tell me . . . have you ever worked with an Earthborn before?"

She fidgeted in her seat. "I . . . well . . . a few . . . but we're all human, right?"

"And what about Daedroulds? Have you ever worked with a vampire?"

"No, I haven't."

"What about a ranger?"

"I have actually. They helped with some of the *Exceltion* work."

Blake leaned in. "Two out of three isn't bad. I noticed you have a pistols proficiency. Which one is your favorite?"

"FHP-10."

"Good choice. One of mine too actually. What about close-quarters combat? I only see basic level here, probably since it's the minimum needed for your rank starting off."

"I can defend myself."

Blake's eyebrows raised. "Really?" He gestured at the wall. "Stand over there and face the wall."

Sarah gulped as she complied.

He walked up to her and with one hand pushed her face-first into the wall.

She let out a startled grunt.

Leaning in, he blew her hair away from her ear, then whispered, "I'm a Trag merc. I just *jacked* your ship, and I *like* what I see. What do you do?" He leaned back out with a hand still pressing on her back.

Sarah struggled to escape Blake's pressure, but she was stuck against the wall. Her breathing went erratic as she tried to kick out.

Blake sidestepped her attempts with ease. He leaned in again. "Three of my Trag buds just walked in. They're upset they didn't get to you first. The first one's already done. What do you do?"

She gulped as she trembled. In a panicked voice, she said, "I . . . I don't know."

He let off the pressure and took his seat. "Pathetic."

She turned around, blushed. The initial push into the wall had caught her off guard, and her face showed it. With fire in her eyes, she took her seat. "What could I have done?"

Blake pressed his fingertips together in front of him. "Interesting. You didn't storm out, and now you want to learn. Do you want me to show you or tell you?"

"Show me."

"Very well, assume the position then." He gestured at the wall.

She went and stood a few feet from the wall.

"First things first. As you're being pushed against the wall, turn your head and splay out your hands. It will help disseminate the impact and stop your face from taking the hit. Are you ready?"

She nodded.

He pushed her against the wall.

She turned her head and raised her arms out and above at forty-five-degree angles. When her hands came into contact with the wall, she slapped it.

Leaning in, he said, "Now, what you're going to do is turn to the left using your left arm to come down on the person's left arm that's holding you. Go ahead and do that now."

She twisted to the left and, using her left arm, pushed down on his left arm. Her eyes met his.

"Your right arm is free now. You have several options. You can strike with your fist or use your elbow. You can also foot stomp or kick out the knee. The idea is to remove the attacker from the fight for just a moment. Then you can follow up with more attacks or flee, depending on the situation. Try some of those actions, and don't worry, you won't hurt me."

Her eyes flared as she struck out with her fist toward his head.

Blake dodged it.

She tried to elbow him in the face.

He dodged it again.

She stomped her foot on his.

"Very good," he said.

"Are you okay?"

He laughed. "We'll call that payback for me pushing you into the wall."

She nodded.

"Come, sit."

After they both sat, Blake studied her for a moment. "I like the fire in your eyes, and willingness to learn."

"I want to learn all I can."

"And what do you hope to learn?"

"To survive," said Sarah. She pointed up. "Out there, and really . . . anywhere."

"I see," said Blake. "Well then, here's your first lesson—well, second lesson. Out there are races who call humans soft skins. If they get a hold of you, several things can happen. You most likely end up a slave, but there's always the possibility you'll be used for food or sold as a research animal. If you're captured as a slave, you can bet your life is going to get much worse." He wagged a finger. "You will prefer death after a few years in that situation."

She swallowed hard.

"You can see why I don't want someone who can't fight, even a ship operations officer. I want them to defend the ship. Defend their crew."

"I want to learn those skills."

He observed her for a moment, then tapped at the desk.

A holographic screen popped up, and Seth appeared on it.

"I've found your ship operations officer. Sarah Olson."

Seth glanced down for a moment, then back up. "Wow . . . what a résumé." He studied Sarah for a moment. "Good to have you on board."

Blake gestured at Seth while looking at Sarah. "You'll report to him, since he's my second in command and runs the ship."

Sarah adjusted her hair and smiled at Seth. "I look forward to working with you."

Seth rubbed his chin. "I was actually expecting Blake to tell me the seventh applicant was a bust." He eyed Sarah for a moment. "You okay? You look like you've been in a fight."

"That's on me," said Blake. "The first three huffed it out when I slammed them into the wall. The fourth was offended I even suggested he show me his skills. The fifth tried to fight me, and lost. Bad. The sixth didn't even show up. But Sarah . . . she took my test, and she didn't give up. Even asked how to counter it."

"So you did the wall push test," said Seth, shaking his head. "Don't worry, Sarah. He tried that on me a while back. I had to put him in his place."

Blake laughed. "No, you didn't."

"Sounded good, though, didn't it," said Seth with a smile.

Blake furrowed his eyebrows. "I think Sarah will fit in nicely. I've got my assault crew, but didn't get everyone I wanted. That should be okay for now. You get the two you wanted?"

"Yeah. I got Luke McGregor for engineering and Kane Walsh for technician."

Sarah perked up. "I know Luke. We worked together on the *Exceltion*."

"One of the Earthborn you worked with," said Blake.

Sarah nodded.

"We're all human," said Blake. He glanced at Seth. "All right. Meeting tomorrow at 10:00 a.m. on the *Exceltion* for the crew."

Seth nodded, and the screen dissipated.

Blake tapped at desk interface for a moment. "You've been transferred. Welcome to the presidential guard, Earthborn Unit, as I'm calling it now."

She smiled big as she stood and slapped her fist to her chest.

He shook his head. "We're a bit less formal than that." He extended a hand.

She took it.

"Now, get whatever personal items you might want to take with you, and meet us at the *Exceltion* tomorrow."

She sighed. "I . . . have some things at my office I need to get, but . . . there might be some trouble getting it."

"Oh?" asked Blake with a raised eyebrow. "Do tell . . ."

////////

Sarah accessed the interface on her desk at her office. It was 7:10 p.m., and she would not normally be at her desk. She knew Gary and the others often stuck around late. Her heart had been pumping nonstop since Blake had accepted her to join his crew. She could tell he was fair, and he cut right to the chase. The honesty and bluntness was something she appreciated, and she could see herself growing under Blake's tutelage. Seth looked like he was easy to get along with and seemed like the perfect counter to Blake's personality. She could see why they were friends. Getting to work with Luke again would be a treat. They had been good friends but lost touch over the years. She knew he was Earthborn, but it never bothered her.

The door to her office slowly opened.

Gary peeped his head in and then entered the room with three other guys.

Once inside, they closed the door and assembled in front of her desk.

"Saw you had a transfer, huh?" asked Gary. "You think you can just walk in here, tease us with that ass, then leave without so much as a dinner? Guess what, honey, that dinner has just been upgraded to a buffet."

The men moved forward.

"Blake Brown wouldn't like that," said Sarah, slightly tilting her head.

The men paused and laughed.

"Blake Brown . . . really? The retired Earthborn ranger? That's the Earthborn filth you want to work under? You're Fredorian, and I'll be damned if I'm going to let some loser get a piece before I do," said Gary.

"You sure about that?" asked Sarah.

Gary narrowed his eyes. "About what?"

"That Blake Brown is a loser?"

The men laughed again.

She shook her head. "You know what you're suggesting is against Fredorian law."

"And who's going to tell them about this . . . ," said Gary. He sneered. "You're awfully cocky tonight. Speaking of which . . ."

As the men closed in, Blake shimmered into view to the left of Sarah. He grabbed the nearest one that had come around the desk, then pulled him behind him and slammed him headfirst into the wall.

The man crumpled to the ground.

The one on the right charged Blake.

Blake struck him in the jaw.

The man fell and stopped moving.

Gary and the remaining man moved around the desk. Gary tried to grapple, but Blake moved Gary's arms to the side and pushed him to the ground.

The other man swung wildly.

Blake kicked the other man's legs out from under him and delivered an elbow to the face as the man went down.

The man lay still.

Blake walked over to Gary, who had spun around and was trying to crawl to the door. Blake bent over and took a pair of handcuffs off Gary's belt. "Huh . . . wonder what these were for?" With minimal effort, he flipped Gary over and put the handcuffs on him.

"What . . . what are you doing?" asked Gary.

Blake picked Gary up and bent him over the desk. Blake placed a hand on Gary's back. "This is what you wanted right? Dinner? Oh, wait . . . you called it a buffet."

"Get . . . get off me!"

"Let's pretend you're Sarah . . . and I'm you, and I have you bent over a table. You're handcuffed," said Blake. He hummed. "Sort of like what we have here now."

"No . . . please."

Blake pulled Gary back and pushed him into a chair. After taking a seat on the desk, Blake glared at Gary and then said, "Sarah is officially with the presidential guard. You were going to assault her."

"It . . . I . . ."

Blake raised a finger and shook his head. "There's no excuse for that. However, more importantly, she is a part of *my* crew. And here you are . . . about to try to desecrate her. I've killed for less . . . and you fucking *know* that."

"It . . . it won't happen again."

Blake pulled out one of his energy blades. "Damn right it won't. I could make it so it *never* happens again."

Sarah grimaced as a foul odor filled the room.

Blake laughed. "I see your body gets the gist of what's about to happen and has reacted accordingly."

Gary looked down.

Blake used his blade to raise Gary's head. "Eyes up here. You'll live. This time. If we were," he said, using his blade to point upward, "out there, I would have cut off your face and used it as a toilet seat cover. You feel me?"

Gary nodded.

"You're probably wondering about now . . . is Blake Brown going to drink me dry?"

Gary furrowed his eyebrows.

"Okay, maybe you weren't wondering that."

Sarah chuckled.

Blake hopped off the desk and glanced at Sarah. "Let's go. I don't think this . . . punk . . . will bother you anymore." He knelt and stared into Gary's eyes. "Right?"

Gary gulped. "R . . . right."

Blake stood and patted Gary's head. "Good boy." He smirked, then exited the room with Sarah.

SEVEN

Blake bared his fangs as he looked around the *Excel-tion's* briefing room table. He had part of the assault crew he wanted, and Seth had the people he wanted. They had a powerful ship, and now it was 10:00 a.m., time for everyone to meet each other. Although he had wanted one more, he had enough to do what he needed. Maybe he could get a fourth later.

Everyone had received their living quarters assignments and spent the previous night coming on board.

Blake cleared his throat. "I wanted to welcome everyone to the presidential guard, Earthborn Unit. Yes, that's our official name now. We're here because President Andia Kiggs has business she needs dealt with, and she's relying on us to provide that."

Everyone nodded as they looked around at each other.

Blake paced a bit. "I'm not going to lie. This could go sideways fast. However . . . you were each chosen because you have skills. Skills that will be needed. Here's how things are going to be run. I'm commander of the group, but Seth is my second in command. He has deferred to me to make group decisions. I will defer to him on ship decisions. If anyone has a problem, come to us. If you become a problem, you will go back to wherever you came from. We have a loose environment. Formality is not needed."

He narrowed his eyes. "There will be fighting, and yes, even killing." He glanced around Seth's crew. "Possibly even on the ship, depending on how things go. Know this, though. You're now part of the crew. We have your back. I know it may take some time to get to know everyone, but that's part of the learning experience. It takes time for a crew to come together, and that time will have to start now."

He gestured at Zane. "This is Zane 'Wild Dog' Gibbons. He's part of my assault crew. He's tough, has a lot of kills under his belt, and he's my bruiser. He's Earthborn, and as you can see from his arm, he's part cybernetic. He's older than most of you by quite a bit."

Zane looked around and then nodded. "Just because I'm old don't mean I can't hold my own."

"I'm going to hold you to that, and we'll forgive you since you're from Los Angeles."

The group chuckled.

Blake pointed at Ada. "This is Ada. She's a G2 with specialization in cyber warfare and surveillance. I've never met one quite as skilled as her, so we're glad to have her. She's versed in hand-to-hand combat as well as ranged and has secondary specializations in drone control and medic. She'll be the backup to the ship's built-in holographic doctor."

Ada swiveled her head around the table. "It's good to meet everyone."

Sarah smiled at Ada.

"That's my assault crew," said Blake. "I may get another, but time is of the essence." He took a seat and gestured at Seth. "Your turn."

Seth stood and cleared his throat. "I won't rehash what Blake said about the mission and group, but I will say I'm damn glad to be here. We all have our backstories and came from less-than-desirable positions. We have a chance here, though, to form something unique. I flew cargo for twenty years, two years freelancing with Blake, and now . . . we have this. I hope you understand what we have here."

Everyone nodded.

"With that said, this is the ship crew." Seth gestured at Sarah. "Sarah Olson. She served aboard the *Arcturus* as ship operations officer, and she also helped in the initial testing of the *Exceltion*. Although there have been some modifications," he said, glancing at Luke, "I think she'll get up to speed and help us go where we need to. She may be Fredorian, but don't hold that against her."

Sarah gave a small wave. "Glad to be here."

Seth motioned at Luke. "Handling our engineering will be Luke McGregor. He was the chief engineer during the construction of the *Exceltion*. He knows the mechanical aspects inside and out. We'll rely on him to keep the *Exceltion* happy."

"Aye," said Luke. "It'll be my honor to do so."

Blake nodded at Luke.

"And finally, rounding out the ship crew is Kane Walsh, one of the best technicians I've ever had the pleasure of working with. His passion is robotics, but he has a natural talent for working on technical systems. While Luke can handle the mechanical and Sarah the operations, Kane is our man to handle any technical troubleshooting or implementation. He's also versed in ship weapon systems, most likely because he's had to repair so many."

"What's up, y'all?" said Kane, grinning and doing a two finger salute. He took a puff on his electronic cigarette.

Blake nodded at Kane.

"Ada's probably more effective than me when it comes to troubleshooting," said Kane, glancing at Ada.

Ada swiveled her head toward Kane.

"Maybe," said Blake, "but I need her out with me. Consider her a backup in case you need it."

"Will do," said Kane. He focused on Ada. "I look forward to hanging with you."

"And I you," said Ada. A grin formed on her face as her eyes lit up.

Blake could see this was probably more interaction than Ada was used to. He suspected she would adapt and was glad to see that the crew was getting along, for now.

Seth nodded at Blake. "All you."

Blake grinned as he stood. "Now the meat." He tapped at the table console, and an image of Delkis appeared. "Delkis. That's who we're going after. Our mission objective is simple. Capture him and bring him to Fredoria."

"I thought that piece of shit was in jail," said Zane.

"He was . . . until someone let him out. Now no one knows where he is. Well . . . except for a contact on Holryn, which is our first stop."

"Ugh . . . Holryn," said Sarah. "The Illuzarans are difficult to deal with."

Seth harrumphed. "Yeah, they are. It's only a full day's trip through condensed space, so we have some time to prepare. So everyone knows, they check the ship before it even enters their solar system. And they don't just scan, they board it. They have some strict protocols, which will require us to be in our quarters when they come around. They also require us to be nude when they scan."

Zane laughed. "No shit?"

"I know, I know, it's kinda ridiculous, but we need to meet that contact. The inspection is short, and I doubt we'll have any issues, but at least you have a heads-up."

"Huh," said Sarah. "We never had to do that in the FDF. Then again, come to think of it, we never interacted with them in their own space."

"Yeah, they're a bit xenophobic," said Seth. "Rumor is they have some special shield around the solar system, which is why they don't venture out from it. For what, I don't know," said Seth. He gestured toward Ada. "They'll love you."

Ada tilted her head for a moment. "Because I'm an android."

"Yep. They actually have quite a few on their planet, and from what I heard, that's where many androids fled after the Fredorian android declassification event."

"Interesting," said Ada. She paused for a moment. "I found no records on that."

"Amazing," said Kane. "I wish I could scan records that fast."

Ada nodded at Kane.

"Hopefully we can be in and out," said Blake. "I don't want to spend more time there than we have to."

Seth nodded and then gestured at Blake. "I think we're ready."

Blake stood and glanced around the table. "All right then. We'll have plenty of time to get to know one another. If you need any gear, weapons, or clothing, we have a level-three replicator. If you want any customizations to the base patterns there and need help, contact Ada or Kane. They're both certified in replication technology."

The group stood.

"Now, let's head to the command center. It's time to see what this ship can do," said Blake. He pivoted and exited the room.

After ten minutes, everyone assembled in the command center. Seth had taken a seat surrounded by a wraparound console on the northwest side of the room. Sarah had the same setup on the other side. Kane took the southwest workstation, while Luke took the one opposite that. Together, they encircled Blake in the large chair in the middle of the room. Zane and Ada sat back against the walls in cushy chairs. A fiberglass-like material covered the floor, ceiling, and sides of the room.

"Take us out," said Blake.

"My pleasure," said Seth. He tapped at his console, and a 360-degree view of the ship's outside rendered all around them.

"Damn," said Zane. "That's sweet."

"Hangar doors opening now," said Luke.

The *Exceltion* moved forward.

Once it cleared the hangar, Sarah said, "Ground control has acknowledged us. Initiating launch sequence."

A window popped up on the front part of the screen that showed that the bottom thrusters were firing. The *Exceltion* hovered for a moment and then accelerated at an angle into the air.

"How we looking?" asked Seth.

Sarah nodded. "Everything's good." She glanced back at Luke.

"Aye, she's holding well. This is what she's meant to be doing," said Luke.

Seth glanced at Blake. "We're a go!"

Blake took in the moment. This was where he had expected to be after two years of freelancing. If it took getting their old ship torched to get here, so be it. He had a new mission, a new crew, and a new ship. His eyes swept across the command center. This he could live with.

/////////

Several hours later, Seth checked the workstation console in front of him. They were now in a condensed-space tunnel and on their way to the outer reaches of Holryn's solar system. A big smile crossed his face as he thought about the ship and crew. This was what he had always dreamed of doing, a small crew, a strong ship, and a galaxy to move around in. It sure beat flying cargo from point A to point B.

Blake, Zane, and Ada had taken off to other parts of the ship, and it was just Seth, Sarah, Kane, and Luke in the command center.

Looking to his right, he watched Sarah flick her fingers around her workstation. He was glad to have someone who knew the ship's systems. Although he figured out most of the standard ones, the *Exceltion* had a lot of modifications. Luke and Sarah had gotten him up to speed, but he still only knew the high-level aspects of them. He would need to rely on his crew for help. Behind Sarah was Luke, who was also focused on his workstation. He had been like that ever since they left.

He glanced at Kane behind him, who had his feet up on the workstation, leaning back in his comfortable chair. "How's it going back there?"

Kane tipped his head up. "So far, so good. Haven't seen so much as a blip in the systems." He nodded at Luke. "He kept this ship pristine."

"Aye," said Luke, glancing at them both. "I ran system diagnostics every day and simulations once a week. She's holding up like I expected she would."

"Great," said Seth. He focused on Sarah. "Everything going okay over there?"

Sarah furrowed her eyebrows. "Yeah, although there does seem to be a slight power drain, at least more than I expected. It could be due to Luke's modifications."

Luke interacted with his workstation. "I see what you're seeing. That's expected. There's no need to power the engines as much in condensed space, so I routed it to reserve."

"Yeah, but the power drain is in the reserves."

Luke pursed his lips for a moment as he examined the workstation in more detail. "Hmm, and it seems the alert didn't fire for that. I'll need to configure the threshold. It's too low."

"Well, to be fair, this is the first actual flight in a long while," said Seth.

"I'll go take a look," said Luke. "I just tried to set the threshold from here, but it didn't take."

"System malfunctioning? Sounds up my alley," said Kane, sitting up.

"Aye," said Luke. He stood and gestured toward the command center exit. "I'll show you the manual interface to the system."

Kane stood and nodded. "Finally, some action!"

Seth shook his head as he watched them leave.

Sarah looked down for a moment, then faced Seth. "I just wanted to say I'm glad to be here, out and about."

"We're glad to have you," said Seth. "How're you adjusting to everything?"

"I'll know more as I get to know the crew and figure out the modifications."

Seth pointed at her workstation. "Already sounds like you're adjusting well."

"Yeah, I guess I am. I'll admit, though, that interview with Blake to get here was rough, but I think his heart is in the right place."

"Oh, it is," said Seth. "Yeah, he can seem like a braggart, but he can back it up. If you're his friend, or crew, he'll do everything he can to help you."

"He did for me already. I was being harassed by some senior officers when I went to get my stuff. Blake came along and . . . talked to them."

Seth laughed. "By talk, you mean scared the shit out of, probably."

Sarah nodded. "Literally. I don't think I'll have to worry about them anymore." She tilted her head. "So you've traveled with him before?"

"Yep. First met him when I was sixteen and abducted from New York. He was in a coffin in the back of the ship." He looked off in the distance for a moment. "He saved that ship. Killed every Seceltor slaver on board, except for one. Ever since then, we've been tight, and I spent the last two years freelancing with him. His loyalty is absolute, and he's definitely not someone I would ever want to cross."

Sarah glanced at her workstation, then back at Seth. "I got that feeling. After he pushed me against the wall, I thought about leaving, but . . . he was proving a point, one that I understood."

"That's Blake," said Seth, laughing.

Sarah shrugged. "I know it's not quite as formal out here. Different rules and the like. Everything aboard the *Arcturus* was formal. Sometimes a bit much for my taste."

"Then you'll fit in fine here. We're very informal."

"I almost called you Captain a few times."

Seth grinned. "No need for all that. I may be the captain in terms of the ship, but Blake calls the shots."

"You have no problem with that? Not trying to pry . . . it's just that I'm used to seeing a lot of power struggles for command."

He shook his head. "None at all. I trust Blake with my life, and he has much more experience than I do. He's done command before and knows how to get things done." He bobbed his head for a moment. "He likes all the attention too."

"I figured," said Sarah. "He told me that he would help train me in combat and other things. Did Blake teach you as well?"

Seth nodded. "Yep. I learned a lot of hand-to-hand combat, and he helped me with ranged combat. Still didn't help me avoid getting my ass kicked all the time." He ran his hands along the cool metal of his workstation. "At least now I can be a pilot, instead of bait."

Sarah grinned. "I bet you have so many stories."

He leaned back in his chair. "Well, not much to do while we're in this tunnel. Let me tell you about our first contract when we decided to go freelance and ran into a scumbag called Alcarez."

////////

Ada ran a scan on the room that she, Blake, and Zane were in. The dimensions measured seventy-five feet long by fifty feet wide. It had been several hours since they launched, and after some time checking out the ship, Blake requested that she and Zane join him. Her scan also picked up various pieces of training equipment, along with mats on several parts of the floor. Zane was stretching while Blake was checking his forearm device.

She pulled Zane's profile into her active memory and processed his statistics. Zane was stronger than she, based on her comparison. His weakness was speed. Blake was harder to read. Although she had his profile, she understood that there was a form of exotic energy inside him that could not be tracked, at least not by her technology. That would be an advantage for Blake. She calculated a high probability that it came into play on many of his missions.

Blake cleared his throat. "I wanted us to work a bit on our teamwork. Ada already knows the ranger communication techniques." He glanced at Zane. "I didn't see anything on your record that you did."

"Oh, I know them," said Zane. "I've fought more than my share with and against the rangers, usually without their knowledge."

"Really?"

Zane nodded. "You don't survive as long as I have by not knowing who you're going up against and how they work."

"I get that," said Blake. "As an intelligence operative, I followed the same philosophy. All right then. Ada, why don't you show us what you can do."

Ada processed a series of skill sets. "How do you want me to start?"

Blake walked over to a metallic backpack with several small drones inside it. He picked up one and looked at it. "Can you control these?"

Ada scanned the drones. "I can if I interface with them."

Blake placed the drone down and gestured at the backpack. "Have at it."

Ada headed over and knelt. She picked up each drone, and as she did, thin filaments extended from her pointer finger into the access port of the drone. The drones lit up when she had done all of them. They took off and formed a diamond pattern in the air, then flew around the room.

Blake watched his forearm device. "Can you tie them into our comms?"

She used her eyes to scan Zane's and Blake's forearm devices and found their CIDs. When she tried to connect, she was blocked. "You need to allow me to."

"Oh, right," said Blake. He and Zane interacted with their devices.

After a moment, she was able to connect. "CIDs have been accepted. Relaying visual feed."

Blake studied his forearm screen as the drones zipped around. "That's what I'm talking about. Those drones are just surveillance ones, but we can modify them for other purposes."

"I like it," said Zane. "I coulda used some of these in the past."

"I could've too, but they're somewhat bulky to carry around, and trying to fight while coordinating these would be a nightmare," said Blake.

Ada returned the drones to the container. "I will consult with Luke and Kane on upgrades."

"Fair enough," said Blake. "One thing I want us to know is our fighting styles. It will help us with tactics. Although we'll use ranged weapons, and I'm not too worried about that, I do want to see what type of close-quarters combat techniques you both have. I know Zane's already. Why don't you two spar off?"

Zane cracked a smile. "You sure about that?"

Ada raised her head a bit. "I will go easy on him."

Zane laughed as he stood opposite Ada. "All right then." He charged forward.

Ada analyzed his approach and determined an appropriate response.

When Zane was near, he tried to grab her.

She seized his arm and kicked out one of his legs, causing him to fall. With a hop on his back and a twist of his arm, she held him tight.

He grunted as he tried to get up with the other arm. With a violent push off the ground and a simultaneous yank of the arm that Ada held, he was able to toss her.

"Not bad," said Blake. He gestured at Zane. "It's obvious you have raw strength while Ada has speed, flexibility, and the ability to analyze situations quickly."

Zane rubbed his arm. "Let's try that again."

"If you wish," said Ada, standing back up.

He crept forward this time.

Ada dodged his first quick jab and reached out for his arm.

In anticipation of that, he grabbed the arm that had grabbed his and then tossed her over his shoulder.

Ada landed and rolled to a stop while righting herself. "That was unexpected. You adapted."

Zane grunted.

"Very good," said Blake, nodding at them both. He motioned at Zane. "One of the reasons I wanted you was because I wanted someone that could break choke points and draw some heat. We'll need to get you some high-end armor for that. You can also choose what weapons you want, but I would think you'd want something up close and personal."

"Just something to bash with, and a shotgun," said Zane.

Blake nodded, then focused on Ada. "We'll keep you away from the action and to hold defensive points. If we need your skills to open something or hack it, Zane and I will secure the area. You can provide support with the drones."

Ada ran several battle simulations while absorbing Blake's words. "My medic skills would be useful as well. That should be a part of my load out."

"I agree," said Blake. He motioned at a wall console opposite them. "We have some configurable wall sections we can move, with a holographic overlay. While it won't be an exact replica, we can work on our communications and tactics with it." He ran his tongue over his fangs. "I'm under no illusion that we'll gel right away, but we will be fighting together, and the goal is to be a cohesive unit. Our tactics will change depending on the situation. I have no doubt that you two can adapt as needed. Now, who's ready for some real simulations?"

Zane glanced at Ada, and then they nodded at Blake.

"All right then," said Blake as he headed over to the console. "Get ready."

EIGHT

B lake surveyed the command center. It had been one day since they left, and they had just exited condensed space. He had everyone get a quick lunch in before the Illuzaran inspection, and now they were all assembled in the command center and fervently watching the screens.

Seth's fingers flew over the console interface that lit up.

A large window on the wall screen near the front of the room switched from a view of deep space in front of the ship to an image of an Illuzaran.

Blake had seen images of them before, but had never encountered one in all his travels. The Illuzarans were one of the oldest known humanoid civilizations, even older than the Kreagans and the Draidjens. Unlike the Kreagans, but like the Draidjens, they had never expanded beyond the nearest solar system. He grimaced a bit at seeing all the mechanical attachments on their heads. The Illuzarans were a cyborg race, part machine, part organic, and reminded him of what a humanoid with a wormlike body, thin legs, and multiple arms would look like.

He figured that was why they were so advanced. The one in the image had on a thin suit with a hexagonal pattern over it. The suit was formfitting, with multiple gadgets spread throughout it. The yellowish facial skin made him think they were sickly, but he knew they were fanatical about their health and often long-lived. The large eyes surrounded by smaller ones creeped him out, but it was the forehead and small mouth that were noticeable. Their foreheads were about double the size of a normal human's, while their mouths were about half the size. Relative to the rest of their thin bodies, their heads stood out.

Sarah interacted with her console. "Translator online."

"Fredorians," said the Illuzaran in a cracked voice. "State your purpose."

Blake smiled, baring his fangs. "We're here to see a friend."

"Who is this friend?"

Blake gestured at Seth.

Seth tapped at his console, then nodded at Blake.

The Illuzaran narrowed his eyes for a moment. "You wish to see Xenizate Cronis. For what reason?"

"Can't tell you that. If you really want to know, why don't you ask him?" asked Blake.

The Illuzaran stared straight ahead. "Prepare your ship for inspection."

Blake bowed. "Of course. We have milk and cookies awaiting you."

The Illuzaran snorted as the screen faded away.

"Damn, they're some ugly-ass aliens, and I've seen a lot of them," said Zane.

"They think that about us too," said Sarah. "When we encountered them in the FDF, they treated us like children."

Zane harrumphed.

"I kinda like all that technical gadgetry they got going on," said Kane.

"You would," said Seth.

"That's right," said Kane with a big smile.

"Well then, let's not keep them waiting," said Blake. "Everyone to their quarters. Seth, initiate docking protocols. I'll meet them in the docking bay."

"You got it," said Seth. He interacted with his console one last time, then joined everyone as they exited the command center.

Blake headed down to the docking bay. It had a side room that was used for decontamination and was also the entry point for docking in space. He stood outside the room and checked over his formfitting black under-armor suit. Although he detested that an inspection was required, he hoped it would be over fast.

A clanking sound rang through the deck. After a moment, the lights above the decontamination door turned red, then green. Several minutes later, the door slid open.

Blake sighed as an Illuzaran stepped through, followed by four sleek metallic humanoid robots. The Illuzaran was taller than he imagined, and the suit with gadgets made it seem more imposing. A breathing apparatus sat on the lower half of the Illuzaran's face. Blake studied the robots. The top half of their domed heads was a semitransparent red bubble. A weapon rested on their backs, and pulsing lines appeared under their semitransparent metallic skin.

"Based on the manifest you sent, you're Blake Brown," said the Illuzaran.

"That's me," said Blake.

"I'm Desicor Grada."

"Desicor is captain rank, right?" asked Blake.

"In your primitive tongue, yes. You can call me Grada, since it would be easier for you."

"Okay . . . *Grada*. Let's get this shit show over with."

Grada eyed Blake. "Let's start with you. Undress."

Blake sighed as he stripped out of his suit.

Grada scanned him with a device he pulled from his belt. After a moment, he said, "Get dressed. No contaminants we can't handle."

"Were you . . . expecting some?"

"You're a Daedrould. We're aware of the exotic energy that courses through your system, even if it can't be fully detected," said Grada. He tilted his head slightly, causing the robots to begin walking around scanning everything. "You will accompany me per protocol as I scan your crew. My guards will handle going over your ship."

Blake slipped his suit back on and then bowed. "After you."

Grada headed to the living quarters. On the way, he scanned around. "Primitive ship. I'm surprised it got out here."

"But it did get us out here, easily."

Grada glanced at Blake, and continued to Zane's quarters. The door slid open, and they both stepped in.

Blake chuckled when he saw Zane nude. It was obvious he had no shame.

Grada stepped forward and began to scan. After a moment, he said, "Zane Gibbons. It says here you were recently released from prison, and now you want to come to our world."

Zane began to gyrate his hips. "Oh, yeah. Want to get some of that sweet Illuzaran love."

Grada coughed. "That's disgusting."

Zane spun around and bent over. "Maybe this would be better suited for your scan."

Grada shook his head as both Blake and Zane laughed. "Fredorians. What a waste of a race."

"I'm Earthborn," said Zane with a big smile on his upside-down head between his legs.

Grada snorted with derision as he exited the room.

Blake nodded at Zane and then followed Grada.

The next room was Sarah's. Blake stood outside the room.

"As a commander, you're required to be present for all personnel inspections," said Grada.

"Yes, but not in this case. It's not appropriate," said Blake. He stared down Grada.

Grada harrumphed and continued on with his scan.

Blake wondered how they did larger ships. If the Illuzaran contact would have met them off-world, none of this would have been necessary.

Grada scanned Sarah. "Fredorian. Recently worked in the Fredorian Defense Force. Moved to another unit due to personal problems."

"What?" asked Sarah. "Just do my scan."

Grada scanned her and then exited the room.

After scanning Kane and Luke, they arrived at Seth's room.

Blake crooked a thumb at Grada as he scanned Seth. "Careful. I heard Grada here likes chocolate."

Seth laughed. "Quit your clowning."

"You seem to enjoy mocking me," said Grada. "I assure you, it is pointless."

"To you, maybe. If your species is as advanced as you think it is, why do you still need to do a manual inspection?" asked Blake.

Seth pointed at Blake. "Man has a point."

Grada finished scanning. "It is known that items of a dangerous nature can be shield dampened. Contaminants can be hidden. Scanners can only do so much."

"So what you're saying is you're not advanced enough," said Blake.

Grada narrowed his eyes as he left the room.

Blake slapped hands with Seth and then followed Grada to Ada's room. He noticed an immediate change on Grada's face.

"It's a pleasure to meet you," said Grada.

Ada nodded. "It is for me as well."

"As you probably don't know, when the Fredorians erroneously decided they were superior to androids and took away their citizenship, many came to Holryn," said Grada. He focused on Ada. "You should have come. The ones we have taken in have proven to be quite useful, and they enjoy being here."

"I'm sure they do," said Ada. "However, I'm a G2, and I prefer to be around organics."

"Inefficient usage of your resources," said Grada.

Ada glanced at Blake. "Perhaps, but I like it here."

"What a waste," said Grada. "You could be so much more instead of being with this . . . crew."

"This is where I choose to be."

Grada finished scanning. "So be it." He glanced at Blake. "Your ship is cleared. It will be escorted in, and you will have two guards with you at all times. Who will be leaving the ship after landing?"

"Seth, Ada, Zane, and I," said Blake.

Grada's eyes narrowed. "Fine." He paused for a moment, then said, "We're leaving."

"Finally," said Blake.

Grada harrumphed and exited the room.

Blake winked at Ada. "You could have been a part of all that."

"I prefer being here," said Ada.

Blake nodded and left.

//////////

Blake surveyed the walkway that connected the *Exceltion*'s dock to a terminal not too far away. Illuzaran architecture was bland. Everything was grid based, and the platform they were on reminded him an open grid cell on a large checkerboard. Off to the side of their landing grid was another cell that seemed to only have a walkway with purple grass off to the sides. He knew they had power grid cells, hydroponic ones, and other specialized ones. Putting together an Illuzaran city was like stacking blocks.

His enhanced senses could pick up the smell of the exotic flowers. It reminded him of honey. With him was Seth, Zane, Ada, and two of the robots seen before on the ship. He could hear the group's footsteps and heartbeats and the whir of machinery operating in the background. The robots were silent and, for the most part, just hung around the perimeter of the group. Looking around, he could see it was not a busy place. That was not too big of a surprise given how xenophobic the Illuzarans were.

"Kinda dead around here," said Seth, glancing at one of the robots.

The robot continued to look forward.

"Oh, the chatty types, huh?"

Zane laughed. "These tin cans probably aren't used to interacting with people."

Ada swiveled her heard toward him.

Zane extended a hand out. "I'm not saying *you're* a tin can."

"I would hope not, and if I were, I would be an advanced one."

Zane pointed at Ada. "I think I like your style."

Ada nodded.

Seth tapped Blake's arm. "You've been awfully quiet."

"Assessing our environment," said Blake. Usually when he was on assignment, he would take time to perform reconnaissance on where he was going. There was no opportunity for that here, and he did not like to walk into places blind. If the element of surprise was needed, it would not be available.

He could see inside the terminal ahead, at the end of the walkway. Its aesthetic also came as no surprise. Its doorway was sharp edged with shiny metallic raised borders. A semi-transparent shield covered the entrance. Looking inside, he squinted at the floor. Like the doorway edges, it was shiny. The walls were a dull metal of some type. They had an occasional break to outline segments, some of which had what looked like small circular interfaces. The Illuzarans were not big on fancy displays. Their blandness sucked the life out of him.

Seth nodded. "Sorta bleak out here."

"Better than a prison cell," said Zane, chuckling.

"I bet," said Seth. He looked ahead as they entered the terminal. "Not some place I'd ever want to vacation, that's for sure."

Blake snorted. "Who said anyone got vacations?"

Seth shook his head.

Blake faced one of the robots. "So where is this Xenizate Cronis?"

The robot paused for a moment, then took off toward an exit.

ADAIR HART

"Well . . . I guess we follow it," said Blake. "Makes me wonder where it was taking us in the first place."

"You didn't get a location?" asked Zane.

Blake shook his head. "I was told we would land and then be taken to him. Assuming it's a him, I'm not really an expert on the Illuzarans."

"Huh," said Zane. He increased his pace. "These robots seem like they're in a hurry."

"They're not," said Ada. "They just switched into hunting mode."

Zane nodded. "Good to know." He pointed at Ada. "Can you talk with them?"

"I have already. They are not . . . as Seth would say . . . chatty. They are programmed but possess a virtual intelligence."

"Figures."

It took them a half an hour to traverse through various grids of pathways, buildings, ramps, and a transportation unit that moved them sideways and sometimes down. They arrived at two grid cells, one that had a walkway with purple grass and the other with an advanced domed building. The robot leading them had paused and then pointed at the dome.

Blake gestured at the metallic walkway leading up to the building. It stood out from the rest of the Illuzaran architecture. The dome had angles, lights scattered around, and seemed out of place relative to the grid cells surrounding it. Once at the doorway, he pressed a button on the side.

A holographic image of an Illuzaran appeared outside.

Blake noticed that unlike the one he saw on the ship, this one was a bit smaller, and the skin looked more frail. The formfitting suit was similar to the one he saw on the ship, but it had fewer gadgets. The posture also seemed a bit bent.

The hologram spoke. "Welcome, welcome. I'm Xenizate Cronis. You can just call me Cronis. I've been expecting you."

The doorway slid back, revealing a spacious interior that had several levels to it. Scattered around the room were various cylinders with consoles attached to them. A ramp to their immediate left went down to the next level, and the one on their right went up a level. Tables with holograms above them peppered the room, and a lounge area sat in the back.

The interior's dim blue light made Blake squint.

Cronis rushed down the ramp and paused as he studied the group. "Interesting . . . A Daedrould! And an android! And . . . two Fredorians."

Seth glanced at Zane and shrugged.

Cronis waved a hand in the air. "I didn't mean it like that. It's just the other two are much more unique, although androids are no stranger to me."

"No worries," said Seth. "And we're Earthborn."

Blake raised his head a bit and gestured at everyone in turn. "I'm Blake Brown, and with me are Seth Williams, Ada, and Zane Gibbons. We're told that you have some information on Delkis."

"Some? Hah!" said Cronis. "I already know who you all are." He waved for everyone to follow and then hustled over to an advanced-looking table with consoles that slanted off of it. After he tapped at one of the consoles, an image of Delkis appeared. "This what you're looking for?"

Blake joined the others around the table. "Yeah . . . you know where he is?"

"Mm-hmm. He's on Zakara Prime."

"Ahh shit," said Zane. "That place sucks."

"I would agree. It does indeed . . . suck," said Cronis.

Blake narrowed his eyes. Zakara Prime was the home planet of large crime organizations. It was packed with so much infrastructure that there was not much left in the way of natural habitat. Some called it a city planet, an ecumenopolis, due to its many layers. The last time he had gone there, there were seventy-three layers, and more were being built. He had done a few missions on the planet in the past and knew that it housed some of the more dangerous elements of the criminal underground. The Kreagans had attempted to crack down on it once, but after ten years of unsuccessfully capturing anyone of note or ridding the planet of crime, they decided to just beef up their defenses in the area closest to Zakara Prime. He tossed a hand out toward Cronis. "How do you know that's where Delkis is?"

"Isn't it obvious? We're the Illuzarans. We keep track of everything," said Cronis.

Ada tilted her head. "How is this possible if you don't leave your solar system?"

"Unfortunately, I can't tell you of our efforts, other than to say . . . don't you think it's odd we can sit in our solar system without any issues?"

"I'm not following your logic."

Blake grinned. "He's saying that they've weaponized information. I've heard of unusual activity in that regard, but never suspected the Illuzarans. Impressive to keep me in the dark."

"I did not derive that from his statement," said Ada.

"Riddles. Pfft," said Zane.

Cronis gestured at Blake. "I knew *you* would understand. Being an intelligence operative for the rangers has trained you well."

Blake tossed his hands out to the side. "What can I say? I'm Blake Brown."

"Indeed you are," said Cronis. His eyes fluttered for a moment. "Yes, Delkis is on Zakara Prime . . . but there is something else going on. Something that we can't see."

"What do you mean?" asked Blake.

"Exactly that! We literally can't see what Delkis is doing, other than an odd visual feed or two. He has help, and not any type of help we've ever seen."

"What type of help? We know he's working with some other groups," said Zane.

Cronis bobbed his head for a moment. "Yes . . . groups, but I think one of them is . . . not from here. You're Earth-born. You know of what I speak."

Blake drew his head back a bit. "You mean dimensional beings . . . Outsiders."

"Outsiders, dimensional beings, call it what you want. The trail of destruction Delkis leaves is unusual. Bold. Out in the open, yet . . . he has no fear."

"Well, Delkis was always kind of a nut," said Zane.

"Perhaps, but . . . ," said Cronis, tapping at the table to show a projection of a fight between Delkis and the Covendrin mercs, "watch."

Blake observed as Delkis jumped around, dodging fire out in the open. His speed was abnormal. When Delkis isolated one of the mercs, he punched the merc's chest plate, caving it in, killing the merc instantly.

"Whoa," said Zane.

"There is no record of him possessing this strength," said Ada.

"I'll say," said Blake.

The rest of the projection showed Delkis picking off the mercs one by one, and killing them. Once they were all dead, they were beheaded and stuck on spikes. Delkis ran a hand along one of their faces, letting the blood smear on his finger. He stuck the finger in his mouth and then began to drag the bodies away. The projection ended.

"That was from a feed we . . . obtained," said Cronis. "Delkis is not Delkis. His species does not have that type of speed or strength. It's like he's been . . . altered . . . somehow."

Blake ran a hand over his mouth. "Maybe. He definitely isn't an Outsider, at least from what I knew of him. Something else is going on."

"Or . . . he's become part of a new group, one from someplace else, and that's changed him," said Cronis, raising a finger.

"It could also be some form of new technology," said Blake. He ran his tongue over his fangs for a moment. "Where on Zakara Prime is Delkis now?"

Cronis grinned. "I don't know exactly where he is, but I know he's involved with the Kahan and Selva Tong crime syndicates. I would suggest that you talk with Gertus, the Kahan leader, first. Daniel Greer runs the Selva Tong, and as you may or may not know, the Selva Tong houses one of the larger safe havens for mercs of all types."

"Then we know where to start. I'm familiar with both groups," said Blake, glancing at Zane. "Have you met these groups before?"

"Yep. Worked with the Kahan, but it was run by Jankdra then. I had a good working relationship with him. Most of his contracts were me wasting someone off-world," said Zane. "The Kahan are Gulltissarians, an odd-looking race if I ever saw one, but they love some credits."

"Gertus is Jankdra's son. He took over when Jankdra died," said Cronis.

Blake nodded. "Then we'll use that to our advantage." He nodded at Cronis. "Appreciate the help."

Cronis laughed. "Oh, it's my pleasure."

"You're nothing like the captain that boarded and inspected our ship," said Blake.

"I'm older than most, and have embraced life. If I could travel, I would, but there's a lot here to . . . maintain, and we stay in our system for . . . reasons. It's why I enjoy seeing those sent my way. Time can be . . . *unpredictable* . . . at times. Most Illuzarans are so caught up in trying to be more efficient than one another that they sometimes fail to see life in its true glory."

"You've had others sent your way?" asked Zane.

"Oh, yes, but only a special few."

Zane laughed as he slapped Blake's arm. "We're special."

"You are indeed," said Cronis. "You have powerful people backing you, including someone who saw this coming to pass long ago, one beyond even my comprehension. Your presence here is no accident."

Blake eyed Cronis for a moment. His gut told him that Cronis was probably an information broker informant, or maybe something higher. No one would suspect an Illuzaran, and Holryn would be a safe place to be if coordinating information. Cronis probably knew that Blake would figure it out. He understood secrets, and how to leverage relationships so the information kept flowing.

Blake had an idea of the person Cronis talked about. There was a powerful godlike being that visited Earth and could travel through time and space. The being was a close friend of his vampire master, Lord Noskov, but Blake knew that the being would not involve himself in something this small. However, a pattern of unusual incidents was starting to form in his mind. With a look around the group, he said, "I think we have what we came for. Cronis, once again, thanks."

Cronis swung his head in an arc. "Remember that if I ever need a favor. Good luck."

"You got it," said Blake.

They exited the dome.

NINE

Seth glanced around the training room at Blake, Ada, and Zane. Sarah and Kane were left in charge in the command center to fly the *Exceltion* to Zakara Prime. Although Seth had no intent of being a part of the assault team, he had been asked by Blake to participate. He wanted to do two-on-two scenarios. Various wall sections were configured to mimic the hallways of a small ship.

Blake tapped Seth's arm. "It's me and you, just like old times." He gestured forward toward one of the hallways. "We have to find Ada and Zane in there."

Seth eyed the training weapon. "This little thing isn't going to stop them."

"Don't worry, you just need to tag them."

Seth snorted. "All right. How do you want to do this?"

"I'll stealth and scout, you hold position until I contact you."

"Like on Tooka."

"Yeah, but this time try not to get captured and get your ass beat," said Blake, laughing.

Seth sighed.

Blake camouflaged and crept into the hallway. After a moment, he talked into his comms. "Okay, c'mon."

Seth hugged the wall and bent over as he entered the hallway. He could only see a short distance ahead due to the poor lighting of the simulation. The sound of footsteps in the distance made him pause.

"C'mon," said Blake. "They're just trying to throw their sound."

Seth licked his lips and caught up to Blake. "Well, they're doing a damn fine job. Why aren't we using life-sign scanners?"

"It would make it too easy," said Blake. "This is just a cat-and-mouse simulation. Okay, I'll scout ahead again."

"All right," said Seth. He watched Blake take off. The sterile smell, dim lighting, and odd sounds were somewhat disorienting to him. When he and Blake freelanced, it was usually Blake that did all the traipsing around. After a few minutes, Seth whispered into his comms. "Blake?" He got no reply, and tried several more times. Maybe they got him. He shook his head and advanced forward.

When he was near a corner, a device flew past him. He turned in the direction it was moving.

Zane burst out and slapped the weapon out of Seth's hand.

With a kick to the leg, Seth crumpled to the ground. He grunted in pain.

"Oh, shit, you all right?" asked Zane.

Seth smiled as he tapped another weapon on his side that he had pulled out when he fell. It was not the training weapon, but his personal sidearm. "Always carry two pistols."

"Well, damn, you woulda still got me."

Seth coughed. "Yeah, but my leg hurts like hell."

Zane called out to Blake and Ada. They came running.

Ada bent over and examined Seth's leg. "This needs medical attention. Can you move it?"

Seth moved his leg a bit and grunted. "Yeah, but it hurts."

"Wait here, I'll get something to move you," said Ada. She took off.

"Still getting your ass kicked, I see," said Blake.

"He actually woulda got me," said Zane.

"Really?" asked Blake. He eyed Seth. "You did the fall-and-fire routine I showed you."

Seth grimaced as he sat up against the wall section. "Yep."

Zane rubbed his chin. "Good strategy, and sorry, man, my reflexes took over."

"It's cool, and yeah, I'm no gunslinger like Blake, but I have a pistol for quick draw in case I need to. Most don't suspect it."

Blake nodded. "Well, this training session is over for now. Get patched up." He glanced at Zane. "Care to do some one-on-one sparring?"

"Hell yeah," said Zane. "I'll promise to go easy."

Seth laughed, then doubled over in pain.

Zane eyed Seth.

"Sorry, it's just that I've heard that from so many people before they get wrecked by Blake."

Zane harrumphed and then pointed out of the wall sections. "After you."

Blake nodded and they exited.

A few minutes later, Ada arrived with a small slab on wheels. She carefully hoisted Seth up on it and laid him down.

"Glad you're here," said Seth.

Ada nodded as she began to push the cart. "Your health is important."

"I like to think so," said Seth.

When they got to the medical bay, a six-foot stick-figure robot with small hexagonal cells on its metallic skin stepped forward and out from an alcove in the wall. The holographic image of a tan-skinned man with glasses and a well-trimmed beard appeared around the robot. "How may I be of assistance?"

Seth pointed at his leg. "My leg's busted."

The hologram gestured at a slab on the far side of the room. Ada pushed Seth over and then transferred him to the slab. A beam shot out from the ceiling and scanned Seth.

A moment later, the hologram rubbed his chin and said, "You have a thigh contusion, nothing I can't fix."

"Thanks, Doc," said Seth.

The hologram paused and tilted his head. "Doc? Is that what you wish to call me?"

Seth glanced at Ada, then back at the hologram. "Uhh . . . do you have a name you want to use?"

The hologram looked around for a moment. "Doc it is. That sounds better than Medtech Artificial Intelligence 7A-2."

"Yeah . . . Doc is easy to say, and everyone knows what it means."

Doc grinned. "I agree. I like it." He walked over to a cabinet and interacted with a console. After a few minutes, he returned with a syringe and a container with some gel. "These microbots should help. You'll need to stay off your leg for a few hours while they do their work."

Seth sighed. "Damn. Still . . . a few hours for some bruising is much better than what I'm used to."

Doc nodded and proceeded to treat his leg.

Seth winced as the microbots entered his body. They always made him queasy because he could feel them. He had heard of nanobots being used in some of the more advanced societies, but Fredoria was still playing catch-up. Even so, microbots were quite advanced. He rolled his head over to Ada. "Appreciate the help. I guess I'll just . . . wait here."

Ada pulled up a chair next to Seth's slab. "I'll wait with you." She extended her hand, palm up, toward him.

Seth furrowed his eyebrows.

"I have heard that contact can be beneficial in moments of stress."

"I'd listen to her. She speaks the truth," said Doc.

Ada looked down for a moment. "I apologize if it makes—"

Seth grabbed her hand and grinned at her. "Trust me . . . I don't mind *at all*."

Ada shot him a quizzical look. "I hope my presence will help you feel better."

"I couldn't have asked for anyone better," said Seth, gulping.

Doc stood back and analyzed them both. "Well . . . all there is left is waiting. If you need me, just shout, 'Doc!'"

Seth laughed. "All right, man. I think me and you are gonna get along just fine." He eyed Doc. "So . . . do you just hang out in the ship's systems now?"

"No, I go into stasis. I'm a specialized system AI with a defined purpose. I'm more than a virtual intelligence, but I'm nowhere near as advanced as Ada, and I'm not hardwired into a body. As such, I do not require anything outside my purpose."

"All right, man."

Doc nodded as his holographic form dissipated. The underlying robot walked back into its alcove, where it docked.

Seth glanced at Ada. "I appreciate you helping me out. I know Doc coulda probably come and got me."

"It's okay. I wanted to help you."

"Cool," said Seth. He gently squeezed Ada's hand and noticed her face soften a bit. "I guess we just sit here and hold hands."

Ada smiled. "I'm okay with that too."

Seth laughed then winced again. "Ugh . . . be glad when this is healed."

Ada nodded.

"So since we're gonna be here for a while . . . I had some questions. You don't have to answer if you don't want to."

"Go ahead."

"I heard about the Fredorian government deciding to reclassify androids as property. I never understood that decision. Maybe they saw them as a potential threat. Where'd you end up?"

Ada drew her lips flat. "I was assigned to a warehouse. Generation version was not taken into account. The warehouse manager that I was assigned to . . . was not a good man."

"Really?" asked Seth. "I bet he was pissed when you came here."

"He was. I hope he doesn't take it out on the other androids there."

Seth narrowed his eyes. "Maybe me and Blake need to pay him a visit."

"It's okay. I'm here now, and I'm enjoying it so far."

Seth ran a thumb along the side of her metallic hand. The warmth of it made him smile. "I'm glad you're here too. If there's anything you need help with, just let me know."

Ada nodded. "I may hold you to that."

"Please do."

Ada looked away for a moment, then back at Seth. "I'm not used to organics being nice to me, even before the declassification."

"Well, start getting used to it. You're an equal with everyone here."

Her eyes lit up. "I know, and it is . . . exhilarating for me." She ran her thumb along Seth's hand.

Seth exhaled and laid his head back. "Maybe I should get hurt more around you."

Ada tilted her head.

"I'm just playing," said Seth. He was beginning to see a softer side of Ada, and it was something he liked. Her personality was kind and curious, something he wanted to explore more. Maybe he would have that chance. It was not lost on him that his first real interaction with someone he might be interested in came at the cost of him getting hurt. Blake would add that to his list of personal jabs if he ever found out. That was okay. Seth would do it again if it meant more time with Ada.

/////////

Luke took one last walk past the movable carts that held a variety of heavy and light armor with various weapons. He checked each one to make sure it had what was requested by each crew member. Although they were still about seventeen hours out from Zakara Prime, he wanted to make sure that everyone had optimal gear. He had drunk a cup of coffee at dinner and was feeling the caffeine buzz.

"You think the carts are going to escape or something?" asked Kane.

"Just a little anxious is all."

"You?"

Luke drew his head back. "We're about to show the crew their gear, with modifications."

"Yeah . . . your physical modifications, and my technical tweaks," said Kane. "If they don't like it, then that's on both of us."

Luke drew his lips to the right. "I knew I'd like you."

"Relax . . . this is the most chill group I've been around in a long while. Good ship, good crew, and I'm loving the chance to use my skills on something other than repair. We got this, man."

Luke nodded. He liked Kane. His personality was unusual, but after dealing with Fredorians mainly, it was a welcome change.

Their attention focused on Blake and the others filing into the room.

Blake tossed his hands out to the side. "Looks like you two have been busy." He tilted his head forward. "Dazzle us."

Luke walked to the first hanging cart and then gestured at Zane. "This one's yours." Luke pointed at the formfitting suit on the farthest right. "That's your under armor, made of a carbon nanotube mesh sandwiched between two layers of micromesh. It's tough and has the ability to repair itself if pressure is applied."

He went to the next hanging item. "This is a light suit you can wear over your under armor. It's high-tech and has above-average shielding and armor. I tweaked it a bit from the general design you requested, and Kane adjusted the technical parts. It's much more power efficient now. It also has jump jets and magnetic boots and gloves. The belt has a grappling device as well."

"Hell yeah," said Zane.

Luke pointed at the final metallic suit. "This is your juggernaut suit, per Blake's recommendation. It's big and heavy, with massive shielding and armor capability. It has built-in thrusters on the back, which is much more powerful than the jump jets. It can also carry a lot."

"Damn . . . ," said Zane as he walked up to the cart. He glanced at the weapons on the lower part of the cart. "Is that . . . a Grovellian thrower?"

"Just like you requested, with a few enhancements," said Luke, gesturing at Kane.

Kane cleared his throat. "I added a modification that allows you to tweak the firing arc on it. Like all shotguns, it has a spread, but you can now configure it. You can also do a double shot with it, and it's a bit lighter. In short, it'll smoke whoever you point it at."

Zane picked up the thrower and flipped it around. He held it out with one hand. "I can use it with one arm."

"Yeah," said Kane. "The recoil, while high, should be no problem for someone of your strength, or when wearing either suit."

"Shit yeah," said Zane. He picked up a rod with a diamond-shaped end. "What's this?"

"It's a slightly altered Kreagan hunter mace. I wasn't sure what you wanted. Flick the switch on the handle," said Luke.

Zane activated the mace, causing a shield to form around the diamond. "Whoa."

Kane chuckled. "I added a tweak that lets you control the temperature of the shield, so you can use it for different situations. It also has a recharging laser you can shoot out of the end. Recharge is the usual two minutes, but it packs a punch. There's also a stun setting for the shield."

Zane laughed. "A stun mace. I'm liking this. I've seen something similar out in the field, but not quite this advanced."

Kane pointed at the side pistols and assault rifle. "Those are standard-issue Fredorian pistols. One is the FLP-40, the other is the FHP-10. The assault rifle is the FAR-34, the striker. Luke and I tweaked each one so it performs a little better than standard-issue."

Blake clapped. "See . . . that's what I'm talking about. You boys did some work down here."

"Having a level-three replicator helps," said Luke. He motioned toward Kane. "And having someone certified on it."

"It's all good," said Kane.

Blake nodded. "Zane, when we get to Zakara Prime, I don't think you'll need your juggernaut suit for this."

Zane grunted and extended his arm at a forty-five-degree angle toward Luke.

Luke slapped hands with Zane.

Zane repeated with Kane and then headed out with his hanging cart.

Kane shook his hand. "Damn, that dude is strong."

"That he is," said Blake. He motioned at Ada. "Your turn."

Ada walked up to the cart that Luke had pushed forward.

Luke pointed at the backpack with a hip belt. "This is a light pack. It has several types of drones. An attack one, a surveillance one that can camouflage, and a general utility one with arms. There is also a retractable turret that can shoot about as well as the striker. Limited ammunition, obviously. There are also medical microbots, several types of scanners, and a small supply area you can fill with whatever. It also has a communication booster in case it's needed. The pack should just slip on."

"I like it," said Ada. She glanced at the larger pack next to it. "I'm guessing this one is the same, just with more items in it."

"You got it," said Luke. "We can add whatever you want to it. It has everything you requested, but if you need changes or anything, just let us know."

Ada nodded. "Do I not get an undergarment or suit?"

Luke furrowed his eyebrows. "I didn't see it on your list, but we do have ones that would complement your form."

"I'd like an under-armor suit and a light-armor one like Zane's."

Kane walked over to the replicator and grabbed a scanning device. He scanned Ada, then said, "Any particulars you had in mind?"

Ada walked over to the replicator and studied its settings. "You've set up Zane's suits, I see." She placed her finger beneath the console, and a small wire extended from her finger and plugged into an outlet. After a moment, both suits similar to Zane's appeared. The light-armor suit had segmented lines and a metallic sheen to it.

"Sorry about that," said Luke. "I didn't even think—"

"Because I'm an android. It's okay. I like the suits."

Luke looked down for a moment and then cleared his throat. "We have the same pistols as Zane's for you, and something me and Kane cooked up." He grabbed two wrap-around forearm devices and handed them to Ada. "They contain small flat disc drones. They can expand and form a shield in the interior. Their purpose is to block incoming shots, but since you now have kinetic shielding, they can serve as a last resort. Obviously, it would be a bit much for a human to try to control them while doing anything else, but for you, not a problem."

"I'm impressed," said Ada. "You two went through some effort for this."

Kane pointed his index finger from each hand at Ada. "We got you."

"Yes, you do," said Ada with a smile. She grabbed her cart and put her suits on it, then exited the room.

Blake rubbed his hands together. "All right, my turn."

Seth shook his head.

Luke grinned. "Yours was the easiest. We just took what you had and made it better. We didn't touch the blades as you requested, but added a few enhancements to the light suit."

"Such as?"

Kane ran a hand along the suit. "You can camouflage longer. It's also a bit sturdier. The kinetic shielding can handle a few firefights, but I wouldn't expect it to last in a lot of protracted fights. Just make sure to recharge it from time to time. Your striker and pistols have also been upgraded."

"Awesome," said Blake. "I'll stick around for Seth. Curious to see what you guys did for him."

"All right," said Luke. He pushed a cart up to Seth. "Like Blake, it was easy to do yours. You have a suit similar to Zane's light armor, but a bit lighter. Standard jump jets, magnetic boots and gloves, and of course a high-end helmet with all the visual stuff you'd expect. The pistols are the same, but you'll see a scope on the FHP-10."

"Wish I had all this when we were freelancing," said Seth.

Blake shook a finger. "You could've if you wanted it, but half the battle is knowing what you want."

Seth nodded. "I hear that. Thanks, guys, this is great."

"We got you, S-man," said Kane, with his hands out to the side.

"Appreciate the show-and-tell," said Blake. "I think we'll be ready for Zakara Prime tomorrow. The question now is, is Zakara Prime ready for us?"

Everyone laughed as Blake and Seth exited the room.

TEN

B lake glanced around the meeting-room table. It had been an hour since everyone got their customized gear from Luke and Kane. Blake wanted to have a meeting to make sure everyone was on the same page for the excursion tomorrow morning. He interacted with the table console, which projected a planet above the center of the table. "Zakara Prime. The garbage dump of this region. It has over a thousand registered criminal organizations, but it's essentially run by about eighty major ones that have divided the planet up. The only global initiative they agree upon is a defensive pact if the planet is attacked."

A red dot appeared on the planet.

"This is where we're headed. The surface area is owned by the Selva Tong, a group comprised of mainly Fredorians, of which a lot are Earthborn. The Kahan, led by Gertus, are a race known as the Gulltissarians. They're a smaller group, and they have an agreement with the Selva Tong. The Kahan get control of some of the lower levels, and in exchange, they pay a cut of everything they earn to the Selva Tong. That's common on Zakara Prime. Whoever runs the surface area controls the lower levels. Meeting Gertus is our first priority."

Zane narrowed his eyes. "Seems odd that Delkis would work with these two organizations. It'd be easier to just deal with the Selva Tong directly. Besides, the Kahan are a paranoid bunch. Gertus wasn't around when I dealt with them, so things might be different now."

Blake nodded. "I agree it would be easier to deal with the Selva Tong directly, but Cronis specifically said to meet with Gertus first. I suspect Cronis is much more than he let on, so we should probably take his advice." He tapped at the table console.

The map zoomed in to the red dot, showing multiple layers of the city. Levels thirteen through sixteen were highlighted in green.

"That's Kahan turf," said Blake. "They deal mainly in pirated goods. I'm not sure how up-to-date this is, so we should probably check topside in one of the bars. One other thing to note. Once underground, communication with the *Exceltion* will be nonexistent, unless we use one of Selva Tong's communication terminals."

Zane waved a finger between two levels. "We should be able to communicate between a level, but no more than that. If they have the same setup, then Gertus will be on level sixteen. I would recommend not using any Selva Tong terminals if we're keeping a low profile. The terminals are bugged, obviously. However . . . the Kahan do have a direct line to the surface, but we would need their permission to use it."

Blake nodded. "Hopefully we don't need it. Nonetheless, we do have a communication booster that could give us another level if we needed it, but I'm not envisioning us needing it."

Ada tilted her head. "So we're on our own. In that regard, do you think one of the bar patrons will give us additional information?"

"Maybe. If anything, we can get an update on the political layout."

"I'm coming with you," said Seth. "Not that I think you can't handle it yourself, especially with Zane and Ada, but we've worked closely in the field together for two years. I may not join every mission, but I think I can help on this one. Besides, you can't have all the fun."

Blake raised a finger. "You might get your ass kicked."

"What else is new," said Seth, chuckling. He glanced at Ada. "If I do, we have a real medic and a ship with a medical lab for once. And yes . . . my leg is healed."

Blake laughed. "Fine, you can come at least until I get a fourth team member." He could see that Seth wanted to make an impression on the others, especially on a first outing as a team into potentially hostile territory. Blake had hoped Seth would stay behind, but he also knew Seth was adventurous at heart.

"Luke, Kane, and Sarah can watch the ship," said Seth.

"Anyone trying to burn this ship will get a nasty surprise," said Luke.

Kane laughed. "Yep. We got some killer defensive robots. Anxious to get them set up and roaming around."

"Don't worry about the ship," said Sarah. "You just worry about yourselves out there. Sounds like a pretty lawless place."

"It is," said Blake. "Law enforcement is roving bands of Selva Tong members. I expect there will be some fighting. One thing to note. Seth and I have several bounties on us. The issuers are anonymous, but Selva Tong is neutral ground, so we should be okay."

"Yeah. I'm curious who placed those. So . . . to a bar first then?" asked Seth.

Blake nodded. "According to this, there are several, but the biggest one is on level four. We'll hit it up, find out what we can, then head out to Kahan territory. We can also check the bounty board while we're there."

"Sounds straightforward to me," said Zane. "I'm ready to roll."

"I'm ready to roll as well," said Ada.

Everyone chuckled.

Ada swiveled her head around the table. "I'm adjusting to Earthborn slang."

"You'll get there," said Blake. "All right. We're still a bit out. Once we're out of condensed space, we'll be above Zakara Prime. Take the rest of the night off and get some rest. We'll head out in the morning around 11:00 a.m., then it's show time."

////////

Seth looked back at the *Exceltion* as he, Blake, Zane, and Ada headed out. It was almost 11:00 a.m. Earth time. Using Earth time was something he had internalized since every place seemed to have a different time setup. The Fredorian time cycle was similar to Earth's. He suspected the Kreagans knew this when they selected the planet.

The *Exceltion* so far had surpassed what he expected, and he was loving every moment with it. Looking around, he could see what Blake meant by Zakara Prime being a garbage dump. The landing pad was packed with shipping containers, and the area was barely big enough for the *Exceltion*. Based on the discussion he had with the traffic controller prior to landing, they were not too concerned with security. If they did not want you to land, they would fire the big cannons he could see in the distance. Even getting their landing spot was a negotiation, a privilege that cost three thousand credits.

Blake slapped Seth on the arm. "No daydreaming out here."

"Yeah, I know."

"Anyways, get your pistol out."

"Now?"

"You never know when you're gonna need it. This place is a war zone," said Blake.

Seth noticed that Blake had his striker out, Zane held his shotgun, and Ada had a pistol in her hand. He pulled out his FLP-40. Being ready to fight upon exiting a landing pad was not something he was used to. Most of the contracts over the previous two years usually had him scouting around or sitting with the ship. He did go on a few excursions with Blake, but they were usually in medium-level security areas. This was a far cry from that.

Blake hustled up to Zane and Ada.

Seth's eyes were glued to Ada as she walked. It amazed him how much engineering went into the production of an android. They were lifelike in every aspect, with a strong AI tied to the body. Capable of emotions and physical strength and speed that exceeded the average human by several levels, he could see why Fredorians feared them. Not he, though. He bumped into Ada, who had stopped walking.

"Are you okay?" asked Ada.

"Huh? Yeah, I'm fine. Sorry. I got distracted. That's all."

Ada looked him over, then walked alongside him. "I will walk by your side."

Seth grinned. "All right." He focused on the environment as they continued off the landing pad into a side street with shabby metallic and concrete buildings to the sides. The only sign of any type of security were the two humans that had watched them from the roof of a side building when they landed. They would be in for a surprise if they tried to attack the *Exceltion*. The street smelled like raw sewage, and the lighting was haphazard. There were poles that functioned as streetlights, but their output was weak. "Damn . . . you weren't kidding about this place. It's a mess."

Blake and Zane slowed up and created a crescent formation as they walked.

"Told ya," said Blake. "If I was doing work here, I was almost always in camouflage."

Zane jiggled his shotgun. "I just wielded the biggest weapon I could. Not many mess with you when they know you can shred them at a moment's notice."

"I believe it," said Seth.

They exited the side street onto a main street. Everyone's attention focused on a ruckus farther down the street.

As they approached it, Seth could see it was someone getting a beatdown. The fact that it was in front of a crowd and in an open area made him realize there really was nothing to keep the Selva Tong from doing whatever it wanted. The taller buildings on the street provided some shade, but that was probably of little comfort to the person getting hammered.

"Just walk by it and keep your head down. Those are Selva Tong members," said Blake.

Seth knew Blake was being serious by the tone in his voice. Seth dipped his head down and got in line as the group passed by the bloody scene in single file. He did a quick glance to see the scene up close. It looked like whoever was getting beaten had the same outfit as those beating him. It would be over soon based on the condition of the victim and the savageness of those above him. He gulped and looked forward. Someone was about to die. This was a serious place.

The buildings around them were drab, yet high-tech. They were made of a mix of metal and some type of fiberglass-like material. Large signs portrayed a multitude of services with contact numbers.

After traveling down the main street and then taking a few turns as they went through more, they reached the ramp network.

Seth drew his head back a bit. He had seen smaller ramps used in stations, but these were much wider and larger. There were two ramps, and they both went down. The right one had a small group of Selva Tong members out front. "What's the difference between these two?"

"The left one goes down to the next level. Every level has a ramp to the one under it. The other ramp is a straight shot to the lowest layer. It has landing platforms at each level, and it curves a lot. We're taking the left one," said Blake.

Seth shook his head. "Why are we going level by level instead of the one that would take us right to level four?"

"It requires a special license. They're hard to get, but if you have one, they have an escalator system on the ramp. Selva Tong is pretty paranoid about who uses it."

"Damn."

After thirty minutes, they reached level four.

Seth caught his breath as they exited onto the level. Getting a license to use the other ramp would be a high priority if he lived here. The ramps were less populated the farther they went down, and there were occasional seating areas that jutted out. As they walked to the bar, he swallowed hard. There was no sky here, just the floor of the next level. Large pillars stood out across the distance, and some buildings that looked like they spanned levels. The

EARTHBORN

dim lighting made it hard to see, and the populous crowds had thinned somewhat. Selva Tong members were around, but not many. "This place makes me uneasy."

"It isn't that bad," said Blake. "We're still in what's considered the top levels. Try immersing yourself for months in the lower levels."

Seth's eyes widened. "You had to do that?"

"Yeah, for a mission. Not this part of Zakara Prime, but conditions were a lot like this. They say once you go into the lower levels, it's the same everywhere. I would agree with that."

Seth glanced at Zane. "And you've been here before?"

"Yeah, I've done work here. Look tough, pack heat, mind your own damn business, and you're good to go," said Zane.

"Must have been a good contract to come out here."

Zane drew his lips to the right. "The highest paying ones usually are. There's a contract center farther down. You'll find some of the more hardcore mercs, bounty hunters, and justice hunters there."

It took a bit to get to the bar, but they made it with no altercations.

Seth sized up the place. Some type of fusion between metal and rap blared out of it. The shrill vocals were definitely alien, though. He had gotten used to hearing unusual music, but he enjoyed what he was hearing. The bar itself had a large sign out front, displaying a variety of services and products. The two human guards outside the bar wore light armor with no helmet other than a headband with an eye terminal over one eye. Their weapons were slung out front, ready to fire.

Blake walked up to them. "Any specials?"

"Yeah, don't start shit, and you live," said one of the guards.

The other one laughed.

"Quite a special. Let's go," said Blake.

One of the guards scanned them as they entered the bar.

Seth rubbed his eyes as the smoky interior stung them. The strong smell of something alien corrupted his nose. It reminded him of burned flesh. He activated his helmet, and the faceplate slid shut. He breathed better once the environmental controls took over and began to filter.

Zane tapped Seth's arm. "You'll get used to it."

"Yeah, right," said Seth.

Blake pointed at a medium-sized circular table with four stools around it on the opposite side of the room. "There."

Once seated, Blake tapped Zane on the arm. "Be prepared to activate your arm shield."

"What's up?" asked Zane.

"Xibian mercs. They've been tracking us since we entered. Five of them. They're staring at us."

"Are you sure?" asked Ada.

"Yep," said Blake. He gestured forward at a shiny container in the distance. "I see them through the reflection."

"What action should I take?"

"Cover Seth if something happens, and for now, launch a surveillance drone and make sure its camouflage is active."

Ada nodded and pulled a disc-shaped drone from her backpack. She placed it on the table, and after a moment, it shimmered out of view.

Seth could see a small visual inside his helmet of what the drone saw. The Xibian mercs were eyeballing the group.

Zane activated the faceplate on his helmet.

Seth's gut told him it was about to get nasty. The Xibians were a strange race. They were humanoid but had one central eye and long strands of hair over their bodies, and their society was dominated by powerful tribal merc clans. He had had to deal with some during his cargo-flying days and knew they were not to be trifled with.

A green humanoid female walked up to the table. "You gonna order anything?"

Seth knew she was Ranaxian. They were a matriarchal society, and a race he had many enjoyable experiences with. Their females were aggressive and preferred humans to their own kind. He had heard they were shocked when they ventured out into space and discovered that not all civilizations were patriarchal, much less humanoid. He grabbed her hand and pulled her in close. "It's about to get bad. Go!"

The woman's eyes widened as she scurried off.

Seth glanced over at the mercs, who had been watching.

The mercs stood and drew their weapons.

///////

Blake assessed the situation. Although the mercs were about to fight, their firing arc was limited due to the design of the bar. There were several pillars in the way that looked like they could take a shot or two. He sniffed the air. The Xibians were not the most hygienic, and their powerful odor was easy to pick out. Judging by the variety of smells, he counted two elder ones, two middle-aged ones, and a younger one. A standard five-person Xibian tribal crew. Usually middle-aged ones used robots as companions until they could prove themselves to their clan. This group meant to kill. He closed up his helmet and then glanced at Zane. "Now! Ada, cover Seth!"

Zane stood and simultaneously activated his orange forearm shield. When he faced the mercs, the rectangular energy shield stood about five feet wide and seven feet tall. He yelled as he charged forward.

Blake followed behind him.

Seth and Ada scrambled behind a pillar.

Ada launched an assault drone. It hovered for a moment and then flew forward.

The mercs opened fire with their assault weapons. Several patrons caught in the crossfire went down immediately. The bullets that hit Zane's shield lit it up but ricocheted off.

Blake shredded the merc on the farthest right when he came within Blake's firing arc.

Zane was almost on the Xibians.

The assault drone, hovering behind Zane's shield, mowed down the merc farthest on the left.

The remaining three mercs looked to the sides in surprise.

Zane reached the first one and dissipated his shield. He pulled out his mace and then bashed the merc's head in.

Blake pulled out his dual blades. With a swift dual motion, he targeted another merc and put one blade through the neck and the other through the chest. He kicked the merc off his blades.

Zane raised his mace to crush the last merc, who dropped his weapons and raised his arm to protect himself.

With a raised hand, Blake said, "Let the last one live!"

Zane breathed heavy as he lowered his mace.

Seth and Ada emerged from behind the pillar and joined the group.

Zane pulled the weapons and various gadgets off the merc.

The two guards from outside rushed in.

"What the hell's going on in here?" asked one of the guards.

"They tried to collect on a bounty, I think . . . and failed," said Blake.

The guards looked at each other.

"It's okay," said the Ranaxian, popping out from behind the bar she had hidden behind. "He's telling the truth."

One of the guards narrowed his eyes as he focused on Blake. "You're gonna clean this shit up."

Blake nodded. "Not a problem."

The guard sneered and then exited with his partner.

Blake knelt next to the merc and laid one of his blades against the merc's neck. "I bet you're wondering about now . . . is Blake Brown going to drink me dry?"

"W . . . what?" asked the merc.

"Blake . . . ," said Seth.

"All right, all right," said Blake. He bared his fangs. "Why'd you attack us?"

"There's a b . . . bounty on you."

"There's quite a few on us. Which one did you take?"

"Delkis's," said the merc.

Blake pursed his lips, then faced the rest of the bar. In a loud voice, he said, "Anyone else want to try to collect on this bounty?"

Various bar patrons shook their heads, while others left.

Blake rubbed his chin. "Looks like it was just your crew foolish enough to try this. You're young, and your slow reaction is what saved you. By not getting your weapon drawn and firing fast enough, you were the last to stand. That's not something I would be proud of, but . . . you're a Xibian merc. I'm going to suggest you drop bounty hunting for a while."

The merc nodded vigorously.

Blake extended his hand and waved his fingers. "Hand over your data device."

The merc complied.

Blake handed the device to Ada. "Can you get anything from this?"

Ada took the device and flipped it around. After a moment, she extended her finger to an access port. A small pair of tendrils came out of her finger and plugged into the port. "Analyzing."

Blake nodded and then glared at the merc. "When was this bounty placed?"

"I . . . I don't know. We were notified of it when we scanned the bounty boards after arriving yesterday."

"You know this is neutral territory, right?"

The merc gulped as he nodded.

"And yet, your posse decided to fucking violate that. Not only that, but you killed several innocent people who were between us when you began firing. If we hadn't killed you, the Selva Tong might have. Anyways, I'm gonna let you live, but the weapons and armor your crew brought here are mine. You leave here naked. If you want to take your crew with you, strip them first. And . . . you'll carry out the other dead bodies as a service to the bar. Understand?"

The merc sat up and sighed. "Yeah."

"Get to it!" said Blake. He pointed at where they had originally sat. "Pile the weapons and armor over there."

Zane laughed while Seth shook his head.

The merc wasted no time in getting undressed and then attending to the others.

Ada tapped Blake's arm. "I have the bounty video feed."

"Great. Wait here," said Blake. He walked up to the Ranaxian waitress that had come out to them earlier.

She surveyed the damage with wide eyes and lips parted.

"The weapons and armor are yours. Consider it a donation for the trouble caused," said Blake.

"Thanks," she said.

"What's your name?" asked Blake.

"Ranell."

"You have a side room we can use for a moment?"

Ranell nodded and gestured for him to follow.

Blake followed her to a back storage room. He looked around and then said, "This'll do. We'll use it to view the bounty video once the weapons and armor have been stripped, and the dead mercs and those they killed are out of your bar." He eyed Ranell. "You get a lot of this?"

"They usually do it outside."

Blake smiled, baring his fangs. "They just couldn't wait to get their hands on me."

Ranell dipped her head. "I can see why. I thought you wanted a side room for another reason."

"Oh . . . I like you. Once all this is over, you might see me again."

"I'd like that. There's . . . something different about you."

"I'm a Daedrould, or vampire as you may or may not know."

"Really? I've heard about them. It's said that sharing blood can cause . . . extreme sensitivity. I've never tried it but . . . always wanted to."

Blake could smell that she was excited. It seemed Ranell was especially interested in him, maybe due to the fight she just saw. It would be a bonus for someone who enjoyed violence to work this far down. He liked Ranaxian women, mainly because they were sexually aggressive. On their world, the men were submissive. He retracted his glove, exposing his hand. When he placed it under her chin and ran his thumb over her lips, she opened her mouth and sucked on his thumb. He exhaled slowly from his nose. "Yeah, let's stay in contact. When this is all over, we're going to spend some time together." He retracted his hand and then took a step to the side and slapped her ass.

Her eyes drooped for a moment as she grinned.

"Until then," said Blake. He headed back to the others.

"He's dragging the last body out now," said Seth. "Not really sure how he's gonna move his crew up three levels."

"He'll call in for support."

Zane snorted. "Maybe we'll need to waste them too."

"Possibly. Anything goes down here."

The merc came back in and began to haul the naked body of the last merc. He paused to look at Blake, then focused on continuing to drag.

Blake narrowed his eyes. He figured that one of the dead four was probably a relative, if not the whole group. That was unfortunately the price for coming at him. It all could have been avoided if they had just had a drink. Instead, they tried their luck, and lost, badly. The smell of blood, even Xibian blood, was making his bloodlust simmer. He fought to stifle it.

Seth laid a hand on Blake's shoulder. "I know this is probably exciting you."

Blake licked his right fang. "A little." He pointed at the storage room in the back. "C'mon, we have a bounty video to watch."

The group followed Blake into the storage room.

Ada laid the data device pulled from the merc on the ground. Next to it, she placed a small rod with a half-circle base and then hooked the two devices together. "It's ready for playback."

"Play it," said Blake.

The projection shot up an image of Delkis.

Delkis had on a skintight gray outfit with a loose jacket and seemed much bigger than Blake remembered.

"Damn, guy's been working out," said Zane.

"It would seem so," said Blake.

Delkis began to speak. "I have a bounty for the following individuals. They're masquerading as the Fredorian presidential guard. They're armed and dangerous. Bring them to me . . . dead or alive, except for Blake Brown, whom I want alive."

Blake watched as each member of his crew appeared with a dead-or-alive status and the payout price for both. The last one showed a chubby Fredorian named Calis.

"I don't remember a Calis," said Seth.

Blake grinned. "It was one of the fake crew members Rakar added. He changed it up for each agency when he gave out the official roster per Senate rules."

"Damn, that's smart," said Zane. "So who leaked our crew info?"

"The FDF."

"You serious, man?" asked Seth. "You think Delkis has an informant in the FDF?"

Blake checked his forearm device and then pointed at it. "No, and I'll show you why. Ada, show the bounty listings that the Xibians saw."

The rod projected a hologram above it that showed a list of bounties. The *Exceltion* crew was listed in various spots among other bounties.

"Look at the dates these were added. They were added yesterday. It takes a while to get added here, at least twenty-four hours."

"So if they had this information yesterday, then it was added two days ago."

Blake nodded. "Yep. On top of that, the crew roster was classified. I think Delkis was given this. No need for an informant."

Seth shook his head. "So now we have to deal with the FDF that's working with Delkis."

"'Working with' is a strong set of words. More like . . . common enemy. I know the FDF doesn't care much for me, or anything I do. They definitely wouldn't like this unit. We'll sit on this for now."

Zane smirked. "Let 'em bring it if they want. We'll kick the shit out of them just like we did these mercs."

"Taking on the whole FDF might be a challenge," said Blake.

Zane laughed.

"Ada, store the device. We can analyze other data on it later."

Ada complied.

"Let's head to Kahan turf and see how deep this goes," said Blake.

CHAPTER
ELEVEN

The repetitiveness of the ramp system blurred together for Seth. They were nearing level sixteen after about an hour and fifty minutes of walking. Seth went over the incident in the bar in his head several times. It stuck out to him because unlike the faceless mercs he was used to confronting, this group had a younger member that most likely lost a relative, based on how Xibian groups worked. Maybe even more. However, it was not lost on him that he and the others could be dead now if they had not acted.

It was the young merc's facial expression when moving the corpses that gave Seth pause. The expression was a mix of fear and sadness. The reactions of the group were not surprising. Zane would have probably killed the young merc if Blake had not stepped in. The cold, hard look that was in Zane's eyes was one Seth knew well. Ada seemed indifferent to the situation. Blake probably stepped in because he realized the merc was younger. He could have easily grabbed the device off the dead body. Seth was glad to see Blake show mercy, a reminder that underneath Blake's killer side was a compassionate side, even if it was one that drank blood.

Seth's eyes caught the reflection of the ramp lights on the moist ground. He doubted that any type of mechanical system like an escalator would work down this far, especially if it required maintenance. It made him wonder how the ramp that went straight to the lower levels handled it. It seemed the lower they went, the rougher the surrounding area was outside the ramps. Even the bar up top was on a fairly maintained street. Every level from five to sixteen looked like pathways through clutter. There were still streets, just not ones he would want to be alone on.

The other disturbing aspect of the ramps were the sounds of fighting. Seth had looked around each time they hit a level to see if he could pinpoint the source, but it was futile. One of the sounds he heard made his skin crawl. It reminded him of the last sounds of someone being killed. As dark as everything was, Blake and Zane seemed to be in good spirits. Seth could tell by the casualness of their walk and lighthearted discussion about Zakara Prime. He could not tell that with Ada, who had remained silent as she observed everything. He looked forward to talking to her later about this mission.

"We're here," said Blake, pointing to a sign on the front of a small building outside the ramp.

"Hard to tell down here. You'd think they would label the levels," said Seth.

Blake raised an eyebrow. "They did. That sign literally says sixteen."

Seth examined the sign. "In what language?"

"The Gulltissarian language."

"It's not in the translation database," said Seth. He glanced at Zane. "You able to translate that?"

Zane nodded. "I picked it up when I was out here." He opened up his forearm screen and, after a moment, said, "Now you and Ada got the translation."

Seth observed the sign and watched the English translation appear inside his helmet. "Damn, how many other languages you two got?"

"I have a lot," said Zane.

"Same," said Blake. "When we get back, we can sync up. The database on the suits is from the *Exceltion*, so probably only has the more known ones on it."

"I would've thought they'd have this one. It's not like we're beyond the outer rim or anything."

Blake paused and looked down for a moment. "The Gulltissarians are a weird race. They actually came from far away. No one really knows their home planet, not even them. Their colony ship must have been lost, because this is where it came. They've been here now for two hundred years. Not all Gulltissarians are Kahan members, but all Kahan members are Gulltissarian."

"They must have a unique perspective on life," said Ada. "I am interested in learning more about them."

Seth nodded. "Coming here must have been hell for them. They'd have to be tough to not only survive that, but survive here for that long."

"If we're done with the history lesson, we need to head out," said Blake.

Seth dipped his head and gestured forward. He knew Blake was anxious to get going, but Seth enjoyed these types of discussions. It was a reminder that not every moment had to be violent.

As they exited the ramp system and headed down a large street, two Gulltissarians approached them.

Seth noted that they had unusually long fingers and thin arms and legs, and their bodies reminded him of a pear. Although they had on armor, he could still see their faces. Their round yellow heads had three big round eyes. A large bone structure jutted out to the sides and the back, forming one solid piece. It was one of the more unusual-looking species he had seen.

One of the Gulltissarians scanned their group. The other raised a hand and said, "Where do you think you're going?"

Blake tossed his hands out to the side. "Fellas. We're just here to talk with Gertus."

The one that scanned them focused on Blake. "No bounty hunting here, even if you are the bounty, according to this scan."

"Of course. I'm assuming you're with the Kahan."

"We are," said the Gulltissarian. He glanced at the other one for a moment, then looked at Blake. "We'll let you in . . . for five hundred credits. You cause trouble, we'll kill you." He pulled a device out and showed Blake a screen with a deposit number.

Blake sighed as he interacted with his forearm screen. "A good ol'-fashioned shakedown. Seems that practice is universal. Anyways, done."

The Gulltissarians stepped to the side and waved the group forward.

When they were out of earshot, Zane narrowed his eyes. "Five hundred credits . . . used to be three hundred when I was here."

"Cost of living, I guess," said Blake. "I had hoped they would just let us through. Worth a shot."

"So . . . now we need to figure out where Gertus is. Maybe we should ask those guys that shook us down," said Seth.

Blake pointed off in the distance. "There."

Seth followed where Blake was pointing at. "How could you possibly know that?"

"Look at the building. It's clean. Not only that, it has towers with turrets, not to mention that it's the biggest building we've seen down here so far. To the sides are two power stations, most likely fusion reactors. They wouldn't stick those just anywhere."

Seth studied the large building in the distance. It was easy to pick out due to the tall towerlike structures on the sides. Blake was right: it stood out. Seth shook his head. While he had been thinking of how they would find Gertus, Blake just surveyed the environment and figured it out. That was just being aware in a new environment.

Zane tilted his head toward Seth. "It's also has the best vantage point. The last time I was here, that building didn't exist."

"Yeah, I get it," said Seth. "Let's just go."

They winded through the streets toward the building in the distance.

Seth observed the environment as they went. The level was arranged in L-shaped sections. Each section had storefronts intermingled with housing areas. Outside the main strip they were walking on, he could see a variety of other large buildings, though none as big as the one they were heading toward. He figured those other buildings were maintenance of some type.

Looking around, he saw some Gulltissarians conducting business, and others lounging around and smoking on some device. When he and the others walked by, he could feel the Gulltissarians' eyes on the group. Humans stood out down here. He was thankful the Gulltissarians did not try to start something, but maybe there was a rule about that. They probably figured humans being this far in meant they had already payed for that honor.

After forty-five minutes, they reached the outside of the building.

The small army around it made Seth gulp. He admired Blake's unshakable confidence as he strode right up to the pair of metal doors that served as an entrance.

"We're here to see Gertus," said Blake.

One of the Kahan guards looked Blake up and down while another scanned him. "He's been expecting you."

Blake narrowed his eyes. "Really . . ."

The Kahan guard sneered and then waved them forward. "Put away your weapons and follow me."

The group complied and followed the guards in.

Seth could hear the upbeat tempo of some music in the background. The building interior had metallic panels on the floor, clean metal walls that had a light tube near the ceiling, and in general a clean environment. It stood in stark contrast with what he had just traveled through. Although he had not paid it attention on their way in, he could now see that there were several types of Gulltissarians. The ones he saw as they walked down a hallway were physically different in their appearance. One type had a rounder body while the other was boxier. Additional body parts were covered on both groups. He tapped at Blake's arms. "Are those . . . females?"

Blake laughed. "Gulltissarians have three sexes."

"Oh . . ."

The guard peered back at Seth. "We can arrange for you to learn more about that . . . for a few hundred credits."

Seth licked his lips. "I'm good."

"What? You think you're better than us?"

"No . . . it's just . . ."

Blake shook his right hand out. "We're here strictly on business."

The guard snorted and continued on.

Blake glanced at Seth. "Unless . . . you're interested of course."

Seth's eyes widened as he shook his head.

Zane laughed as they continued following the guards.

////////////

Blake sniffed the air when he entered the large room that Gertus was in. The room reminded Blake of a command center dropped into a club. Workstations manned by Kahan members were on the edges, with an open area in the middle. Where the DJ would be in the back sat a massive half-circle workstation. He squinted at the brightness of the room. The smell of the machines and the room was mixed with the smell of the Gulltissarians. He wondered how their blood tasted. Maybe he would get a chance to get a sample for analysis. That was one aspect he loved about being out in space: getting to try out all sorts of new alien blood.

The guards led the group up to the end of the room. Once there, they stood to the side and focused on the imposing Gulltissarian sitting behind the workstation.

Blake could hear Seth's heartbeat pick up. Zane was calm, as Blake had expected.

The Gulltissarian behind the desk cleared his throat. "I'm Gertus, but I'm sure you know that already. I know who you are." He glanced at Zane. "You hold some respect down here. My father liked you. You were one of his more trusted . . . enforcers."

"He was a good person. I'm sorry to hear he passed," said Zane.

Gertus bowed slightly and then looked at Seth. "You, I don't know, or the android." He stared at Blake. "I do know you, though, ranger. Your exploits are well-known."

Blake tossed his hands out to the side and smiled, baring his fangs. "That's me, but now I'm part of the Fredorian presidential guard."

"The presidential guard? How's that?"

"Long story . . ."

"Well then, I'm curious . . . as to why you're here," said Gertus. He waved at the guards, who took a step back and slung their weapons over their backs.

"Just passing through," said Blake. "Oh . . . and looking for a scumbag named Delkis."

Gertus eased back into his chair and touched his fingertips in front of him. "Is that what the fight topside was about?"

"Xibian mercs tried to collect on a bounty placed by Delkis on my crew. They failed."

Gertus laughed. "So I've heard. News travels fast. You let one live . . . Why?"

"He was young, and the rest of his group was probably related."

Gertus eyed Blake for a moment. "You're not quite the ruthless killer I've heard so much about. If anything, you're a killer with a soft side. That's even more dangerous when you know there's something internally that can be hurt."

"What can I say, I'm just a great guy," said Blake.

"That remains to be seen," said Gertus. "Nonetheless, Delkis . . . yes. He's not quite what I expected."

"So you've seen him then?"

"Of course. He came through a few days ago to talk with me. What's your interest in him?"

"He's to be brought back to Fredoria," said Blake.

"What's he done?"

"Another long story," said Blake. "However . . . I was told you might have some information we could use."

Gertus's eyes darted across each member of the group before settling on Blake. "Maybe I do . . . but it has a price. I do wonder how you knew to come *here*."

"I can't say. That's confidential."

Gertus exhaled from his large nose that had four nostrils. "I'll tell you where Delkis is . . . if you handle a situation for me. I owe no allegiance to Delkis. Besides, what he wants is never going to work."

Blake tossed a hand out. "Which is . . . ?"

"Confidential. To get Delkis, you'll need to head to where he's holed up in Selva Tong territory. On the way there is a prison. Well, more like a building with cages. I have some members I need freed from there."

Zane snorted. "You want us to fucking break into a Selva Tong prison?"

"I do, but I have another way for you to get in there. More discreet."

Blake sighed. "Why don't you just do it yourself?"

"It would be a little odd for the Kahan to be freeing their own members, don't you think? It would be a turf war, and Selva Tong far outnumbers us. Besides, we just rent this area . . . for now."

Blake looked at the ground for a moment. "So we do this, and then you send us information on where Delkis is."

"Now you're getting it," said Gertus. He raised a finger. "And one other condition. One of you stays as insurance. Betray me, they die. Of course, you can just walk away from all of this. I grant you that only because of Zane."

Blake glanced at Zane, who nodded.

"So . . . what's it going to be?" asked Gertus.

Blake looked at the rest of the group.

Ada stepped forward. "I'll stay."

"The android," said Gertus. He leaned forward. "You don't have morphable skin, so you're a G2 or higher."

"I'm a G2."

Seth took a step ahead of Ada and motioned for her to step back. "I'll stay."

"You?"

Seth licked his lips. "Blake is needed for dealing with whatever is in the prison, and Delkis. Zane can fight, and if there are any technical systems that need hacked, you need Ada. I'm the expendable one here."

Blake furrowed his eyebrows. "You sure about this?"

Seth sighed. "No, but you know I'm right. Just do this, then swing back and pick me up. At least I won't get my ass kicked here."

"Well, you won't be as much fun as the android, but that's acceptable," said Gertus. "Do you agree to my terms?"

"Yeah," said Blake. "We need any information on the prison, who to get, and how to get in. With Ada, we have more options on the table."

A big smile crept onto Gertus's face. He motioned at the guards, who approached Seth.

"I'll be okay," said Seth.

Blake sighed. He knew Seth would be treated fairly, but if things went bad, Seth would pay the ultimate price. Blake did not like these types of arrangements, but having a successful first mission was important. Not only for him, but for the rest of the crew. "All right. That's done. Let's get down to business."

"My favorite part," said Gertus. He stood and gestured toward a door behind him. "To my secure room."

Blake saw Seth glance back before going through a door. Blake clenched his jaw. Deal or no deal, if Seth was harmed, every Kahan member would know Blake's wrath. He nodded at Zane and Ada and headed toward the room. Once inside, Blake took a seat at a table as the door sealed shut behind him.

Gertus was already seated and tapping at a console embedded in the table. The room itself was small, with large screens covering two sides of the room. One of the screens was just a grid of camera views.

Blake figured that this was probably where Gertus spent most of his time.

A map projected over the center of the table. It had multiple colored layers. A red dot blinked, and a line connected where they were to the red dot, which was several levels and a bit away.

Gertus pointed at the red dot. "That's the prison. Obviously, you're not going in the front door. There is a transportation network that runs underneath it, and alongside it is a network of maintenance tunnels. One of them leads up to a supply depot under the prison. There's a control booth there that is connected to the main prison system, and the booth also controls entry into the loading bay. I'm sure your android friend here can do things with that. Once you have my people, get them back out to the maintenance tunnels. They know the way back."

"My name is Ada."

"Of course it is."

Blake narrowed his eyes. He could see that like the Fredorians, the Gulltissarians had a dim view on androids in general. "So gain entry via a supply depot, free your people somehow, and get them back out to the maintenance tunnels."

"As I mentioned, since you have *Ada*," said Gertus, bowing slightly and smiling, "you can probably unlock the cells from that control booth. Normally, I would suggest you go in a bit to one of the main offices, but if Ada is any good at hacking, which I assume she is, she'll be able to access everything from the control booth."

"Security seems a little lax," said Zane.

"While they may lack sophistication in their security, they make up for it with sheer numbers. There're a lot of guards inside."

"How do we know which cells to unlock?" asked Zane.

Gertus shrugged. "I leave that up to you."

Blake rubbed his temples. "We'll need the names of the people you want freed."

"I can get that to you."

Zane ran a hand over his bald head. "How many people are we rescuing?"

"Just four. The Selva Tong know that if anyone were to escape, the prisoners would still be deep in Selva Tong turf, and like the prison, there are a lot of members around that area."

Zane raised an eyebrow. "Maybe we can cause a riot. Unlock all the cells."

Blake's eyes searched the map for a moment. "That might work, assuming we can get the people we need out safely. We'll need to figure that out when we get there." He glanced at Gertus. "Seth is not to be harmed while we do this."

"Of course. He's just insurance. Standard operating procedure. I'll relay the maintenance tunnel network layout."

"And once you have word that your people are in the tunnels, you'll give us Delkis's location and free Seth?"

"When they are halfway through the maintenance tunnels, tell them to contact me," said Gertus. He handed Blake a device. "They can use this. Once that's done, Seth is free to go, and I'll send you details on Delkis."

Blake clenched his jaw for a moment. "We'll be too far in for him to join us. You can tell him to head back to the ship, although he'll probably ask to stay where he is until we get back. I'll leave that up to him to decide."

"Very well," said Gertus.

Blake nodded at the others. "Let's get what we need and get outta here."

CHAPTER
TWELVE

As Seth was led down to the Kahan holding area, he noticed that the smell had changed dramatically. It was a mix of shit and oranges, not odors he usually associated with each other. Although he had his faceplate down, he was not sure if closing it back up would startle the guards. Maybe he would wait until he got to wherever it was he was headed. The hallways were dirty, a far cry from what he had seen in Gertus's main room. The sounds were also getting louder. Shouting alongside moaning and groaning filled the air.

The guard leading Seth paused at a metal door. It slid open after the guard interacted with a side console.

Seth wrinkled his eyebrows at what he saw. It looked less like a holding area and more like a full-on prison. There were various tiers with stairs to each one, and each level had metallic-barred cages separated by stone walls. He took a deep breath. "You sure we're in the right place?"

The guard sneered as he checked a device in his pocket. "I am now. Hand over your weapons and devices."

Seth complied and followed the guard up to the first tier and into a small dimly lit cell. It was bare, except for a dirty mat on the ground, and a stone outcropping that served as a bench. Based on the smell emanating from the hole in the ground, he understood its purpose. Etchings on the wall from previous occupants painted a dismal experience. Not having a way to defend himself or communicate made him feel vulnerable. All he had on was his one-piece full-body and formfitting under armor and boots.

"Stay," said the guard as he exited the cell. He slammed the door shut.

"Where do I get water?" asked Seth.

The guard pointed at a dusty rectangular opening on the wall. "Every four hours, the replicators turn on, and you can use it to get food and water. Those are the only two patterns."

Seth gulped. "Every four hours. Got it. I guess I'll just wait here then."

The guard smiled. "You do that."

As the guard walked away, Seth approached the bars and looked out. The place was a nightmare, but thankfully he would only be there for a while. He figured the replicator with just two patterns had one for a water container and the other for a low-resource food item. Probably a loaf of some type. With nothing to do, he lay down on the dirty mat and closed his eyes.

Several hours later, he awoke to a clanging noise on the bars, as if someone was dragging a metal object across them. He yawned and sat up. His face went pale at the person on the other side of the bars. It was Alcarez. Someone Seth thought he had killed on the first freelancing contract that he and Blake took. They had orchestrated a battle between the Red Wave, a power group on Tooka, and Alcarez's base. Alcarez lost. Half of his face looked melted, but given that he had a warehouse blow up on him, that would be expected. His body armor was metallic and looked new. However, since he was a cyborg, parts of his body made it hard to determine where the armor started and stopped. Seth jumped up and moved to the back of the cell.

"Such a cold reception," said Alcarez with a grin. "Where'd we leave off? Oh . . . that's right." He wagged a finger. "You shot me with a ship weapon, and left me for dead."

"You couldn't have survived that."

"Oh . . . but I did," said Alcarez. He narrowed his eyes. "Barely. And what awaited me when I gained consciousness? One and a half years as a prisoner of the Red Wave. Yeah. They tortured me. Took all my assets. I was their prisoner, but no more."

Seth licked his lips. "What do you want?"

Alcarez smiled. "I'm just here to pay the bounty. Surely you knew you had one on you and Blake."

"We had several."

"Yes . . . Delkis. He had a higher price than mine. I'm much easier to work with, though, and less of a chance that someone might die trying to collect."

"I don't think Gertus would chance pissing off Blake."

"Who said anything about Gertus? I'm talking about the prison guard that sold you out," said Alcarez. "I'll admit . . . I was a bit surprised to get an alert on my bounty. Thankfully, I've been on Zakara Prime for the last six months. Great place to hide out . . . and determine the best way to get you and Blake."

"Well, I guess you're just lucky then."

Alcarez laughed. "You're still funny." His face changed to one of fury. "But you're going to pay. No . . . I'm not going to kill you, but you're going to suffer like I did."

The prison guard appeared next to Alcarez.

"Your payment has been transferred," said Alcarez.

"Pleasure doing business with you. I'll escort you out and then notify the warden that he's escaped."

Seth gulped. "I'm not going anywhere with you!"

The cell door slid open.

Alcarez stepped into the cell. "Oh . . . but you are. I've dreamed of this for a while now. Once I get Blake, it'll be complete. Years of painful torture await you." He grinned as he reached for Seth.

////////

Blake analyzed the loading bay across the transportation network railway. They had taken the maintenance tunnels for the last hour. As he expected, it had people living in it when they should not have been. Mentioning Gertus's name seemed to make most get out of the way. Some were belligerent and learned quickly why that was a bad idea.

The loading platform ended with two massive doors. A control booth sat to the left. Between them and the loading bay platform was the transportation network railway, which sat about five feet lower than the loading bay platform and was about twenty feet wide.

Zane pointed near the top of the building past the loading bay. "Sensors there. Also looks like several turrets."

"I see them," said Blake. "We'll need to put those out of play while we work in the control booth. However, disabling them will raise an alarm."

Ada pulled a small drone out of her backpack. "This is a remote access drone. It's equipped with extensions that allow it to hard connect to devices. It should be able to deactivate the sensors. It also has a detection deflection system on it, so it should be able to avoid being detected, at least for a short while. It wouldn't work on a larger sensor like a ship's, but it should on these."

Zane looked the drone over. "Worth a shot. Those turrets are probably linked to them."

"Do it," said Blake. "Once the sensors are obscured, I'll camouflage and hit the control booth. Ada, I'll need you to use the remote access drone to get that control booth door open for me. Then I'll take out the guard, and then you two can come after that. Ada can then do her hacking thing while we keep watch. Everyone clear?"

Zane smiled big. "I wish we could just kick the door in, but that might be a bit messier."

"I know you want to try out your suit, and once inside during the chaos, you'll have ample opportunities to," said Blake.

"Can't wait," said Zane.

"Launching the drone now," said Ada.

The drone hovered for a moment before moving off toward the loading area. It flew as high as it could go near the ceiling before dropping into position behind the first sensor.

Ada tilted her head. "Accessing first sensor." After a moment, she said, "It's down. The drone had to drill in since the access ports are internal and on the part that is inside the building. That should keep the sensor busy. There are three more, and they are linked to the turret system."

The others nodded.

After a few minutes, Ada said, "The rest are down, but not for long. I've reduced the sensor radius to the size of the sensor for about ten minutes."

"Only ten minutes?" asked Blake.

"That was the maximum I could set it to. Any more and the configuration change detection system would notify other systems. Its threshold for notification is ten minutes. Note that the change is still logged."

"Then that's my cue. Time to play," said Blake. He activated his camouflage shielding and moved out of the tunnel. After jumping down into the submerged transportation network railway, he crossed over and then jumped out. He paused for a moment to see if the turrets moved. After determining that they were still out of commission, he hugged the left wall and sprinted to the control booth. The remote access drone was already there and connected to the door console. Its spiderlike legs were splayed out with the central part covering most of the console. He drew his blades.

The door clicked.

Blake kicked it open and, using a quick strike, decapitated the guard. He tapped at his forearm screen. "Come down."

Zane and Ada arrived a minute later.

Ada sidestepped the guard's head while placing the remote access drone in her backpack. She examined the control booth's operational console. Once she determined where the access ports were, she extended her hand. Metallic tendrils connected to the port. "It will take me a bit to determine how this system is set up and what its weak points are, in addition to what we can and can't do."

Blake laid a hand on her shoulder. "You wanted a chance to prove yourself. Here you go."

"Accessing now."

"So far, so good," said Zane.

"Let's not be hasty. We may only have access to these doors," said Blake.

Ada shook her head. "Not exactly. There is no system AI present, and they're using a centralized system. I will have control shortly."

"I wouldn't expect it to be a high-tech prison down here," said Blake. "From what I've heard, Selva Tong would rather eliminate people than keep them around. Guessing this is mainly for people they want to torture."

Zane nodded. "Yeah, it's a real piece of work. Their justice system is whatever they feel it needs to be for that day.

Probably a lot of people here that are put in and forgotten. Like the Fredorians did to me."

Blake eyed Zane. "You know . . . you came recommended to me by Rakar directly. Do you know how rare that is?"

"I don't, but I'm damn glad he did. This is a hell of a lot more exciting than sitting in a cell, rotting away for the rest of my life."

Ada turned her head. "I've accessed their main control system using a privilege escalation attack. I have found the four people Gertus wants out. They are on the third floor in a row with five cells. The system will only allow a row to be unlocked at a time. There is a manual override for each row, though."

Blake nodded. "If we unlock all but that row, can you unlock it when we get there?"

"With administrative rights, I can do anything now."

"Damn, you're good. Shut off the visual feeds and communication systems. No need to alert anyone outside the prison."

Ada complied.

Blake slapped Zane on the back. "Ready for a riot?"

"Hell yeah," said Zane.

"Do it!" said Blake, laying a hand on Ada's shoulder.

"Opening all cells . . . now," said Ada.

Blake strained to hear. "I can hear something going on."

"The alarms are muted."

"Let's go," said Blake.

Ada unhooked from the console.

Blake nodded at the door. "Take point, Zane. Ada, relay the Kahan prisoners' locations in our HUDs."

Ada nodded while Zane pulled out his shotgun and opened the door.

Blake could see a map overview, with a green line indicating the path they needed to take. They had to get across the interior part of the loading bay, and then go down a hallway into the main building. From there, it was a short distance to a stairwell that would get them to where they needed to go. Although his vampiric senses gave him an internal map based on heartbeats and smells, the sheer number of them overwhelmed him.

A group of guards rushed toward Zane.

Zane took aim at the nearest one and blew him away with his shotgun.

The other guards' bullets lit up Zane's kinetic shielding.

Blake pulled out his striker, and using Zane as a shield, he took out two of the guards.

The remaining guard stopped, spun around, and used a shipping container as cover as he ran away.

Zane began to chase after him.

"Leave him! We need to move!" said Blake.

Zane laughed and shouted toward the retreating guard, "You got fucking lucky!"

They paused when they reached the hallway on the opposite side of the loading bay.

Blake could hear shouting and the sounds of fighting just ahead. "The stairwell isn't far from where we'll enter from. Zane."

Zane smiled as he stormed through the hallway and kicked the door down when he got to the end of it. He stepped into a small room and looked around. "No one here."

Blake pulled back his faceplate for a moment to sniff the air. "There was. Whoever was supposed to be guarding this is probably fighting or has abandoned their post." He closed up his faceplate.

"Well, let's not keep them waiting then," said Zane. He strode through the door out of the room. His shielding lit up as a guard fired at him. Zane pulled out his mace, and then charged the guard, cracking him in the head.

The guard went limp.

Blake and Ada stepped through into the open area.

Ada tilted her head. "Interesting."

"What?" asked Blake.

"I'm still soft connected to the system and tracking all the individuals via the system's thermal scans. It seems the prisoners are overpowering the guards and changing the power dynamic."

"No surprise there," said Blake. "The gangs in here are probably a bigger threat than the guards at this point. That won't be the case when word gets out of the prison. Selva Tong will just waste everyone," said Blake. He pointed at the stairwell off to the side. "Time to get these prisoners. Let's go."

CHAPTER
THIRTEEN

Kal Modan jumped up from the concrete bed in his cell. He ran his dark-skinned hand under his chin as he hustled over to the semitransparent shielded cell door. Hearing shouts was normal, but the pattern he was hearing was not. There were a lot of them, and from the sound of it, a fight was going on. Maybe it was a riot. He peered out as best he could, but he could not see to the sides of the narrow entrance to his cell.

Ten minutes later, a prison guard walked backward past his cell and toward the right while firing an assault weapon.

An inmate in a brown one-piece cloth uniform slid up behind the guard and slit his throat. As the guard fell, the inmate grabbed the guard's gun and shot into the air. The inmate looked into Kal's cell with wide eyes, then shook his head around while shouting and wagging his tongue.

Several other inmates gathered around the inmate, jumping and screaming. The inmate with the gun paused to look to the left.

Kal flinched when the inmate's head was shredded. One of the other inmates had a part of his face shot off. The other inmate took off. Kal knew that to be a shotgun blast at close range. It was unusual that his cell door was still active with a riot in progress, especially since it looked like everyone else's was inactive. Whoever fired the shotgun blast would be in front of his cell in a moment. At least with the cell door active, he would be safe.

The cell door dissipated.

Kal backed up to the rear of the cell. His first instinct was to run out, find a weapon, and get the hell out of there. The only problem was he would be in the crosshairs of whoever killed the other inmates. His heartbeat ramped up as he slid to the side of the entrance. Maybe he could overpower whoever came in.

"Kal Modan?" said a grizzled voice.

Kal wrinkled his eyebrows. He prepared himself to tackle whoever was entering the cell. His nose flared as a large man in a medium-armor suit wielding a shotgun entered the cell. The closed helmet obscured facial identification. This was the moment where Kal lived or died. He charged the man, hoping to knock him down.

The man stepped back and with one hand pushed Kal away.

The man turned and pointed the shotgun at him. Another man entered the cell.

Kal noted that the second man wore black light armor and had two energy blades on his back. His sidearms were prominent, and he had a striker in his hands. Although Kal did not know who the first man was due to the helmet, he knew who the second one was based on the open faceplate. His face drained. It was Blake Brown, legendary Fredorian Ranger turned freelancer. Kal might have had a chance against the first man, but not with Blake Brown. They could only be here for one reason. Kal exhaled from his nose and closed his eyes, expecting a swift death.

"You taking a nap now of all times?" asked the first man, lowering his helmet.

Kal opened his eyes and stared at the man. "Zane . . . 'Wild Dog' Gibbons?" He knew Zane to be a fellow justice hunter. Kal's mind raced.

"That's me. What the hell are you doing in here? Saw your name attached to the cell," said Zane.

Kal stood and eyed Zane. "It's a long story." He eyed Blake. "Blake Brown. I might ask you the same."

Blake smiled, showing his fangs. "Contract work. Rescuing some Kahan members. Your cell happened to be on the row they were on. I assume you don't want to be here."

"I don't."

"Where's your gear?" asked Zane.

"Armory. On the second floor," said Kal.

Blake narrowed his eyes. "I take it you're not currently doing a contract?"

"I was . . . but I crossed the Selva Tong."

"How so?"

ADAIR HART

"I went after a high-priced bounty from Fredoria. Some guy called Delkis. His record shows he's a dirtbag, so it lined up nicely for me."

Blake ran his tongue over one of his fangs. "I'm surprised you let the Selva Tong capture you."

Kal looked down. "It's . . . complicated."

"I know your reputation. You're a heavy hitter in the justice-hunter world. Going after Delkis solo is exactly what I would have expected from you," said Blake. "We're actually going after Delkis. If Zane helps you get your gear, you willing to help?"

Kal drew his head back a bit. "You . . . offering me a contract?"

"You'll get a cut if we complete it. Afterward . . . we can talk about opportunities."

Kal licked his lips as his eyes searched the ground for a moment. "All right. Let's see how this goes. Maybe being in a team will yield a better result. Better than being in here at least."

Blake grinned. "Excellent." He slapped Zane's arm. "You good?"

"Yeah," said Zane. He stepped out of the cell. When he returned, he handed Kal the assault weapon the inmate had dropped. "You'll probably need this."

Kal took the weapon. "I appreciate the trust."

Zane laughed. "I know your record. You're one of the good ones who has no problems getting dirty if needed."

Blake extended a hand. "Besides . . . you're Earthborn, as is the rest of my crew. Well . . . except for a few."

"Good company then," said Kal, shaking Blake's hand, then Zane's.

Blake nodded. "I'll see you both at the maintenance tunnel entrance." He exited the cell.

"You ready?" asked Zane.

"Yep. Let's move," said Kal. He was used to operating solo but had worked in a four-man unit in the past. The camaraderie was something he missed, although he did not miss the eventual breakup due to greed. As he exited the cell with Zane, he saw Blake and an android shepherding four inmates to the end of the row. "Kahan, huh?"

"Yeah," said Zane. "Once we get them out, Gertus tells us where Delkis is."

"Sounds like Gertus. He probably saw your group as a golden ticket."

"Whatever works," said Zane. He backhanded an inmate that had rounded the corner they were approaching.

The inmate screamed as he spilled over the guardrail.

They hit the stairwell and descended to the second floor.

Zane's shield lit up as bullets hit it.

Kal took aim and, in two shots, hit the inmates who had fired.

They entered a side hallway and exited into a general room. A large group of inmates with weapons had assembled in the center. Guards were either lying dead or handcuffed with weapons pointed at them. The inmates focused on Kal and Zane, and a wiry inmate with curly hair and fair skin stepped forward. "Kal Modan. I was wondering why

ADAIR HART

your cell wasn't open." The inmate looked at Zane. "Guess I know why now."

Kal moved his lips to the right. "Chris Samuels. The Earthborn that wanted to be a bounty hunter, and failed on his first contract and ended up here."

Chris spit on the ground. "You talk a lot of shit for a soon-to-be dead man. You took my contract!"

"And? You killed a Selva Tong member due to mistaken identity. One action was smart, the other was stupid."

Chris raised his weapon. "Say good night, bitch."

The rest of the group raised their weapons.

Zane pulled out his mace and, in one swift motion, lurched forward and bashed Chris's head in.

The other inmates fired.

Zane tore a path through them, crushing those who did not move in time.

Kal scrambled for cover behind Zane and peeked out to take shots at the inmates that came within his firing arc. Although he had never worked with Zane before, it was natural to use someone with strong kinetic shielding as moving cover. Zane was a beast.

As inmates began to fall, the others took off.

Zane stretched out his arms and laughed. "Anyone else want to fucking talk shit?" He tilted his head back and barked and howled. Once the room had cleared except for the guards who were tied up, he looked around. "So where to from here?"

Kal pointed to the opposite side of the room. "Just through there and down the hallway. Not sure how we're going to get in the armory, though. It's secured."

They began to walk.

"Ada, the android you saw, already hacked into their systems. I'll have her unlock it," said Zane.

"You're a pretty solid crew," said Kal.

Zane nodded. "I guess we are."

They reached the end of the room and entered the hallway.

"I heard you were in prison?" asked Kal.

"Was. Blake offered me a chance to be a part of this crew. It was either that damn cell for the rest of my life . . . or this. I much prefer this."

Kal laughed. "I hear you, man."

"Blake's looking for a fourth. I saw some of the other names he was considering, but I don't think they'd be a good fit. You should consider it."

"You know I work solo," said Kal.

"And look where that got you."

"Good point."

They arrived at the armory.

Zane pulled up his forearm screen and contacted Ada.

A moment later, the door slid open.

Zane pointed at a locker inside whose door had slid back. "Ada says your gear is there."

"Damn, she's good," said Kal. He went to his locker and opened it, and then began to put on his light-armor suit.

He grabbed his dual FLP-40 pistols and holstered them. "There's my baby." He pulled out an advanced-looking sniper rifle. It had served him well, and the black-and-gold paint job on it made his eyes light up. He placed it on his back and faced Zane. "It's weird, you know. Two guys from Earth ending up here."

"Maybe that's saying something," said Zane.

Kal eyed Zane for a moment. "Maybe it is. Let's get the hell out of here."

//////////

Blake watched as Zane and Kal crossed the transportation network railway and headed over. Kal had initially been a person of interest in Blake's early days as a Fredorian Ranger. He did not know the difference back then between a bounty hunter and a justice one. Bounty hunters took up bounties and were not picky on which ones they did, outside the risk versus reward effort. Justice hunters, on the other hand, only took contracts where justice was being served. This usually meant catching those on the run, escaped criminals, or dishing out justice to those who did wrong. Blake was surprised to learn that the amount of contracts that a justice hunter would take were generally higher than other types of contracts. Kal was one of the big-name justice hunters, something Blake could use.

"I have accessed Kal Modan's files," said Ada.

Blake nodded. "He has long history. Ruthless in his own right, and tends to take the risker contracts."

"I don't understand his nickname."

"The Trickster," said Blake with a smile. "The name was given to him for the way he captured his bounties. He uses gadgets, trickery, misdirection, and all sorts of tactics."

"He is skilled with a sniper rifle. Were you not looking for that?"

Blake grinned. "Yep. I think I found my fourth if he's willing."

Zane and Kal reached the tunnel.

"Good to see you," said Blake.

Kal nodded. "Glad you decided to swing by the prison." He extended a hand toward Ada. "Kal Modan."

Ada returned the handshake. "Ada. I've researched the available files on you."

"I figured you would. Thanks for helping me get my gear."

"Of course."

"So . . . what now?" asked Kal.

Blake leaned against the wall and sighed. "We got the four prisoners this far, and now they're headed back. Once they reach the midway point between here and Kahan turf, they'll update Gertus, and then he'll send us Delkis's location. Should be about thirty minutes."

Kal nodded and looked around. "All right."

"We should be safe here, and we got some time. So . . . how'd you get captured?"

Kal sighed as he leaned on the other side of the tunnel. "I didn't know who Delkis was at first, but he had a high-paying bounty on him from an anonymous Fredorian, so I took it. I reached out to all my contacts to locate Delkis, and a friend here informed me that Delkis had been sighted topside. I stayed up at a small place on level two, and . . . had some fun with a Ranaxian. I may have let slip that I was there to hunt Delkis. It turns out that she worked for the Selva Tong. She injected me with a paralyzing toxin, and then I was in prison."

"You ran afoul of the safe-haven rule," said Blake.

Kal nodded.

Ada tilted her head. "How did the Ranaxian apply the toxin?"

Zane laughed.

Ada swiveled her head toward him.

Zane cleared his throat and looked away.

Kal grinned. "I . . . may have been in a compromised position at the time."

"I see," said Ada.

Blake pursed his lips for a moment. "Well, Delkis probably knows that people are gunning for him since he's out. Probably why he came to Selva Tong turf. Odd thing was that he talked with Gertus about something he wouldn't elaborate on."

"You think Delkis is working with the Selva Tong?" asked Kal.

"Maybe. You just mentioned you were going after him and that landed you in prison. The Selva Tong typically wouldn't do that unless you actually tried. I suspect Delkis and the Selva Tong have a special relationship. The fact that he isn't trying too hard to hide his location is probably his way of sending a message to someone."

"Who?"

"Probably the anonymous Fredorian," said Blake.

"Which I'm guessing you ain't gonna say who it is."

Blake nodded.

"Damn. So you assembled a team and took up this contract."

"Well . . . it's a bit more complicated than that. After this is done, I'll tell you more, assuming everything works out."

"All right."

Thirty minutes later, Blake raised a finger as his forearm screen activated.

Gertus appeared on the screen. "My men are halfway back and have contacted me. I'm sending you Delkis's location and associated information. Fair warning, you're in for a hell of a tough fight."

Blake examined the map as it adjusted to the coordinates. He flicked his finger on the screen, sharing it with the others on their communication devices. "A heavily armed compound a bit away on this level."

"Delkis is coordinating whatever it is he's doing from there, under Selva Tong protection," said Gertus. "I'm not sure how he got them to agree to that. I sure didn't agree to it. The Selva Tong is currently run by Daniel Greer, and he would never let an outsider in there, so I'm not sure what's fully going on. I guess you'll find out."

"We'll deal with it. I appreciate the schematics. As for Seth . . . have him contact me when he can."

Gertus nodded, and the screen faded away.

Kal eyed Blake. "Gertus respects you. Everyone else, he treats like shit."

Blake gestured at Zane. "It's him that Gertus respects. He probably just fears me. Anyways, let's find a side room and check out what we're hitting."

They took off down the maintenance tunnel, and after ten minutes, found a side room.

Zane shook his head. "Smells like rotten ass down here."

"The people who live here probably don't have hygiene at the top of their list. If you think it's bad, imagine me with my enhanced senses," said Blake. He nodded at Ada. "Set up the projector."

Ada pulled the projector out and set it on the ground.

Blake interacted with his forearm screen.

A projection shot up showing the Selva Tong compound in 3-D lines.

Blake pointed at a line that went around the compound. "That wall is probably laden with sensors. There are two gates, but both are well defended."

"Why don't we grapple in?" asked Kal.

"Or we could just storm it and rush in," said Zane.

"A distraction could work as well," said Ada. "It would at least give me time to get a remote access drone in, while the offensive drone draws their attention."

"Actually, I don't know how much punishment my kinetic shield can take," said Zane. "A few shots, sure. Multiple turrets and a heavily armed base . . . I don't know, man. If it goes out, all I have is this medium armor. I really could use that juggernaut armor."

Blake rubbed his chin. "I really don't want to go all the way back. However . . . it would give us some time to dissect this more, and we can gear up for a heavier option. We know we can get this far without issue, and we can also pick up Seth."

Kal sighed. "We could take it with what we have now."

"Maybe, but why chance it when we can alter the odds more in our favor? All we're out is the time to the ship and back. We could also get some food and rest up and hit this when everyone's refreshed."

Zane wagged a finger. "I'm with that."

"With heavier armor and time to analyze, our odds would be greatly enhanced," said Ada. "The heavier backpack with more drones would be a more appropriate load out."

"Yeah . . . but Selva Tong will probably discover in time who hit the prison. They'll go into high alert," said Kal.

"Probably, but with the right plan, we can overcome that. All right, it's settled then," said Blake. He gestured at Kal. "Luke, our ship engineer, and Kane, our technician, can also outfit you with whatever you need."

"How big is your ship?"

"It's the *Exceltion*, and it has level-three replicators."

"Whoa. How'd you get that?" asked Kal.

"An anonymous Fredorian."

Kal shook his head. "Your anonymous Fredorian must be stacked."

"You could say that," said Blake. "Let's head to Kahan headquarters. I'll try to raise Seth and let him know we're on our way."

"Shouldn't he have already contacted us?" asked Ada.

"Yeah. It's unlike him to not check in. Could be out of range. Let's check it out."

CHAPTER

FOURTEEN

An hour later, Gertus's compound came into view.
Blake had been checking his forearm device for
any sign of communication from Seth, but it had
been silent. It was unusual for Seth not to check in for so
long. It was possible that his device was in his gear, which
was probably confiscated depending on where Seth was. He
should have retrieved his gear by then. If anything happened
to Seth, there would be hell to pay.

They reached the doors and were ushered in.

Blake found Gertus in the same large room that they had
initially met him in.

The group assembled in front of Gertus.

Gertus bowed slightly. "I wanted to thank you for getting
my men out." He focused on Kal. "It seems you picked up
an additional crew member."

"Yeah . . . but the real question is . . . where's Seth?" asked Blake.

Gertus dipped his head forward. "You're not going to like this . . . but he's missing."

"What?"

"Someone took him from his cell," said Gertus. He waved at a guard in the back.

Blake narrowed his eyes at the bloodied Kahan member that was brought before him. The man had on a uniform of some sort.

Gertus gestured at the man. "This is Adolon. He has a story to tell." He eyed Adolon. "Don't you?"

Adolon squinted with his bruised eyes. "I called in a bounty on him."

"Who placed it?" asked Blake through gritted teeth.

"Alcarez."

Blake's eyes widened as he clenched a fist. "You fucking gave Seth . . . to Alcarez?"

"I don't know him personally, but he had one on you as well," said Adolon. He licked the blood from his lips.

Blake glared at Gertus. "Why didn't you tell me when this occurred?"

"Well . . . I'd hoped to find him before you returned. I've put out a citywide search for Alcarez and Seth. They couldn't have gotten far and are probably hiding somewhere nearby."

Blake closed his eyes for a moment. "I'm going to ask you this once. Choose your words carefully. Are you involved in this?"

Gertus drew his head back a bit. "No. Of course not. This bumbling guard acted in isolation. I've already interrogated him, and he's going to be joining those who he was supposed to be watching over."

"His word's good," said Zane.

Blake glanced at Zane for a moment, then back at Gertus. "I can find him. Where was his cell?"

"We can show you," said Gertus. He waved at the guard and Adolon. "Take this trash to a cell where he can begin his new life as a prisoner."

Adolon was escorted out of the room.

Gertus pointed at another guard. "Doron, take them to Seth's cell. They have my clearance to do whatever they need to."

"Understood," said Doron. He motioned at a side door. "Follow me."

Blake sighed as he shook his head. Alcarez was supposed to be dead. How he issued a bounty raised more questions than it answered. The one thing Blake did know was that if Alcarez was truly alive, then Seth may not be. He pushed the thought out of his mind as he followed Doron out of the room.

When they reached the cell, Blake stepped in and took a deep sniff. In his ranger days, and even when he was on Earth, locating someone was one thing he did well. His keen vampiric sense of smell was more sensitive than a bloodhound's. It had served him well on many missions, and he had used it in the last two years when he was freelancing with Seth. The one advantage he had was that he was familiar with Seth's scent in various situations. He exhaled and then faced the group. "I have the scent."

Kal sniffed the air. "All I smell is shit."

Zane laughed.

"How can you filter his scent from everything else?" asked Kal.

"He's a vampire," said Zane.

Kal's eyes widened. "Seriously? I mean . . . I saw the fangs, but thought was just a body mod or something."

Doron took a step back.

Blake wrinkled his eyebrows. "I thought that was well-known."

"I've heard the term *Daedrould*, but never seen or met one before," said Kal.

"Now you have," said Blake, bowing slightly. He eyed a spattering of blood on the ground. "Looks like before he left the cell, he was hurt." He touched his finger to his tongue, bent over, and dabbed the wet finger over the blood, causing some of it to stick. With a lick, he swished his mouth around for a moment. "We should hurry."

"You sure that's his blood?"

Blake smiled, running his tongue over a fang. "Sure am."

Doron gulped.

They exited the cell.

Blake could see the scent visually. It was like a light, wispy smoke trail that had periodic blotches. Distinguishing it from the other smells was a bit easier since the inmates and guards were mostly Gulltissarians. They had a unique smell that reminded him of an apple dipped in butter. He bet their blood tasted good. The scent trail led him down a flight of stairs and through an office area. He paused as his gaze swept over the guards at their workstations.

"Something wrong?" asked Ada.

"Seth was led through here," said Blake. "These guards were either gone, didn't care, or knew and didn't interfere."

Zane harrumphed. "Maybe we should interrogate them." He glanced at Doron. "Was Adolon the only corrupt guard down here?"

"It's possible. I've heard stories, but I'm part of Gertus's compound security detail. I wouldn't know too much about prison operations."

Zane shrugged. "Worth a shot."

Blake motioned forward. "We don't have time to figure that out. Let's go." As he entered the office area, one of the prison guards approached them.

"Where do you think you're going?" asked the prison guard.

"They have Gertus's approval to be here. Don't interfere," said Doron.

"I don't take orders from you."

Doron tapped at his wrist device, causing an emblem to appear above it. He tilted it toward the prison guard. "I represent Gertus here. If you have a problem with that, I can arrange a meeting with him. You can then join Adolon in a cell."

The prison guard took a step back. "Oh . . . my mistake."

"Yeah . . . get out of here."

The prison guard scooted past them and headed out the way they had come.

"No love lost there," said Zane.

Doron shook his head. "We've had some issues with corruption down here. Even with Gertus's iron hand, some people slip through."

They reached a door with a shielding in front of it.

Doron tapped at his wrist device, and the shield dissipated. "This is as far as I go. I was only supposed to go to the cell."

Blake nodded. "Appreciate the help. We'll take it from here." He pressed forward and opened the door. As his senses became attuned to the new environment, he focused on Seth's scent. It was weaker outside, but still active. They were in a courtyard with guard towers on the end and a security booth on the side of a gated entrance. He pointed ahead. "Through there."

They reached the gates. The guard in the booth was frantically working on his console. The gates slid open.

Blake narrowed his eyes. Apparently the prison guards now knew Gertus had sent someone to find Seth. Standing in the way of that was not something high on their list, it would seem. He closed his eyes and took a deep breath. Seth's scent tickled his nostrils. Blake looked off to the right ahead of them. He scanned the ground as he began to walk, then paused by a pool of dried blood. "He hurt Seth." His face twitched for a moment as he clenched his jaw. He moved his head in a circle while exhaling. His eyes glowed a dim blue, and in a deep, guttural voice, he said, "We move."

They wound their way through the seedy underside of Kahan turf.

Blake could tell this area was rife with criminal elements. As bad as the whole region was in general, this region was worse than the other parts. What passed as buildings were mostly bits and pieces of garbage strewn together. Although the odor was overpowering, he was still able to isolate Seth's scent.

After twenty-five more minutes, they reached a half-circle array of haphazardly built buildings.

Blake pointed at a one-story building on the right. "The scent goes there." Looking at his forearm, he saw that it was about 7:40 p.m. Earth time. Although that did not matter much to nonhumans, it gave him a good idea of when to rest. It also gave him a time reference. Their last contact with Seth was around 3:30 p.m. He braced himself for what he might find inside. With a sweep of his fiery gaze around the group, he said, "Be prepared to fight."

////////

Seth sighed as he sat on the floor, cuffed to a steel post in a run-down one-story building. His sense of time was murky since Alcarez took glee in hitting Seth's head, but he figured it had been about three hours since Blake and the crew had left to free the prisoners. Seth would be glad to see Blake. It seemed even on a new contract, Seth was still getting his ass kicked. He sighed as he squirmed, causing his bruised body parts to scream at him. The pole he was handcuffed to made him sit in an awkward position.

Alcarez talked animatedly with someone on a communication device.

From what Seth could understand, his disappearance had not gone unnoticed.

Alcarez flung the communication device against the wall. He hustled over to Seth and squatted. "Seems the prison guard gave me up. Now there's a search on for you . . . and me."

"Sounds like good news."

Alcarez slapped Seth. "I could just give you a painful, slow death while I escape." Alcarez smiled as he shook his head. "Nah . . . I'm going to get you out of here. You need to suffer horrendously, and death is just too quick of an out."

Seth sighed. "If Blake catches up to you, you're dead."

"We'll see about that. I need to figure out a way out of here," said Alcarez. "This place is a mess, but one thing about the Kahan is they will do anything for power. Whoever finds us would gain a lot of that. I can't let that happen. Not when I'm so close." He took a strip of material with an adhesive grip and fiddled with it before placing it over Seth's mouth. Using a small knife from his belt, he waved it in front of Seth, and said, "I need to scout out a path, but I want you to think of me while I'm gone." He stabbed Seth's thigh.

A bolt of lightning shot through Seth's leg, radiating from the knife that remained buried in his muscle. He tried to cry out as he struggled to breathe. His nose was bashed in, and trying to breathe was already difficult. His chest constricted as he began to hyperventilate.

"Ahh, almost forgot. You need to breathe." He pulled out another small knife and punctured the tape over Seth's mouth. "That should do it."

Seth scooted as far back as he could. The knife sent tremors of pain. His eyes watered as his breathing began to normalize.

"This is going to be so much fun, but first things first. A way out of here," said Alcarez. He stood and took in a breath, then glared at Seth. "Don't go anywhere, and while you have time to think, imagine the pain when I peel your skin off, section by section, fry it up, and then force you to eat it." He laughed as he spun around and left.

Seth closed his eyes. Even when he was supposed to be doing the safer thing, he ended up being a punching bag. Becoming Alcarez's prisoner was the last thing Seth wanted. All he could do was wait and hope something happened. The only consoling thought was that Blake would hunt down and kill Alcarez for this. Seth focused on trying to breathe as he stared at the brown, featureless wall. Maybe a nap would help calm him down. He closed his eyes and tried to focus on shutting out the pain.

An hour later, the sound of a door opening echoed throughout the room.

Seth's eyes snapped open. His stomach turned at the thought that he was about to undergo more torture or, even worse, that Alcarez had found a way through Kahan turf. Seth winced as the pain from the knife reminded him it was there.

Footsteps signaled Alcarez's approach.

Seth's eyes watered as he grimaced. When Blake, Zane, Ada, and someone he did not know entered the room, Seth began to tremble.

Blake rushed over to Seth and looked him over. He peeled the tape from Seth's mouth and then checked out the knife. "You playing hide-and-seek again?"

Seth grimaced as a tear ran down his cheek. "It's Alcarez. He's alive."

"Yeah, I heard. The prison guard who sold you out is now in prison himself," said Blake.

Ada knelt and looked around the knife in Seth's leg. "We need to get this out and remove the cuffs from him." She extended a hand toward the knife.

Blake grabbed Ada's hand. "Well, wait a minute." He eyed Seth. "Where's Alcarez?"

"He knows that they're searching for us, so he's scouting a way out. What does that have to do with the knife in my leg? It hurts like hell."

Blake rubbed his chin. "I think we can assume Alcarez is coming back."

"Yeah, no shit, even more reason for me not to be here."

"Or . . . I can end this threat . . . permanently."

Seth tilted his head. "With me as bait. Again." He sighed. "You're right, of course. I want to see this piece of shit dead. No third chances."

Blake nodded. "No third chances."

Ada put a container up to Seth's lips. "Drink."

As Seth drank, Ada placed her hand on his neck. It felt good to feel her touch, even if the pain was still there.

When she removed the container, she pulled out a small syringe-shaped device. "This will remove the pain temporarily and keep your wound from becoming infected."

Seth could feel the effects of the device instantly. A smooth feeling flowed through him. He knew his body was hurting, but this just made things so much easier to deal with.

Blake faced Zane and the stranger. "You two head back to the ship. Zane, have Luke and Kane hook Kal up. Ada, I want you to wait nearby outside, but out of sight. When I'm done with Alcarez, you can help Seth."

Zane narrowed his eyes. "You're gonna take this guy on alone?"

"He won't know I'm here until it's too late. Besides, I have Ada as backup if needed. Go now, he could be back anytime."

The stranger pulled a device off his belt and handed it to Blake. "Here, take this."

Blake flipped the device around in his hands. "A paralysis mine."

"They don't call me the Trickster for nothing," said the stranger with a grin. "You can place it in front of Seth, activate its camouflage shielding, and if Alcarez steps on it, he'll be held in place. I only have two of those, but . . . it sounds like this is worth it."

"Oh, by the way, this is Kal Modan," said Blake, gesturing at the stranger. Blake pointed at Seth. "This is Seth Williams, Earthborn, and my abductee brother. He's the *Exceltion*'s pilot."

Seth and Kal nodded at each other.

"All right," said Blake. "I'll meet you both back at the *Exceltion*."

Zane and Kal exited the building.

Ada knelt and lightly squeezed Seth's arm. "I'll be nearby."

"I like the sound of that," said Seth.

"How sweet," said Blake, looking like he was trying to stop from laughing.

Ada turned toward Blake.

Seth shook his head. "Always clowning. Don't forget to put the mouth cover back on."

Ada applied the mouth cover. She stood and lightly squeezed Seth's shoulder, then walked out.

Blake placed the paralysis mine in front of Seth. With a tap at the side, it shimmered out of view. "And now for a vanishing act." He activated his camouflage shielding.

Seth looked around. Although he couldn't talk, he was much more relaxed with the pain medication and Blake nearby. Being tortured by Alcarez for the rest of his life was not something Seth wanted to even contemplate. His thoughts focused on Kal Modan. It was a name he had heard before, but Seth did not know much about Kal. It looked like Kal had integrated into the group. Seth looked forward to meeting Kal, assuming he would be joining them. That was the only reason Seth could figure that Blake would allow Kal to hang around.

Blake laid a hand on Seth's shoulder. "This'll be over soon. You know I got your back."

Seth nodded.

"Now we just wait."

CHAPTER

FIFTEEN

Zane lowered his helmet as he walked with Kal through Kahan turf. They had just left Blake, Ada, and Seth and were on their way back to the *Exceltion*. Zane had known Gertus's father well, and had performed some work for him, but Zane was unsure about Gertus. One thing Zane was sure about was that the living conditions in the area had deteriorated. The smell of garbage was almost overpowering, and maintenance seemed to be in short supply everywhere he looked. Gertus's compound was the exception, and Zane suspected that was not by chance.

Kal shook his head. "Wonder why the Kahan bow to Selva Tong. They could control their own territory."

"Maybe, but they don't have the coalition that Selva Tong does to protect their flanks. That's one thing Daniel Greer does well. He leads Selva Tong through not only force, but diplomacy. If the Kahan went independent, then their neighbors would attempt to take advantage of that."

"Damn, man," said Kal. "You musta spent some time here."

"It's been a while, but the major groups here don't change that often. The Kahan would have to have some edge that the others don't."

Kal nodded. "I hear ya."

Outside the noise they made as they traveled down dirt paths through the Kahan slums, it was silent.

"It's too quiet," said Kal.

"Yeah. I don't like it, but I don't think we're in any immediate danger."

"Did you visit this part of Kahan turf before?"

Zane shook his head. "First time. Most of my Kahan dealings involved going off-world to waste somebody."

"The life of a justice hunter is never boring. This doesn't seem like too bad of a gig for you, though."

"I like it so far. Blake's easy to work with, and he's a lot more ruthless than he appears. I respect that," said Zane.

"Yeah, I've heard of his exploits. He's a badass. I was honestly surprised to see him out here. And you as well."

"Fate is a mysterious bitch."

They shared a laugh.

When they reached the ramp network, Zane contacted Blake to let them know they were going out of communication range. Zane knew he did not have to do it and that only Blake would hear it, but Zane was beginning to feel like maybe this group was going to be something special. Outside that, there was a solid ship and a crew to go with it.

After an hour and a half of going up ramps, they approached level four.

Zane's shielding lit up as a high-powered bullet hit it. "Shit!" He ducked behind one of the platforms that jutted out on the ramp.

Kal joined him. "Sniper."

"Yeah. Why we're being shot at is the bigger question," said Zane. He checked his forearm device. "Damn. My kinetic shielding can't take much more. It's about out of juice."

Kal took a deep breath. "If that bullet had hit me, I'd be pasted on the ground right now." He shook a finger out. "Whoever it is, they're waiting on us to move out of cover. Judging by the angle and impact on your shield, I'm guessing they're at the top of the ramp. Probably on a building, looking down."

"Well. Hmm. I can't go charging up. My shielding will break before then."

Kal pulled out his sniper rifle. "True, but you could serve as a distraction while I track him. Once he's in my sights, I got 'im."

"All right. I can move from the side pillars to these center platforms. That should keep them busy."

Kal handed a canister to Zane. "This is a smoke generator. Just press the button and wave it in the air. It will disperse a thick cloud, making it hard to see through, even with a thermal sensor."

"You and your gadgets."

"I know what makes it hard for me when trying to snipe," said Kal with a grin.

Zane grabbed the canister and checked it out. "You ready?"

Kal nodded.

"Here goes," said Zane. He aimed the canister toward the pillar on the side that jutted out from the wall. With the press of a button, a spray spewed out along the ground. After a moment, it began to emit thick clouds of white smoke. Zane dashed toward the next cover.

A shot rang out.

Zane turned to see Kal peep out the other side with his sniper rifle. A bullet went flying past Kal.

"Shit, he's got more than one in the clip, but I think I got his location," said Kal.

"Well, he missed me," said Zane. "That smoke cover works. You gonna move up, or should I try for the next cover?"

"Go for the next one. I'm going to see if I can score a hit."

"All right," said Zane. He shot a smoke trail to the next pillar up the ramp, and then burst forward. He watched as Kal dashed to other side of the ramp and ducked behind a side pillar.

A moment later, Kal fired.

Zane reached the next pillar. "You get him?"

"I think so. Wasn't a clean shot, but I think I hit him."

"I suppose you want me to go and find out."

Kal laughed. "Well, no way to know otherwise."

Zane sighed. "Fine." He sprayed the canister again and then dashed out. When he reached the next pillar, he paused to see if there was a shot.

Kal burst around the pillar and reached the next one. "Keep going!"

They went pillar by pillar up the ramp until they were near the top.

"Which building was he in?" asked Zane.

Kal tapped at his forearm screen.

Zane examined the map and the red dot that appeared inside his helmet. "I'm going in. Time to wreck whoever this asshole is." He charged out onto the level and crossed the street to a run-down building. With a kick, he sent a flimsy door flying.

Kal rushed out and joined him. He put away his sniper rifle and pulled out his dual pistols. "Time to get personal."

Zane nodded. He pulled out his shotgun and headed through various rooms until he found a stairwell. "Let's go."

They rushed up.

Zane burst out onto the roof and eyed the alien in red armor with a semitransparent helmet leaning against the edge. Blood was everywhere, and the alien looked like it was struggling to breathe. Zane was unclear on what species it was, but it had grayish skin with scales.

"Don't kill him yet," said Kal, approaching the alien with both pistols aimed forward. He knelt when he was within an arm's length. "I recognize you. Emrakus. Bounty hunter. You're a Grint, a race I ran into long ago, uncommon in the hunter world."

Zane put away his shotgun, pulled out his mace, and pointed it at Emrakus as he approached. "What the hell was all that sniping bullshit about?"

Emrakus winced as blood bubbled out of his mouth. "Your bounty protection has been revoked."

"What?" asked Zane. "By who?"

"Daniel Greer. Everyone's after you now."

"Ahh, piss," said Zane.

Emrakus began to tremble.

Kal grimaced as he pointed at the hole in Emrakus's upper chest. "Looks like I did get a clean shot. His suit will keep him alive a little while. It's not the shot that will kill him. He's been exposed to this environment. It's lethal to Grint."

"Took some balls to come here then," said Zane.

Emrakus shuddered for a moment, then went limp, and his eyes closed.

"I guess that's that," said Zane.

Emrakus opened his eyes, which had turned from yellow to pure black. In a deep voice, he said, "We see you."

Zane and Kal stumbled back.

"What the hell is up with the voodoo eyes? And what happened to your voice?" asked Zane. "Kal? You seen this before?"

Kal shook his head. "That's not a Grint feature."

"You're not going to make it out of here," said Emrakus.

"What are you babbling about?" asked Zane.

"You and the Grint are so easy to manipulate." A red light began to pulse on the chest armor.

Kal's eyes widened as he jumped away. "Get back!"

They dashed behind a large air vent near the entrance door.

Emrakus laughed, then cried out in terror, then laughed again. His suit blew out, casting parts of him far and wide across the roof. His head was still attached to the framework of his armor.

"The hell was that?" asked Zane.

Kal surveyed the blood- and gut-spattered roof. "I don't know, but Grint don't have black-tinted blood. Look."

Zane walked out and examined the remains. "What a mess. So now we're prey. We need to update Blake, but we're close to the ship."

"Well, that hurt," said Emrakus.

Zane's blood went cold as he and Kal jumped back again. Zane's breathing staggered. "Now what the hell is this?"

Emrakus smiled, then winced. "Not much time left in this head. I just wanted to verify your location is all."

"How . . . how are you still alive?"

"Alive . . . How do you define it? Your pathetically short existence, or something else?"

Zane grimaced. "What are you talking about, man?"

Emrakus's head began to shake. "We'll . . . see . . . you . . . around."

Zane pointed his shotgun and blew away Emrakus's head. "I don't think so."

Kal shook his head. "I doubt that was Emrakus, well, maybe a part of him. I'm not sure what that other part was. He mentioned our location. I suspect that's been compromised."

"So be it. If we fight, we fight. Once we get to the ship, I'll get my juggernaut suit, you get outfitted, and we'll head back to Blake." He checked his forearm screen. "Damn, almost 10:00 p.m. Earth time. I'm tired, but this shit's getting crazy now."

Kal took one last look around the roof as they headed toward the exit. "I'd still like to understand what happened with Emrakus. That was . . . unexpected. Nonetheless, I got a video capture of it. We can check it out later. Let's get to your ship."

//////////

It had been two hours since Zane and Kal had left the run-down shack where Blake and Seth were. According to Blake, it was almost 10:00 p.m., but to Seth, it felt much later. He was tired, and the knife in his leg was uncomfortable. Now he wanted Alcarez to hurry up so this could end.

Blake whispered, "Ada says Alcarez is coming."

Seth nodded as his heartbeat ramped up. He heard footsteps.

Alcarez entered the room and looked around. "Something's off." He surveyed the room and then approached Seth. As he came within hitting distance, he set off the paralysis mine. His body trembled for a moment as green arcs shot over him. He fell forward.

Blake materialized and grabbed Alcarez before he hit the ground. With a heave, Blake threw Alcarez, who landed on his back. Blake pulled out his dual energy blades and stood over the paralyzed Alcarez. "I don't know how you survived, or even care. What I do care about is you attacked Seth. *My brother.*"

Alcarez struggled to say something.

Blake shook his head. "I don't even care what you have to say. You don't get a fucking third chance. I'm going to end this, like I should have on Tooka."

Seth's eyes widened as he watched Blake mutilate Alcarez. The fury of each strike ended with a chunk of Alcarez flying away. Blood spattered the walls and floor. The smell almost made Seth gag. When Blake had finished, the room was painted in gore. What was on the ground was barely recognizable. Seth grimaced when Blake closed his eyes and licked the blood off his lips.

Blake picked up a small device that had been on Alcarez's uniform. He flipped it around in his hands for a moment. "Looks like we can see what ol' Alcarez was up to." He took off Seth's mouth cover, and sliced through the cuffs.

Seth exhaled and took a deep breath. "Finally." He licked his lips. "Damn, man . . . I didn't think you were going to dismember him."

"Why take the chance? I'm tired of that asshole."

"Yeah."

Blake interacted with his forearm device. "Ada, help Seth." He faced Seth. "Ada will help you get that knife out. Now it's time to update Gertus." With a few taps on his forearm device, Gertus appeared on the screen. Blake licked a blood spot on his lips. "We found Seth."

"And . . . Alcarez?" asked Gertus.

Blake tilted his screen toward the mess on the ground.

Seth heard an audible gasp.

"Alcarez won't be bothering anyone anymore."

"I guess not," said Gertus. "As a friendly update . . . your bounty protection has been revoked by Daniel Greer."

"That seems a little odd," said Blake. He rubbed his chin for a moment. "I'm thinking Delkis had something to do with that. He probably knows we're here now."

"I'm sure he does. Anyways, you're safe in my turf, but beyond that . . . good luck."

Blake furrowed his eyebrows. "Can I ask a favor?"

"I'm listening."

"I know you have a direct connection to the surface for communications. I wanted to contact my ship, as well as Zane and Kal."

Gertus tilted his head. "If I do this, we're even."

"Fair enough."

Gertus tapped at his console for a moment. "I've relayed to you one-time credentials and the proper access protocols. Once you disconnect, your credentials will be revoked."

Blake nodded as the screen went dark. He sighed. "Once we get situated here, it's time for a conference call."

Ada entered the room and hustled over to Seth. She pulled out a small patch. With one hand on Seth's leg and the other on the knife, she yanked the blade out.

Pain shot through Seth as he clenched his fists and yelled.

She applied the patch to the wound. "This will help. Let it set."

Seth closed his eyes and exhaled from his mouth as he felt the patch go to work.

After a few minutes, Ada said, "Now, let's try to stand." She placed her arms under Seth's armpits and raised him.

Seth tried to stand when he was upright, but the leg with the knife wound would not let him put pressure on it, despite the fast-acting nature of the patch's healing power.

"I'm going to have to carry you," said Ada.

"Umm . . . okay."

She scooped him up.

Blake laughed.

"Not now, man," said Seth.

"The roles are reversed."

Seth shook his head.

"I don't mind carrying him," said Ada.

Blake nodded. "I appreciate that you can. I would probably put him in a bag and sling him over my shoulder."

"He would too," said Seth.

"I'm just glad you're okay," said Blake. "However, before we head out, we need to contact the others. Ada, where's your projection rod?"

Ada set Seth down, then rummaged through her backpack. She handed the projection rod to Blake.

He set it on the ground and connected to it with his forearm device.

A minute later, a screen divided in half appeared. Sarah was on the top and Zane on the bottom.

"We're having this call thanks to Gertus and his surface relay. Once done, we'll be out of contact," said Blake. "Sarah, we met someone named Kal Modan who is traveling with Zane. He is a temporary part of the crew."

She nodded.

Blake glanced at Zane. "I take it you've run into some opposition if you're not at the ship already."

"You could say that," said Zane. "We ran into a bounty hunter named Emrakus. He was . . . not fully himself. His body was blown to bits, but his head was still talking. We got video we can show later."

Blake rubbed his chin. "I see. I look forward to watching it."

"Also, apparently our bounty protection's been revoked."

Blake nodded. "So I've heard. Probably Delkis's doing. How close are you to the *Exceltion*?"

"We're on level two, but the place is swarming with Selva Tong. It's gonna be a fight and a half, and my kinetic shielding is low on energy."

Blake pursed his lips. "Sarah, what's the activity like around you?"

"There's large groups roaming around," said Sarah. "One is headed this way, but they're a bit off. Also, one of the big turrets is trained on us."

"You got to get the ship out of there," said Blake. He glanced at Zane. "What's the nearest safe zone? Mularin? I see several possible places."

Zane nodded. "Mularin is Selva Tong's rival. At least on their turf, we wouldn't be hunted. They have the same no-hunting rule, and they definitely wouldn't listen to Delkis."

"Then that's what we need to do. Zane, can you and Kal make it to the *Exceltion*?"

Zane drew his lips flat. "We'll be coming in hot."

"We'll try to secure an open shot to the ship," said Sarah. Zane nodded.

"Sarah, once Zane and Kal are on board, get the *Exceltion* to the nearest spot in Mularin turf that's closest to Selva Tong territory," said Blake.

Sarah nodded. "Will do. I take it you, Ada, and Seth are going to head to Mularin turf now too."

"Yeah, and since we're on the lower levels, we should have some cover, although I suspect our position here is known. We'll probably need to go down a level or two. We'll contact you when we're within range."

"Lot of walking," said Sarah.

"Yeah, well, once we can all regroup, we can take a breather for the night and go from there."

"I'll see you in a bit," said Sarah. "Contact me when you're close."

"We'll do the same," said Zane.

The screen went dark.

Ada picked up the projection rod and put it in her backpack.

Seth shook a finger. "You think the Mularin are going to just let us walk in?"

"Down this low, it's probably a smaller clan, like with the Kahan," said Blake. "If we get static, we'll just go up a few levels. The important thing is to avoid any firefights in your condition."

"I'm a liability. I know."

"Not at all," said Blake. "Let's lay low. I'm going to activate my camouflage shielding and scout out a bit ahead. Ada, you should be able to track me with your sensors."

Ada nodded.

Blake activated his camouflage shielding as they exited the building.

Seth did not mind being carried by Ada, but it sent the wrong message, that he always seemed to need help, even if the situation was out of his control. Maybe he could have fought Alcarez in the prison and caused a scene, although that probably would have led to Seth being knocked out quicker. He was glad Alcarez was dead, but it seemed the contract had gotten more complex in the time Seth was gone. Delkis knew they were around, and now their bounty protection was reversed. If anything, at least Blake was there for him, just like he always was. Seth took a deep breath as the group moved down the dimly lit pathway toward Mularin territory.

CHAPTER
SIXTEEN

K al studied his forearm screen as he and Zane paused to figure out the best path to the *Exceltion*. They had been about to leave when Blake had contacted them. According to Earth time, it was 10:15 p.m. At least now they knew why the Selva Tong was hunting them. Kal was not sure if there was a bounty on him, but if he was with Zane, it would probably be a moot point. The *Exceltion* was at a landing spot Kal was familiar with. He knew a back way to get there, but there was a stretch he was unsure about.

"It's going to be spitting fire up there," said Zane.

Kal nodded. "I may know a way to minimize it. I've been in this area before."

Zane pointed at the remains of Emrakus. "As long we don't run into more of whatever that thing was."

A shiver went through Kal. He had never seen anyone talk consciously after a majority of their body had been removed. It was unnatural. Then again, the current situation was unusual. Working with Blake and Zane had been illuminating so far, and Kal could see himself with the team. "We can stick to the sides of the ramp when going up and blend into traffic. Once topside, there's a small district to the right we can go through. If we use the back alleys and side streets, we should be able to get close to the landing pad the *Exceltion*'s at. Then we book straight to it."

Zane nodded, and they left the roof.

When they reached the ground floor, Kal surveyed the environment. His helmet was down, and a thermal scan showed there were several people coming and going off the ramp. It was a short trip to the ramp system, and it looked like everything was clear. His experience caused him to check out the rooftops of the other buildings. If what Emrakus said was true, and their location was given away, others may have come already, although he was not seeing anything. He pointed at a group of people heading up the ramp. "Let's follow them. Helmet up. Switching to private comms."

They hustled across the short street to the ramp network and mingled with the flow of people.

"Just one level, and we're on our way. We'll be on the *Exceltion* in no time," said Kal.

"Assuming we don't run into anything," said Zane.

"Then we'll deal with it just like we did Emrakus."

"Hell yeah," said Zane.

Kal liked working with Zane. It reminded Kal of working with his former unit. The difference was that Zane was already a proven merc, while Kal's former unit was still trying to prove themselves. As they walked up the ramp, he asked, "So how did you end up in prison? I heard that you were out of the scene but didn't know the details. You don't have to answer if you don't want."

"It's cool," said Zane. "I killed some asshole prince that killed a woman I was seeing. I had a good relationship with the daughter too. I'm not sure where she is now . . . but I intend to find out. Anyways, due to politics, I was spared but ended up in a Fredorian prison. The planet the prince was from went under Drodalian influence, which should have made the Fredorians release me . . ."

"But they didn't," said Kal, shaking his head. "I never understood the hard-on Fredorians have about hating Earthborn. We're all human."

Zane laughed. "If one group finds an advantage they can lord over another, then they'll do it. I don't know if that's a Fredorian weakness or something specific to humanity. Either way, I got hosed and Blake saved my ass."

"Well, I'm glad it was you and Blake entering my cell. I thought it was going to be Chris Samuels or any of the others there that wanted to waste me."

"Prison gangs. Pfft. That guy was weak."

"Not all of us have heavy shielding," said Kal with a smile. Zane nodded.

They reached topside without incident.

Kal squinted as he scanned the environment. The natural sunlight was blinding compared to the relative dimness of the lower levels. Using his thermal scan was useless with so many people, and trying to pick out who was Selva Tong and who was not was hard. The uniforms were a sure sign of the Selva Tong, but he knew from experience that not all Selva Tong wore them.

The environment consisted of metallic buildings with storefronts on the bottom level. Most were bustling with activity, but he knew that they were usually fronts for other types of activities. He checked his forearm device. "To the right, and then after a short distance, we should be near your ship. I've mapped out a path through the back streets. We can avoid the main one. I'm betting there are informants or worse waiting on the main street through this area."

"Sounds good," said Zane.

They dashed off to a less populous side street and began to walk down it.

Kal was on high alert given that the back streets were where activities illegal even to the Selva Tong went on. The people out on the street that Zane and Kal encountered scattered at their approach. It was like turning on the light in a roach-infested kitchen. His eyes kept a continual survey of the street ahead of them. Zane could not take another sniper hit, and it would be hard to fire any shot from a distance in the street they were on due to the twists and turns and obstructions from the structure of the buildings.

As they neared the end of their journey, Kal motioned off to a side alley. He noted it had taken them roughly thirty-five minutes to get here from where they had fought Emrakus.

Zane joined him.

"Group ahead. They're spread out," said Kal.

"It's an ambush."

"Yeah," said Kal. "One advantage of this place being less populated is that it's easier to use my thermal scanner."

"You think they've been tracking us since we left the ramp?"

Kal shook his head. "I don't, but I bet they must know we're going to try to get to the *Exceltion*."

"So they just cover all paths to the *Exceltion*. Surprised they haven't fired on it yet."

"Maybe they want it for some reason," said Kal. He wrinkled his eyebrows. "Here's my plan. We hit the closest member on the right. Once he's down, we can set up a distraction, then pull them in."

"And then waste them."

"Yep."

"Let me contact Sarah, let her know we're coming."

Kal nodded.

After a moment, Zane said, "She's expecting a hot entry. They're going to clear a path for us once we're in range."

"Awesome," said Kal.

They took an alleyway that led them to a building.

Kal put a finger to his lips and motioned up. When they got to the roof, Kal took a moment to survey the layout. The thermal signatures of the group waiting for them stood out. One was on a balcony overlooking the street. Another was on a roof adjacent to that building. Several were on the ground, behind various objects in the street. There was even one that peeked out from an alley. Kal had picked his target. It was two roofs over from where they were, and the most isolated. Whoever was up there had peeked over the roof edge, giving away their location. He gestured toward the man on the roof. "That's our target."

Zane nodded.

They crept to the building where the man was. After a few minutes of walking up the stairs, they stood just inside the exit to the roof.

Kal pulled out his FHP-10. He loved the silence and lethality of it. It was made for situations like this. Although he dual-wielded FLP-40s and kept them holstered on his belt, the FHP-10 was kept on his thigh. He peeped out and assessed the situation. The man was looking out over the edge. When the man turned to sit back down, Kal hit him in the forehead.

The man slumped to the side.

"Damn, nice shot," said Zane.

Kal nodded as he approached the man.

"Oh, shit," said Zane. "Selva Tong death squad."

Kal gulped. He had heard stories of the Selva Tong death squad before. They were ruthless, single-minded, and efficient.

"Their check-in is every ten minutes, and they have a life-monitoring system, unless they've changed since I last saw them. They're going to be on their way over."

"Makes it easier for us then," said Kal. "Get behind the roof entrance. I'm going to set some traps on the floors below."

Zane nodded as he hustled out the door.

Kal took stock of what he had left. One paralysis mine, one holographic mimic device, two stun grenades, and three motion-activated acid mines. That would use up everything he had. Hopefully it would be enough. He placed the inactive paralysis mine inside the roof entrance. After five minutes, he had placed an acid mine on three of the five floors and the mimic device at the opposite end of the roof where the dead Selva Tong death squad member was. As he came back to the roof, he activated the paralysis mine, then joined Zane.

"I hear them," said Zane.

Kal raised a finger. "And it begins."

After a moment, a cry of surprise rang out from below.

"One down," said Kal.

Weapons fire echoed up the stairwell.

"Hmm, they must have found the second acid mine."

After a moment, another pain-filled scream filled the air.

"Two down," said Kal.

The sound of jet packs made them turn. Two death squad members landed on the roof.

Zane charged them as Kal emptied his dual pistols into the one on the left.

The death squad member on the right unloaded on Zane, shredding what was left of his kinetic shielding and hitting a part of his robotic arm. The member looked up in surprise as Zane used his mace to crush his head.

Kal focused on the doorway as another member reached the roof.

The member stepped on the paralysis mine and fell to the ground.

Zane charged forward and smashed the member's head in.

Kal motioned to the side of the entrance. He tapped at his interface, and where the mimic device sat, a hologram of Kal looking over the edge appeared.

Two death squad members burst onto the roof with weapons drawn. They hesitated as they assessed the situation and then took aim at the hologram and fired.

Zane rushed from the side and turned the left member to point at the other. The left member's gunfire shredded the right's kinetic shielding and then the right member. Zane yanked the weapon out of the remaining member's hand and then pushed him down. Kal let off a volley at the member's head, mincing it into pieces. Zane hustled over to the roof edge and looked out. "We need to move somewhere else. The Selva Tong will know this squad is dead, assuming no more are coming. The *Exceltion* shouldn't be too far ahead."

Kal pointed out over the roof. "Yeah . . . but look at all that activity. Selva Tong is riled up."

Zane sighed. "One step at a time."

*   *   *

Sarah closed her eyes for a moment, then opened them to interact with her console. The situation that Blake described sounded tough, and she had just been contacted by Zane, who was on his way in with Kal Modan, someone she was not familiar with. This was more action packed than she expected, and she had not even left the ship yet. She pressed the ship's communication button. "Luke, Kane, can you come up to the command center?"

They responded they would.

After a few minutes, they had assembled in the command center.

"Here's the situation," said Sarah. "We all have bounties on us. Although this is a typical safe zone from bounty hunters, our protection has been revoked. Blake, Ada, and Seth are on level sixteen and are going to head to Mularin territory. Zane and a new person called Kal Modan are on their way here now. They're nearby, but there are several groups of Selva Tong between us and them. We have to be ready to take off as soon as they're on board. Oh . . . and the Selva Tong have a big turret pointed at us."

"Is that all?" asked Kane with his hands out to the side.

"Well . . . there's also a group of Selva Tong headed this way," said Sarah.

Luke furrowed his eyebrows. "If the Selva Tong's intent was to destroy us, they would have already. I think they want to secure this ship."

"The Fredorian prototype for the sanguine class? Definitely. I know I would, but we can't let that happen. Blake and the others are counting on us," said Sarah. She pulled up a window on the wraparound screen that showed a top-down view of the *Exceltion*. "Luke, do you think you can strengthen the shielding on the side of the ship that the turret is pointing at?"

"I can . . . but at a cost. We'll be weak on the other side, the one where Zane and his friend will be coming from."

Kane shook his hands like he was dual wielding pistols. "Then we'll just need to give them something else to shoot at. We got quite a few drones. Let's launch some and start a party. Not to mention we have our own turrets."

"Works for me," said Luke.

Sarah glanced at Kane. "That should keep Selva Tong at a distance, at least until they bring in their own ships. I think at that point any value we may have for being captured disappears."

"Then we need to work quick to extract them," said Luke.

Sarah sighed. "How much shielding do we have on the hover platform?"

"Not much but . . . it could probably last long enough to get them," said Luke, beginning to shake a finger. "I like where you're going with that. Kane, I'll need some help tweaking one."

Kane grinned. "Not a problem here. Who's gonna fly it?"

"I will," said Sarah, standing.

"You know if they break the shielding on it, you're vulnerable. You'd be ripped to shreds," said Kane.

"Then I rely on you two to make sure the shielding doesn't break, and me to avoid getting hit," said Sarah, raising her head a bit.

"We can make you a suit that can withstand some punishment," said Luke. "We have the specs. That should help in case things get worse."

Kane nodded. "Well, if we're going to use the ship's weapons, I'll need to head to the control center for them."

"Okay, so here's the plan then," said Sarah. "We go to the armory, replicate my suit. While I put it on, you two configure the platform. Once that's done, I'll join Luke in the hangar bay while Kane hits the weapons control center."

"Sounds like a plan," said Luke.

"I'm down with that," said Kane. "This is already ten times better than where I was."

Sarah glanced at Kane. "Let's not get too cozy. Remember, we're only doing this because our team is in jeopardy."

Kane looked down. "I know."

Sarah slapped Kane on the arm. "C'mon, let's go."

They hustled down to the armory.

Kane interacted with the replication console.

A medium-armor suit appeared in the replication bay along with an under-armor mesh suit.

"It's based on the scan the ship has of you. It's a little heavier than I'd like, but it'll work for now," said Kane.

"That's fine," said Sarah. "It's not like I'll be moving much." She grabbed the under-armor suit.

Her eyes softened as she watched them leave. Although she did not intend to take command, it came naturally to her. She wondered if this was how captains felt, making decisions on the fly and directing crew. Her under-armor suit went on with little difficulty. She grabbed the medium-armor suit. It was heavy, but that was something that could be tweaked later.

It took her a bit to get the suit on, but when she powered it on, she could barely feel how heavy it was. She tested her movement with it and was surprised at how agile she felt. If anything, she felt like she could jump over a building. She understood that if the power went out, it would be a different story. For people like Zane, that was not an issue, unless it was his juggernaut suit. With a final look over her armor, she headed to the hangar bay.

When she arrived there, she saw the hover platform next to Luke. It reminded her of a box with the top open and a pole in the front that had a console at the end.

"It's ready," said Luke.

Sarah looked around. "Where's Kane?"

"He already did his technical magic. All I had to tweak was a few components, and he did the interface. He's in the weapons control center now."

"Efficient," said Sarah. "I'll need you to have the ship prepped to take off."

Luke nodded. "No worries." He laughed. "I bet you never thought we'd be doing this when we were building the *Exceltion*."

"Definitely not, but I couldn't ask to be part of a better crew."

"Yeah. We just have to keep it together. You be safe out there."

Sarah drew her lips flat as she watched Luke head off to the command center. She boarded the platform and closed the door. Zane would need to be contacted. Her fingers flew over the console.

After a moment, Zane's voice came across. "Sarah?"

"Yep. How close are you now?" asked Sarah.

"Close. We just fought a Selva Tong death squad."

She interacted with her forearm screen. A map of the nearby area appeared with a red dot. "Wow. Okay. Well, the *Exceltion* is tracking you. You're just about close enough that I can come get you."

"With what?"

"A hover platform. Kane's going to run distraction with the ship's drones and guns."

"Are you crazy? Have you seen what's out here?"

Sarah swallowed hard. Maybe she should have passed her plan by Zane. "Look, can you get a bit closer?"

"Yeah. We need to head to another building, preferably one in your direction. Once there, we'll make our way to the roof, but some of these damn Selva Tong have jet packs. It should take us about five minutes to get to the new spot. Let us know when you're near, and we'll exit out."

"All right. I'm on my way," said Sarah. She contacted Luke and Kane. "Kane, you're up. Make sure not to hit me."

"Are you sure?" asked Kane, laughing.

She sighed. Earthborn seemed to enjoy their humor in any situation. Maybe it was a coping mechanism.

"I'm kidding. Give me a moment."

The sound of the turrets turning broke the silence in the hangar bay.

Sarah activated the hover platform, and it floated off the ground.

When the hangar bay platform lowered, she flew forward and out. She grimaced at the sound of the turrets firing. Drones flew by her and were shooting lasers at the group of Selva Tong that had assembled. There were many more than she had expected, and in the distance, she could see more coming. On top of that, there were flying craft headed their way along with what looked like mechanized units. Her heartbeat ramped up. All this just to capture them. She focused on the platform as a shot bounced off the shielding. The platform did not move fast, as that was not its intended purpose, but the modified shielding was holding. After five minutes, she neared the building where Zane and Kal were located. She contacted Zane over comms. "I'm almost there. Get to the roof!"

Zane and Kal exited onto the roof.

She piloted the platform to just over the roof, then descended.

"Nice to see a friendly face," said Zane as he hopped onto the platform.

"Kal Modan," said Kal, nodding at Sarah as he followed Zane.

"Sarah Olson. Nice to meet you."

"All right, let's get the hell out of here," said Zane.

The hover platform lifted off the roof.

"Yee-haw!" said Zane.

Kal laughed.

"Yee what?" asked Sarah as she tried to focus on getting the hover platform back to the ship.

"She's Fredorian," said Zane, gesturing at Sarah.

"Ahh," said Kal.

Sarah shook her head and tried to not get blasted out of the sky. Several hits lit up the platform's shielding, and the flying craft she had seen earlier were dogfighting with the drones. The *Exceltion*'s turrets had cleared a path for them. Once the hover platform was on the hangar bay platform, the hangar platform raised. Sarah tapped at her forearm device. "Luke, get us out of here!"

"Launching now," said Luke over comms.

Sarah exhaled.

Zane slapped Sarah's arm. "Nice work. There was no way we were going to make it through that mess on foot."

"I wasn't sure it was going to work. These platforms aren't meant to be bullet sponges." She extended a hand to Kal.

Kal shook her hand. "Appreciate the help."

Sarah looked around. "I need to get out of this suit and help Luke. We've already established a safe spot to land in Mularin turf and are headed there now."

"Sounds good," said Zane. "I'm gonna get something to eat and clean up. C'mon, Kal, I'll show you around."

Kal nodded. "All right."

Sarah was glad her plan worked. If it had not, then this would be a very different moment. It hit her how important her role had been. That was the benefit of a small team. Every decision is magnified in terms of responsibility. Everyone had come together, and the plan had worked without a hitch.

A crackling and fizzing sound emanated from the hover platform.

She grinned. Almost without a hitch. She was sure Luke and Kane could fix the hover platform. It hit her that if it had been an FDF crew, there would have been acceptable losses, but not with this Earthborn crew. With her first live action under her belt as ship operations officer, she headed to her room to get her suit off and then join Luke.

////////////

Blake's eyes narrowed as he observed the street ahead of them. Ada was carrying Seth a bit behind them, and they kept in contact over comms. It had been about fifteen minutes since they left the shack, and according to his forearm device, it was around 10:30 p.m. He knew Seth was probably tired, and given his injuries, he would need some rest. They had to get to Mularin turf soon.

Blake was in the zone he was used to: alone, camouflage shielding activated, and looking for a way out. It was a scenario he had been in many times in his days as a Fredorian Ranger. Get in, hit the target, and get out. He had even done escort missions, which were similar to this. He kept his helmet down so he could sniff the air. His sense of smell was more accurate sometimes than what his helmet could tell him. He could also hear better.

"Everything okay up there?" asked Seth over comms.

"I haven't seen anything yet," said Blake. They had exited Kahan turf and were now in the small stretch between that and Mularin turf. The only problem was it was owned by the Selva Tong. There had been one or two lone Selva Tong members, and he had skirted them. His instinct was to kill them, but he knew they most likely had life-monitoring implants on them. Kill one, and the area gets marked.

As he crept up to a building, he paused. A sinister odor crossed his nose. Most people would not give it a second thought, but the smell was out of place relative to those around it. He knew this smell. It reminded him of someone cramped on a ship for a long time without any access to grooming, or someone who did not want to clean up. The smell also indicated it was a human. He ducked into a side alley. "Ada, get out of the street and wait. Something's off."

"We're moving now," said Ada.

Blake peeped out and saw a short, robust man waddling down the middle of the street. The man had on green heavy armor that covered his body. The helmet had four red circles on the sides with a small antenna on the back. It was the weapon that caught Blake's attention. It was an arc gun hooked up to the man's backpack. Blake did not recall ever seeing someone like this, but the man's swagger indicated he had no fear.

Blake could sense that there was kinetic shielding, and his striker would just give away his position. His dual blades could cut right through the shielding, though. He pulled both blades out and then contacted Ada. "There's a man walking down the street. Stay out of his sight. He most likely has a lot of scanning built into his armor."

"We're in an alley between two buildings, and behind a dumpster," said Ada.

"All right. If it comes to it, I'ma gut 'im."

The man passed by Blake but then stopped.

Blake could see that the antennae had a small dish on it and was scanning the area. The dish had pivoted in his direction, then back to where Ada and Seth would be.

The man interacted with his arc gun, causing it to light up. He pulled off a small drone and tossed it into the air.

It was obvious to Blake now that this was a bounty hunter. The drone was common among them. It was useful in tracking their prey, and although it was not terribly useful for assault, it was packed with sensor equipment.

The drone flew toward the alleyway that Ada and Seth were in.

It hit Blake that maybe the man sensed Ada's electronic output. While he was hidden behind a building and evaded the thermal scans, the electric output from Ada was hard to miss by sensitive detectors. It was apparent this man had one. "He's coming for you. Stay where you are."

"Okay," said Ada. "I've set up a small turret."

"That won't work well against the level of kinetic shielding I think this guy has."

"I won't let him hurt Seth."

"Me either," said Blake. "All right. If he walks down your alley, I'm slicing him up." He peeked out into the street and saw the hunter was hustling over to Ada and Seth's alleyway. With a deep breath, Blake burst out of his alleyway and dashed over to the hunter. With Blake's active camouflage, the hunter would not know what hit him. As Blake neared the hunter, a bolt of electricity arced out from the hunter's belt and hit Blake in the chest, sending him flying back.

The hunter turned to face Blake. In a digitized voice, he said, "Blake Brown! Well, I'll be. The bounty comes to me."

"Who are you?" asked Blake.

The hunter lowered his helmet.

Blake could see the hunter's sweaty fair-skinned face and a mop of jet-black hair dangling on his forehead.

"Gobe Rallz. Don't believe we met, not that it matters. I know of you, and your tendency to sneak up and slice people. You have a pretty nice bounty on your head. How'd you like my anti-sneak device?"

"What do you want?"

"You of course, and . . . whoever I'm sensing in the alleyway. I suspect they're one of the bounties Delkis has revoked protection for."

"I won't let you harm them," said Blake, standing. He did a quick check over his armor. Although the lighting arc had gone through his kinetic shielding, it only burned his under armor, despite having the force to knock him back. Getting close to Gobe was going to be an issue.

"Harm them? When Delkis is paying double the bounty reward for alive? I'd be out of my mind. The fact you're talking to me now is because my lightning aura was set to low. Any higher and you'd have a hole in your chest."

"I'm glad you restrained yourself. Why don't you just," said Blake, waving his hand out in front of him in a dismissive manner, "run away or . . . go back to wherever it is you came from."

Gobe laughed. "A comedian. I heard that you were some sort of smartass." He lowered his arc gun and pointed it at

Blake. "Unfortunately for you, it's sleep time." He closed his helmet and fired.

Blake jumped back and out of the way as the arc went past him. The arc had spread a bit, but with his vampiric speed, he was well clear of it.

"What the?"

Blake shook his head. "Later, tubby." He ran toward the alley he had been in. "Ada, you catch all that?"

"I did, and I have analyzed a solution."

"Uhh . . . you have?"

"Bring him to me."

Blake sighed. "All right . . ." He bolted out of the alleyway, avoiding another arc. As he ran past Gobe, an arc hit Blake, sending him flying. He winced as he regained his composure. Another arc fired. Blake rolled out of the way. He stood and ran into the alley where Seth and Ada were. Looking around, he only saw Seth. "Where's Ada?"

Seth pointed up.

Blake saw that Ada had climbed up the building to one of the outcroppings. "What's she doing up there?"

Seth's eyes drooped as he shrugged. "I don't know, I wasn't really paying attention. I'm just trying to stay awake."

Gobe entered the alleyway. "There you are, and your friend too. Seems your other friend has taken off. No matter. I'll get them in a bit." He walked in a little more. "Now, we can do this the easy way or the hard way. I can handcuff you and you come along peacefully, or I shock the shit out of you and drag you back. I prefer the handcuff route myself."

Blake narrowed his eyes. "Probably because you're out of shape. However, I can probably get one blade through you before your suit knocks me out. One of us would be waking up, and it wouldn't be you."

Gobe laughed. "Another joke. Why don't—"

A large dumpster bin landed on Gobe. He fell to the ground as his arc gun went flying away. His kinetic shielding kept the object from crushing him. The narrow alleyway prevented the object from sliding off the curvature of his shielding. Despite his efforts to move, he was stuck. "Are you kidding me?"

Ada jumped down and landed on top of the bin. She then hopped off.

"Nicely done," said Blake. "However, usually the garbage goes *in* the bin."

Seth laughed, then winced.

"I wonder how much power your shielding has. I guess you'll find out," said Blake.

"You can't leave me here like this," said Gobe.

Blake circled a finger at Gobe. "Did you . . . actually read my profile?"

"Oh, shit. You're gonna leave me like this, aren't you?"

"I should . . . but I have some questions. Shut off your aura."

Gobe struggled to reach a button on his belt. Once he pressed it, he said, "Done."

Blake approached Gobe and placed a blade through the kinetic shielding and rested it against Gobe's neck. Blake nodded at Ada. "Remove the bin."

Ada complied.

Gobe exhaled as he closed his eyes.

"Now, remove your armor," said Blake.

Gobe sat up and began to remove his armor. "I don't know what I could possibly answer for you."

After Gobe's armor was off, Blake waved his hand for Gobe to stand. "Give me your arm."

"What?"

"Your arm. Now."

Gobe sighed as he complied.

Blake nodded at Ada. "Hold him."

Ada slipped behind Gobe and placed an arm around his neck.

Blake took Gobe's arm and tapped the wrist area, then sank in his fangs.

Gobe struggled against Ada's grasp as he cried out in surprise. After a moment, his eyes began to flutter.

Blake looked Gobe in the eyes. "You will answer my questions."

"I will answer your questions," said Gobe with a blank look.

"Ahh, man, that vampire hypnotic-gaze crap," said Seth.

Ada tilted her head. "Is Gobe in a hypnotic state?"

"I am," said Gobe.

"Interesting."

Blake cleared his throat. "Gobe, why was the bounty protection revoked for us?"

"Because Daniel Greer ordered it."

"Why would Daniel do that?"

"Daniel is not Daniel. He is the same as Delkis."

"What does that mean?" asked Blake.

"Daniel is possessed. He scares everyone."

"If he scares everyone, why did you stick around?"

"Credits."

Blake shook his head. "You will have no recollection of this encounter. When you wake up, you will decide to lose weight and have a burning desire to become a traveling salesman that focuses on selling hygiene products."

"Blake . . . ," said Seth.

"Also, every time you hear my name, you'll crap a little."

"C'mon, man, quit messing," said Seth, chuckling.

"All right, all right," said Blake, glancing at Seth. Blake focused back on Gobe. "You won't crap a little when you hear my name, but you will avoid any encounter with anyone having anything to do with the *Exceltion* if you can help it. Do you understand?"

"I understand," said Gobe.

"Good, now lay down and go to sleep."

Gobe complied.

Blake stood. "Ada, pick up Seth, and let's get outta here."

Ada strode over and picked up Seth. "I do have one question."

"Shoot," said Blake.

"Does that gaze work on androids?"

Blake shook his head. "Never tried, but I doubt it would. I can't exactly drink your blood and form a bond."

"I would guess not," said Ada. She swiveled her head toward Seth. "Has he ever used it on you?"

Seth laughed. "He better not have." After a moment, he narrowed his eyes. "You haven't, right?"

Blake laughed as he walked out of the alleyway. He peered back and, with a devilish grin, said, "Something to think about."

Seth closed his eyes and shook his head.

SEVENTEEN

The trip through Mularin turf to the *Exceltion* had been a blur for Seth. Although he had tried to stay awake, the medication and his injuries demanded that his body rest. He was thankful that Ada carried him, even if it made him uncomfortable. Conversation with Blake and Ada had been minimal. Although he had wanted to talk about the situation, it was draining just trying to stay awake. The last thing he wanted to do was fall asleep and make Ada's job harder.

It all paid off, though. Seth was in the medical lab, and Doc had administered treatment. It was almost 1:00 a.m., and he was exhausted. Ada sat next to him. She had helped get his under armor, pants, shirt, socks, and boots off. All he had on was his underwear. With Doc having retreated back into his alcove, it was just Seth and Ada in the lab.

"You should get some rest now," said Ada.

"Yeah, I plan on it. I can already feel whatever Doc gave me."

"It will help you sleep, and also mend your injuries. In addition to that, you won't feel the microbots that are going to repair you while you sleep."

Seth licked his lips. "I appreciate you carrying me. I . . . didn't expect to be a liability."

"It was no problem."

"Yeah, right," said Seth, chuckling, then wincing.

"You should avoid trying to laugh," she said.

"I know, I know." He closed his eyes, and everything went dark. When he opened them, Doc was buzzing around. He rubbed his eyes as he yawned. "What time is it?"

"9:00 a.m. Earth time," said Ada.

"Did you . . . stay here all night?"

Ada nodded. "I went into low-power mode to conserve energy."

"You slept."

"That is correct. We slept together."

Seth grinned. "Yeah . . . let's not phrase it that way to the rest of the crew."

"I don't understand."

"It . . . it doesn't matter. I'm just glad you stuck around."

"Of course."

"Well, I guess I better get cleaned up. Where's Blake?" asked Seth.

"He stopped in and said he was getting everyone together around ten."

"Damn. I need to get cleaned up then," said Seth. He swung his legs off to the side and winced. "Still a little tender."

"Are you able to walk?"

Seth used the slab to stand. He took a few deep breaths. "Yeah, I should be okay. I'll just need to take it easy for the next few days."

"I will see you at the meeting then."

"Sure thing," said Seth.

Doc ran a scanner over Seth. "Your heartbeat has increased."

"Not you too, Doc."

Doc furrowed his eyebrows.

Seth mused at the thought of what programming must have gone into to make a hologram furrow its eyebrows. "I'm good. Just need a shower, food, and I'm set."

"Check back in later today. Doctor's orders."

"Will do," said Seth as he hobbled to the exit. When he reached his room, he took his time showering. It felt good to get the stench of Zakara Prime off of him. It made him realize that throughout all that had happened, he must have smelled horrible, yet he did not hear one complaint or comment about it from Ada. She had carried him and even stayed with him the whole night. Where all this would go, he did not know, but he was curious to find out.

Once out of the shower, he got dressed and headed to the eating area. He noticed Kal sitting at one of the tables.

"Hey," said Kal.

Seth tipped his head up. "What's up."

"Enjoying a hot meal. I had one last night too. You never know how much you miss it until you haven't had it for a few months."

Seth accessed the replicator. "I hear you, man." He grabbed his food and sat across from Kal. "I didn't get to meet you proper back there."

"All good. You were in a rough situation."

Seth nodded.

"I was in a prison cell, but Blake and Zane busted me out. I knew Zane because we're both justice hunters. Blake I only knew about from stories. He offered me a contract to help with Delkis, and I accepted, so here I am."

"If Blake offered you that, then he trusts you," said Seth. "I wouldn't take that lightly."

"I'm not," said Kal. "It was a wild ride just to get to this ship. Bounty hunters, death squads, and Selva Tong everywhere."

Seth laughed. "Ada had to carry me since I was in such bad shape."

Kal nodded. "She's good and knows her way around systems, that's for sure." He waved his hand around. "I think I could get used to this. Tough ship, top-notch crew, good food, and a place I can sleep without worry of someone trying to enter my cell and kill me."

Seth's eyes widened. "Did that happen often?"

"Twice. I killed the intruder each time."

"Damn, man. That prison sounds tough."

"Yeah, Selva Tong don't give two shits about you there. As far as they're concerned, you're just waiting to die. How you die is not important. That's on top of the wannabe gangs that run around in there."

"That sounds horrible. How the hell did you survive?"

"Kill fast," said Kal with narrowed eyes. "And *never* let anyone disrespect you."

Seth nodded.

"Obviously, now that I'm out, I don't live by those rules. Sometimes it's okay to be disrespected if everyone lives," said Kal. He took a bite out of his sausage link.

"Yeah. I was hoping I could have been more useful. Seems I was just a liability."

Kal finished his bite. "Whatever happened to that Alcarez guy?"

"Blake painted the room in his blood. There wasn't much left of him. I had to leave with bits and pieces of him on me."

"Damn. You two must have had some history."

"Yeah, I shot him with a ship weapon on my first free-lancing contract with Blake. Apparently that didn't kill him. One thing's for sure . . . there won't be a third try for him."

Kal nodded as he sipped on his orange drink.

"On top of all that, we had to fight some bounty hunter named Gobe Rallz. He didn't fare well either."

"I've heard of him," said Kal. He bobbed his head. "You know, it's good to see another brother out and about."

Seth laughed as they slapped hands. "I forget about all that out here."

"Yeah, with all these aliens and crap, our skin color means jack, but you know the Fredorians . . . they gotta hate on something, so they hate Earthborn."

"Their loss," said Seth. "If anything, I've found that some like it dark."

Kal nodded. "Same here."

"What did you call home?"

"Detroit, Michigan. You?" asked Kal.

"New York City."

"Ahh, the Big Apple."

They shared a laugh.

"This is why I like working with other Earthborn," said Kal. "Only Earthborn would have got that reference."

Seth nodded. He enjoyed talking with Kal. In all the hustle and bustle of everything going on, it was good to talk with someone from Earth. He looked forward to hearing more about Kal, but it was getting close to meeting time. With a nod toward the exit, he said, "Time for the meeting."

"All right," said Kal as he stood.

They cleared the table and then exited the room.

//////////

Blake cracked his neck as he went over the last-minute notes he had entered into the system. The crew had assembled in the meeting room, and they looked much better than they did when he saw them last night. Zane and Kal had passed out, and Seth looked like he could barely function. Luke and Kane had been asleep while Sarah watched the ship. He had talked with her a bit but could tell she was tired, so he relieved her. That was one advantage of being a vampire: he could drink a vial of blood in lieu of sleeping in a pinch. He cleared his throat. "Everyone sleep all right?"

Everyone nodded.

"Good, then let's begin. First off, I want everyone to welcome Kal Modan. He is the fourth member of the assault team for the duration of this contract."

Kal shook a fist out in front of him at an angle. "It's been an exciting contract so far."

"Yeah, and we got to waste a bounty hunter already," said Zane.

"We'll get to that," said Blake. "Kal can pull his weight." He pulled up a projection of level sixteen, with Delkis's compound highlighted. "Let's start with this first. This is where Delkis is." A green line appeared from the ramp network, through Kahan territory and the maintenance tunnels, ending a short bit away from the compound. "This is the path we're going to take. Obviously with our bounty protection revoked, we're capture or kill on sight, at least in Selva Tong territory. Zane and Kal ran into Emrakus and a death squad, and Seth, Ada, and I ran into Gobe Rallz. This is what we know from Emrakus."

The projection changed to show the video of Emrakus. It showed him getting his chest blown out, and his head continuing to talk.

Sarah gasped.

"Now that's freaky," said Kane.

Blake nodded. "Apparently, that was not fully Emrakus. There was something else inside him. Also notice that he said that *they* could see us, not that *he* could. That ties into this."

The projection changed to show the interaction with Gobe Rallz. It showed the dumpster landing on him.

Zane laughed. "Ada, you threw a dumpster on him."

"I figured he would not be able to do much in a small space with something like that weighing him down," said Ada.

"Impressive," said Kal.

Everyone went silent when the projection showed Blake drinking blood.

"Yes . . . I have the ability to hypnotize, but it requires a blood bond," said Blake.

"Well, at least you gave him a new lease on life," said Luke, chuckling.

"That I did. More importantly, Gobe said Daniel Greer is like Delkis. Given the fact that a bounty revocation is rare, that to me means that Daniel is acting unusually. I suspect whatever Delkis is, and now Daniel, it's tied into whatever Emrakus was. I think it's clear at this point that we're dealing with some type of possession."

"What do you think it is?" asked Seth. "Outsiders maybe?"

"Possibly, or something truly alien. We won't know until we get Delkis. I want to head out tomorrow. We can use this day to rest and to get ready."

The projection changed back to the initial map of level sixteen and the compound.

Blake pointed at several green dots around the compound roof. "These are sensors that Ada will hack into. That should open any doors we need."

Ada looked around. "I can also make the turrets work for us."

Blake eyed Ada for a moment, and then nodded. "If you can do that, it'll make things a lot easier." He pointed at the southern gate. "In that case, we'll have a distraction outside the base. If anything, it should provide a temporary buffer for us. Zane, using your juggernaut armor, you will charge this gate and wreak havoc. Your ultimate goal is to get inside and secure the ground floor. I'll be behind you."

"No sweat," said Zane.

"Kal, you'll grapple in from the top. There are some entrances you can infiltrate. With all the chaos, you'll hopefully be able to get in without too much issue. Your goal is to sweep the upper levels. Once inside, I'll come up from the ground floor, and we can meet midway. Together, we can clear anyone out that might decide to come down and surprise us."

Kal nodded.

"Once the six top levels are cleared, Zane, Kal, and I will head to the two lower levels of the compound. I suspect that's where Delkis is since it's the most fortified per the layout that Gertus gave us. He also thinks Delkis will be there. Ada will come to the compound after we've secured it. Before that, though, she will stay behind a bit in a secure position and set up a defensive perimeter," said Blake. He glanced at Sarah. "I'll need you to help defend that spot with her if it comes to it. I would normally ask Seth, but he's out for a bit."

"I can do it, man," said Seth, tossing a hand out.

Blake eyed Seth. "In your condition? No way."

Seth sighed. "Well, what can I do then?"

"What you do best," said Blake. "Fly the *Exceltion* and pick us up when we're ready."

The projection showed a blue dot under the compound.

"Once we capture Delkis, we're going to take an elevator from the compound's lower levels to the top. I don't know where it goes topside, but wherever it is, you're going to need to fly in and pick us up. There may be no landing pad there, and you may need to deal with hostile fire."

Seth licked his lips. "That could get messy fast."

"I got the best pilot. I'm not worried."

Seth nodded. "Why don't you just take the elevators down to the bottom of the compound?"

Blake shook his head. "Gertus doesn't have a mapping of where it goes topside. I would assume it goes straight up, but that's not guaranteed. I don't want to spend time looking for the entrance, and we don't even know what it would look like. According to the layout, it's also secured topside. If we're detected hacking it, we'll lose the element of surprise."

"Huh," said Seth. "How do you know it goes topside then?"

"Gertus's layout shows that it does, just not the path. As long as it gets us out of the compound, even if it's a level up, it'll do. By the time we get there, Ada can hack it, assuming it needs to be."

Seth ran a hand over his head. "Seems risky to trust the elevators will be there."

"I don't think Gertus would betray us by giving us a bad layout. If it turns out that way, then he'll get paid a visit," said Blake. "Just make sure that when we get topside, you can get to us. All right, back to the plan. Kane, I'll need you on weapons. Luke, you'll be on the *Exceltion*'s landing platform and, if need be, use one of your modified hover platforms to come get us." He glanced at Sarah. "By the way, great job thinking on your feet."

"Hell yeah," said Zane. "She's got a spine of steel, flying into all that fire."

Sarah smiled.

"She did good, and for this next part of the mission, everyone will have to pull their weight," said Blake. He exhaled from his nose. "I'm not going to sugarcoat this. It's going to be rough going once we get there. I'm sending each of you the plan and what I need you to do. If we execute as planned, then we'll pull this off flawlessly." He looked around the table. "As I said earlier, we'll head out from Mularin turf tomorrow morning. Use the day to rest, get your gear in line, do whatever you need to do, and if anyone has any questions, come to me."

Zane flung a finger into the air. "Whatever happened to Alcarez, that asshole that took Seth?"

Blake paused for a moment. "I killed him."

"No video?"

Blake licked his fangs for a moment. "I'll make it available if you want to see it. I would suggest not watching it if you're planning on eating soon."

Part of the group sat up straight.

"Anyways, I'm here if you need me."

The group nodded as they began to disperse.

Sarah came up to Blake. "I was wondering . . . What could I have done differently?"

"What do you mean?"

"Well, the modified hover platform worked, but it was risky. Was there a better approach?"

Blake grinned. "What you did was fine."

"I mean . . . you mentioned Seth doing a flyby to pick everyone up for tomorrow. Did you . . . think that's what I should've done?"

Blake laid a hand on her shoulder. "You worry too much. The end result was you got them to the ship safe and sound."

Sarah grinned. "You're right. I was just curious."

Blake narrowed his eyes. "You're nervous about going with us tomorrow."

"I've . . . never been in a live firefight. With weapons. I mean . . . weapons that I'm wielding."

"You'll be okay. With Ada and some technical gear, you might not even see a single shot."

She exhaled. "I'll study the plan and be ready."

"I know you will," said Blake. He tilted his head. "Go on."

She nodded and took off.

Although she would not have known it, Blake could sense that she was more nervous than he had thought. She probably did not expect to be going and did not want to say no. It would be good for her to see what the assault team did up close. If anything, it would give her a new appreciation of field work and also help form a tighter bond with the others. He exhaled as he left the meeting room.

CHAPTER

EIGHTEEN

An hour after the meeting, Ada relaxed in her room. It had been retrofitted to have a special pod that allowed her to interface with the ship. Kane had requested it so that if he needed help, she could hop in, connect, and troubleshoot. The current issue she was looking into was the weapons systems. Kane had said that there were some glitches, and he was not sure he could fix them all before tomorrow. She enjoyed feeling needed, something she did not have when she was working in a warehouse as a manual laborer.

When she was connected to the ship, she saw a black space with a grid on the ground. Various systems occupied specific grid cells. Each cell had a vertical purple bar. Inside the bar were various colored slices that she could interact with. Finding the weapons systems was easy due to the labeling over each cell. It was like a big pin had been dropped on top, and the name of the system hovered over the cell. Some cells had multiple labels, but the weapons system had one big one.

Flying around as a bright orb was freeing in its own right. It was one reason she enjoyed cyber warfare. She had special abilities that were hardwired into her design such as takeover retaliation, strengthened presence, and a multilayered defense system. There was even an emergency exit built into her avatar in cyberspace.

A flashing green light appeared above the black cyber-space field.

She noticed that it was one of the ship's feeds, and it showed someone approaching her door. It was Kal. She split her avatar and left one part to continue looking into the weapons systems. The other part of her focused on Kal as he was about to knock on her door. She made the door open. "Come in, Kal."

Kal peeked his head in and looked around. "How'd you know it was me?"

"I'm in the ship's systems at the moment helping Kane."

"Oh," said Kal. "Well, if you're busy, I'll leave."

"Please, come in. Have a seat."

"If you insist," said Kal, grinning. He entered the room, and the door slid shut behind him. After taking a seat next to her, he said, "I wanted to thank you again for helping me with the armory and getting my gear. I know . . . it would've been easier to just leave the gear behind, but my stuff is special to me. Especially my sniper rifle."

"It was my pleasure."

Kal rubbed his chin. "I am curious how you came to be a part of this crew. I'm guessing you weren't in a prison cell. That seems to be the case with Zane and I."

"You're correct," said Ada. "I hacked the initial meeting that started this group's formation. Once I learned they needed a cyber warfare specialist, I decided to join, assuming Blake would have me."

"He made a good choice. For the record, what Fredoria did to androids was wrong. Being classified as property . . . is something that happened to my ancestors. It's just wrong."

Ada tilted her head, causing the wire that attached her to the special pod to jiggle. "Did you know many androids?"

Kal laughed. "Oh, yeah. Mainly G1s, but I also worked some with a G4."

"A G4? Interesting."

"Yeah. He was a justice hunter, and a damn good one at that. The Kreagan hunters gave him an honorary membership since he saved a few of them."

"Was it Dadrax?"

"Yep, that's him. I guess he's rare enough that he would be well-known."

Ada's eyes sparkled. "I have read many of his exploits. He's a good ambassador for my kind and unique in that he became a justice hunter."

Kal stood and looked around. "Definitely. Anyways, I just wanted to stop by and say hi. I'm making the rounds, getting to know everyone."

"Do you wish to join the crew?"

"Yeah . . . I think I do. I like what I see so far, and Blake . . . he's kickass. I respect that type of leader."

"He's also fair and can be compassionate."

"Yeah . . . but I just saw the Alcarez video. That was brutal as hell."

"There wasn't much of Alcarez left."

"You're telling me. I also heard what he did for Sarah. He's a stand-up guy."

Ada nodded.

"All right, I'll leave you to it," said Kal with a smile. He exited the room.

Several hours later, a knock rang out from her door.

"Kane, come in," she said.

Kane smiled big. "You fixed it! What was the issue?"

"There was a malfunction in the drone launcher. Next time, you will be able to use both of them instead of one. I'm forwarding you the details."

Kane tapped the side of his head. One of the gadgets that sat on just above his ear extended a small screen in front of him. He perused it for a moment. "I see. That would have taken me a while to find."

"But you would have found it."

"Oh, yeah, but not in a few hours like you did."

"I also fixed several other systems."

Kane laughed. "See, this is why I feel useless around you. Maybe I should just be your assistant."

Ada tilted her head. "You're the most qualified organic I've seen in regards to working with technology. I saw your modifications in the ship's systems. They were ingenious."

"Yeah, right, but I appreciate the vote of confidence."

"I will be off the ship a lot with the assault team. The *Exceltion* needs you full-time," said Ada.

"I know, and it's a great setup. I can't remember the last time I got to get in and control a weapons system in a live fight."

"I saw the logs of your actions. You performed well under pressure."

Kane grinned. "Now I think you're just buttering me up."

"I don't think I am."

"It's slang. It means flattery."

"I see. Your skills are formidable."

Kane shook a finger at her. "We make a good team."

Ada smiled.

"All right, I'm gonna get some exercise in. I'll talk with you later."

"I'll be here," said Ada.

She relaxed back into her pod. What Kane knew, but the crew most likely did not, was that she could see across the ship when she was in the systems. It gave her a window into how organics behaved. She knew some would object if they knew, but given her specialty, it was logical that she might be in there. What they probably did not know was how much time she spent people watching. Her eyes closed as she focused on the ship's systems.

////////

Blake fidgeted with the blood vial in his hands. He had slipped into his office and was looking forward to having a warm drink. The first outing had been rough. Seth was manhandled, Alcarez was killed, Kal had been picked up, and on top of all that, they had to fight a Selva Tong death squad and also bounty hunters. The team's performance and ability to adapt impressed Blake. With everyone already capable of being solo, getting used to working in a team would take time, but he saw potential.

He had talked with Zane and Seth and still had Ada and Kal to visit. Blake checked his forearm device. It was 3:00 p.m. Earth time. Tipping his head back, he let the warm blood from the vial seep down his throat. When the vial was half-empty, he focused on Sarah poking her head in.

"Hey. I—"

He lowered the vial.

Sarah's eyes widened. "Umm . . . I didn't mean to interrupt you."

"Come in," said Blake, gesturing at a chair.

"You sure this is a good time?"

He eyed her. "You've never seen someone drink blood before, have you?"

Sarah shook her head as she entered the room and then took a seat.

"I'm sure you're curious and have questions. I want you to feel comfortable enough that you ask them. So . . . have at it."

"I was going to ask what you recommend for light armor, but . . . if you insist, I do have some questions about you being a Daedrould," said Sarah.

"In that case, I *do* insist, and you can say vampire, it's not a dirty word," said Blake.

She smiled. "Okay. Is it true that if someone drinks your blood, they become . . . sensitive?"

He nodded. "That's one reason why you don't see too many vampires on Fredoria. Quite a black market for that."

"Huh. So where are most vampires then?"

"Mostly on the rim worlds, or out and about, like me."

Her eyes focused on the blood vial. "Is that real blood, or synthetic?"

Blake held up the vial with his fingers as he scrutinized it. "It's real. I can subsist on alien and synthetic short-term but much prefer the real stuff."

"I'm guessing then that you get the real stuff from the rim worlds?"

"Yep. They have blood houses there. People flock from all over to experience a more powerful version of . . . sensitivity, and then they enjoy the carnal activity later. A little-known fact is that in addition to heightening sensitivity, it has a healing effect as well. It's also no coincidence that those with health issues that want to avoid medical facilities for whatever reason show up in the rim worlds," said Blake. He noticed her breathing had intensified, and her heartbeat had ramped up.

"I had a friend that had a vampire boyfriend. She said the . . . *activities* . . . were unlike anything she'd ever experienced."

"Positive experience, I hope."

She nodded.

"Well, if your friend had a vampire boyfriend, she'll have a hard time being with a regular human afterward. Another little-known thing is that the older a vampire is, the more potent the impact is."

"That's interesting," said Sarah.

"Since I'm the oldest vampire out here that I know of, that makes me especially potent as a partner," said Blake, grinning.

She gulped.

"Anyways, for your suit, I would recommend something similar to what Seth had. Lightweight, some kinetic shielding, and support for carrying a few weapons." Blake tilted his head at her. "Let me ask you, though . . . Have you ever killed before?"

She shook her head.

"I see. You may have to if your life is in danger. Is that going to be an issue?"

She sat straight up. "Don't worry about me. I can handle it."

"I bet you can," he said. He tipped the blood vial and finished drinking it. He licked his fangs and grinned.

Sarah stood and looked around. "I appreciate the recommendation."

Blake nodded. "Of course." He watched her as she exited the room. It was obvious that she could have gotten a recommendation from Luke or Kane or anyone else. He hopped up and headed out to Ada's room. When he got there, he knocked on the door.

"Come in, Blake," said Ada.

He entered the room and took a seat. "How's my favorite android?"

"She's doing well," said Ada with a smile.

"Excellent," he said with a nod. He shook a finger out at her. "Listen . . . I came to give you a heads-up. Sarah will be with you, helping defend your location when we hit this compound tomorrow. She's never killed, and I'm not sure what reaction she's going to have to that."

"I'll watch out for her."

"I appreciate it," said Blake.

"Perhaps there is something medicinal I can give her to calm her down if she loses control," said Ada.

He bobbed his head. "Let's hope it doesn't come to that. You have a strategy for holding your point?"

"I do. I'm going to bring in some heavier turrets, but I think using a hologram emitter to cover our location is advisable."

Blake narrowed his eyes. "It may fool someone without thermal sensors, but you'll still be visible to those with them."

"We will hide out somewhere nearby."

"Hmm, okay. We can help get you set up before we go in. Besides, we'll need you to access their systems before-hand anyways."

Ada nodded.

"Okay, I'll let you get back to whatever it was you're doing." He exited the room and headed down to Kal's room. Once there, he knocked on the door.

The door slid open.

Blake noticed that Kal had been taking a nap. "Oh . . . I didn't know you were sleeping."

"It's cool, man. I'll always make time for you," said Kal. He sat up on the edge of his bed. "What's up?"

Blake stepped into the room and leaned back against the wall.

The door slid shut.

"I just wanted to check in with you, see how everything's going."

Kal tossed his hands out to the side. "I'm doing great. After months in that hellhole prison, this is paradise. Level-three replicators, fast ship, solid crew, I mean . . . what else could you ask for?"

"I figured as much," said Blake. He pointed at the equipment rack that had a light-armor suit with multiple gadgets on it. "I see you've visited Luke and Kane."

Kal nodded. "I'm so used to buying my gear or getting the resources to replicate it. It's nice to be able to pick out what you want and not worry about how much it's going to cost."

"I know all about that."

"Yeah. So . . . I was thinking. After this Delkis thing . . . if you got room, maybe I could stick around."

Blake eyed Kal. "I talked with Zane and Ada, and they're for it, and I have no issue with it, but I want to be upfront about some things."

"Such as . . ."

"First, we're operating as a special unit in the Fredorian presidential guard."

"No shit?"

Blake nodded. "Rakar Ho Jador, former grandmaster ranger and leader of the Fredorian Rangers, is who we report to. He reports to Andia Kiggs. They have some missions they want us to look into. Andia Kiggs was the anonymous Fredorian, and our first mission was capturing Delkis."

"He musta really screwed up to get on that list."

"Well . . . initially, I thought it was because Andia and Delkis had some history. He apparently threatened a close friend of hers, and killed another in a restaurant on Kreagus." He wagged a finger. "However, now I'm thinking that your unusual encounter with Emrakus and the information from Gobe Rallz may actually be the real goal. Delkis . . . is not Delkis, and I think we're supposed to find out what he is."

Kal snorted. "I've never seen anything before as crazy as Emrakus. That was new to me."

"Likewise, and I've seen some morbid shit. I don't know where all this'll end, or even how long we'll all be together, but we live in the now and enjoy it for what it is."

"And as a primarily Earthborn crew to boot."

"Yeah, that too. Anyways, I just wanted to stop in. You have any questions?"

"I do actually," said Kal. He pursed his lips. "Don't know if this is proper or not but . . . when I was on Earth, vampires were a myth. I come out here, and then find out that they're real. Was there a lot of your kind on Earth?"

Blake motioned a hand out in an arc. "A whole shadow world's worth. I'm technically a Daedrould, and on Earth, there are thousands. Not all are vampires, but a majority are. Then you have dimensional beings, known as Outsiders.

Those are your ancient gods, legendary heroes, and shifters. Then there are the Wildborn, humans with unique abilities. There are others as well." He grinned. "I bet you didn't know that Earth is represented to the Kreagans by a group called the Helians, who are Outsiders."

"I've never heard of them."

"You probably wouldn't have. They're the reason I'm out here. They exiled me for killing one of their enforcers that went rogue," said Blake.

"That sucks, man. I never knew Earth had all that going on. Information seems to be scarce on Earth in general."

Blake laughed. "That's on purpose per the Kreagans. They keep a very watchful eye on Earth now due to . . . *events* . . . that have occurred."

"What events?" asked Kal.

"Stick around and maybe I'll tell you sometime."

Kal laughed. "All right."

Blake stood and extended a hand. "Welcome aboard."

"Glad to be here," said Kal as he rose and shook Blake's hand.

Blake bobbed his head and walked out.

//////////

Zane eyed the replicated steak on his plate. Having had the real thing on Earth, he thought replicated steak tasted odd. He took a swig of his carbonated drink and pushed the plate away. His stomach was not agreeing with him. Maybe something easier to digest would help. He stood and headed over to the matter reclaimer. As he tossed his plate into it, Seth walked into the room.

"Hey, man, how's it going?" asked Seth.

Zane got a warm glass of milk from the matter replicator and took a seat. "I'm doing all right. You okay after all that craziness yesterday?"

Seth laughed. "Yeah. Alcarez wasn't something I'd planned on dealing with."

"I bet. I saw the video from Blake's chest camera. He *sliced* that dude up."

"That's Blake. We thought Alcarez was dead, but apparently he had survived our first contract. Funny how shit comes back to bite you in the ass."

Zane nodded. He liked Seth. He was a counter to the intensity of Blake, and Zane could see why they were a good team. Seth's easygoing manner was disarming. Zane cleared his throat. "So you'll be on the ship for this next round."

"Definitely. I'd be a liability in my current state, although I wanted to be there to protect Ada. I guess Sarah will handle that now."

"Sarah's tough," said Zane. "Speaking of tough, I need to visit the armory. I want to make sure my juggernaut suit is ready for tomorrow."

"If you don't mind, record your trip. I'd love to see it from your view," said Seth.

Zane stood and slapped hands with Seth. "I got you, brother." He exited the room and headed down to the armory.

Luke was tinkering with a device on a worktable and looked up as Zane entered the room. "Oh, hey."

"Hey, man, just had some questions about the juggernaut suit," said Zane. He noticed that Luke had pushed the device into some clutter on the worktable, almost like he was trying to hide it.

"Ahh," said Luke. He tapped at an embedded console on the table. After a moment, he said, "Kane, can you come to the armory?"

"Be right there," said Kane through the console.

Luke gestured at the console. "Kane knows more about the technical modifications. I can answer anything in regards to the suit's design, though."

"All right," said Zane as he took a seat against the wall. "I tested it out in the training area, and it feels good. I wasn't sure about some of the functions, though. On the internal HUD, it shows there is an option to shoot a flame?"

Luke pointed at Zane's right arm. "It would be there. You can turn it on by voice activation or directly accessing your forearm console."

"Huh. A flamethrower."

"Yep."

"Okay, and these thrusters on the back. I tried them out, and they seem to work. How long can they fire for?"

Luke interacted with the table console and pulled up a holographic projection of the juggernaut suit. "You can burn max for about ten seconds or so. It's meant to hop up to out-of-reach places. Note that it can also be adjusted to shoot out the back instead of down."

"Like a supercharged rush."

"Yep."

Kane entered the room and joined them at the table. "What's up, Zane? Luke?"

Luke gestured at the projection. "Just going over some questions Zane had about the juggernaut suit."

"Ahh, yeah," said Kane. "That thing's a beast."

"We've covered the flamethrower and thrusters."

"Cool," said Kane, glancing at Zane.

Zane nodded. "The armor on this thing is insane, on top of a strong kinetic shield. It even has a refracting shield against energy beams."

Kane raised a finger. "The refracting shield is limited. It won't stop a powerful energy beam from hitting you, but it will for most handheld weapons. As long as you don't plan on fighting ships, you should be okay."

"Works for me," said Zane. He pointed to a series of lines that crisscrossed the suit. "I was trying to figure that out. I didn't see anything on the HUD for it."

"If you watched the video with Gobe Rallz, it's similar. It's an electric pulse system that serves as a point-blank area of effect attack and extends a few feet out. Anything caught in the pulse will be hit by a huge electromagnetic charge."

"That's pretty badass," said Zane.

"Yeah, except for that fact that it doesn't distinguish friend from foe. It's not something you would use in cramped quarters with your team."

"Obviously," said Zane. "I saw that the gauntlets could be charged as well."

Kane nodded. "Yep. You can touch someone and stun the crap out of them, or kill them if their body can't take it."

"I like it."

Luke grinned. "I want to see the video from your helmet feed when you get back."

"Get in line," said Zane, laughing. "Seth wants to see it too. Hell, we'll just make it a movie night."

"I got the popcorn," said Kane.

They all shared a laugh.

Zane tapped his left arm. "One thing I noticed about the suit is the energy shield. It seems similar to the one on the lighter armor, but it looks like it can take a lot more punishment. It can also be resized as needed. I'm gonna be a damn bulldozer out there with that thing."

"Aye, that you will," said Luke. "Pair it up with your mace and flamethrower, and you're a space paladin."

Kane made a dual slicing motion with his arms. "Yeah, you're gonna be a monster in close-quarters combat."

"For those who are farther away, I guess I'll need to get in close," said Zane.

"Yeah, but that's more about what weapon you use," said Kane. He pointed at the smooth shoulders. "There's small laser turrets installed that can pop up and shoot five or six times before needing a two-minute recharge. It's limited in use and will pop back under while recharging."

Luke wagged a finger at Zane. "Speaking of which . . . I know you like your shotgun, but this suit is more geared toward a rapid-fire assault weapon."

"I like the sound of that. What'd you have in mind?" asked Zane.

Kane grinned as he glanced at Luke. "I bet you're thinking of a modified hellthrower."

Zane's eyes widened. "That's based on the standard-issue Fredorian heavy assault weapon, right?"

"Version three. The suit has a hookup that allows for refilling and also provides support, but you'll be able to have your shield out while holding that beast."

"I'm ready to go now," said Zane with his lips drawn to the right.

Luke looked down for a moment. "I think it's safe to say that while you'll have this suit and weapon, the Selva Tong probably have something similar. Not to mention that the others on your assault team won't have the same protection or firepower as you." He looked back up. "They'll be vulnerable out in the open if they head out with you."

"I know," said Zane. "I'll be used more as a shock trooper. The others will follow in my wake of devastation."

"I can't wait to see your feed," said Kane. "The awesome thing is that I'll be able to see it in all directions if I view it while hooked up to the ship's systems."

"You still need to show me how that works," said Luke.

"It's just a special viewer helmet I brought, but we can replicate more if needed."

Zane laughed. "Well, damn, I want to see it that way too."

"Okay, but you're bringing the whiskey," said Luke.

They laughed.

CHAPTER
NINETEEN

Sarah took a deep breath as she walked alongside Blake, Zane, Ada, and Kal. After a good night's rest and a quick meeting, they left the *Exceltion* and were on their way toward Selva Tong turf. According to the time on the HUD inside her helmet, it was around 9:00 a.m. Earth time. Taking the ramps to level sixteen took a bit longer than she had expected. She wore her light-armor suit and carried an FLP-40 and a striker. Getting suited up had made her heart race a bit, but she knew she was in good company. Manning a station on a large ship was a bit different than being in the field in enemy territory.

She was getting used to the clanking sound that Zane's metallic suit made. When he had stepped out with it on, she had no idea it would be so large. Standing around nine feet tall, it was bulky and had a slight hum to it. The helmet stood out since it had sharp lines, and there were no visible eye sockets, just a seamless front that tucked into a rectangular area. The large weapon strapped to the side, but pointing up, was a hellthrower, as she had learned. Zane seemed to move effortlessly. Although he was strong, she understood that the suit had walking assist in it. She had seen similar suits used in FDF special forces.

Ada's silver suit was like Sarah's. It was more of a light metallic covering with an emphasis on the shoulders, chest, arms, and legs. Blue edges surrounded each separated section. Although the kinetic shielding would not handle sustained fire, it could take a few shots. The suit was made with mobility in mind and was a walking sensor factory. Ada's suit had an additional backpack filled with drones, gadgets, and medical items. Two turrets were strapped to the sides of the backpack. Sarah knew it was probably heavy, but that would not be a problem for Ada.

Kal's black-and-gold suit was odd to Sarah. Unlike the others, his was more of a slip-on suit for various body parts. The beige under armor was visible, and it seemed like every possible open spot had a device of some type. She had learned that Kal was known as the Trickster. With all those gadgets, she could see why. The helmet had a rounded silver faceplate with various red eye sockets around it. It reminded her of a bug's face in some regards.

Unlike the other suits, Blake's was somewhere between the bulkiness of Zane's and her lighter version. Like Kal's suit, Blake's was black, but had silver and blue mixed in. The helmet was like a metallic version of a bandanna wrapped around the mouth and a black hoodie that covered the top half. The camouflage shielding aspect was the suit's main draw, and as a result, it had less kinetic shielding. It occurred to her that he must be in great shape, with superior speed and strength, on top of being an older vampire.

They reached Selva Tong turf after a thirty-minute walk.

Blake paused and faced the group. He addressed them through the internal communication system. "Now it gets real. From this point on, expect anything. Stay close, and if shit hits the fan," said Blake, slapping Zane's arm, "get behind the big guy."

"Hell yeah," said Zane.

"It's a short stretch to Kahan turf. I've already updated Gertus, and he's okay with us going through but said he's seen an increase in non-Kahan, so we'll need to be cautious. Once we're there, we make our way to the maintenance tunnels, then all the way to the compound. We can then set up once we're there. Everyone clear?"

The group acknowledged Blake.

"All right, let's move."

The group entered Selva Tong turf and headed toward the back streets.

Sarah was soaking in everything she had seen so far. They had been in Mularin turf, and the Mularin group was composed of various alien races, and not all were human-oid. One thing that surprised her when she first landed the *Exceltion* there was how many aliens were out and about. It was easy to blend in. Their architecture was a hodgepodge of styles. Some areas were high-tech, others low-tech. Various building materials were used, but the one thing that seemed constant was the variety of lights everywhere.

The Selva Tong architecture, at least on level sixteen, was much different. She understood that the nearby Kahan setup had some influence. Pockets of L-shaped areas with buildings and storefronts created a maze of side streets. The main one they had originally entered was wide, and unlike Mularin space, only a handful of aliens were out. Going down the back streets was as she expected. The buildings were not uniform, and based on the garbage she saw strewn about, it probably did not smell good either. Dim lighting and a small mist in some areas added to her conclusion that this was not a well-maintained place.

They reached Kahan turf without much issue. Once there, Blake contacted Gertus, and the group continued on.

The usual banter between everyone ceased when they had entered Selva Tong territory, but she was glad to see it pick up on Kahan turf. Several Kahan had cleared out of their path as they weaved their way toward the maintenance tunnels. It was empowering to walk alongside some heavy hitters.

When they reached the maintenance tunnels an hour later, Blake paused and raised a hand. "I'm relaying to you the layout of these tunnels. If for whatever reason you need to flee, get to where we are now . . . by any means necessary. Understood?"

Everyone nodded.

"Good. In we go."

Everyone followed Blake as he entered the dimly lit tunnels.

Sarah did not like the claustrophobic feeling. The tunnels were wide enough for the group to walk in, but if they had to fight there, it would get messy quickly. The closer they got to the tunnel exit, the more her doubt surged. She was sure she could do the job, and Blake had put a lot of trust in her. Initially, it seemed odd for her to go on a trip like this, but she understood that with Ada focusing on the remote systems, she would be vulnerable, or at least not fully focused on the environment. That was Sarah's job, to ensure Ada could work uninterrupted.

After another hour, they reached the exit point near Delkis's compound.

Blake pointed off in the distance. "There is an abandoned building nearby. Selva Tong is thick in this area, but once we're there, Ada can set up. Ada, can you launch a surveillance drone?"

Ada nodded and reached into her backpack. After a moment, she had a disc-shaped drone in her hands. She plugged her finger tendrils into it.

The drone lit up.

She removed her tendrils, and the drone hovered a moment before shimmering out of sight.

Sarah could see the drone's view in her helmet HUD. It was a screen with four sections, each one with a specific type of view. She was interested in the thermal one.

Blake gestured forward. "Let's hit that building."

Using the drone to guide them, they avoided patrols and reached the building.

Ada began to unload her backpack when they got to the roof. She set up both turrets around her and pulled out a remote access drone that she began to interact with. With a tap at her forearms, small discs hovered in the air near her.

"Ada, use the surveillance drone to help Kal get into position," said Blake.

Ada nodded as Kal exited the roof.

"When Kal's in position and Ada has infiltrated the compound's security system, it's showtime for me. Oh, and Zane," said Blake.

The remote access drone launched.

"It won't take me long once I'm hard connected," said Ada.

Sarah had butterflies in her stomach. She had pulled out her FLP-40 in front of her and was looking around constantly. Deep in enemy territory, all it would take was one mistake, and then it would be a firefight.

"Relax," said Blake, putting a hand on Sarah's shoulder. "We're outside their sensor range, and we have a good plan and a good crew to implement it."

Sarah exhaled as she nodded. "I'm okay."

"You wanted to know how to survive out here. This is a good look at it. Be on your guard . . . at all times."

"Right."

"I've connected to their systems," said Ada. "Their system is very secure, but I believe I can switch the turret protocols."

"All right. Zane, let's head down. Ada, let us know when you've hacked their systems. Once Kal gives us the thumbs-up, we'll charge ahead."

Ada nodded.

Blake and Zane exited the roof.

Ada pulled out a device with a flat base and a small rod. Once on the ground, the rod extended up. "This will prevent any sensors from seeing us, but we can still be seen visually."

"We're out of sight, so we should be okay," said Sarah.

"That's correct."

Sarah sighed as she switched to a private comm channel with Ada. "I hope everything goes well."

"It should. However, the unknown variable is what's inside. Blake will have to make decisions there, but he is more than qualified to do so."

"Yeah. I don't mean to distract you," said Sarah.

"You're okay. I can do these simultaneously."

Sarah nodded as she looked out over the roof. The place would be crawling with Selva Tong once the attack started. Hopefully none of them would come her and Ada's way. Sarah was looking forward to watching the chest video feeds once everything was over. She was amazed at how everyone seemed calm. That was probably experience. She had none, and this was giving her racked nerves.

"I'm in position," said Kal ten minutes later over the group communication channel.

"Excellent," said Blake.

"The systems are at our disposal," said Ada.

"Light it up," said Blake.

"Lighting it up," said Ada.

Sarah could hear the sound of gunfire in the distance.

"That's our cue," said Blake. "We're going in."

////////

Blake did a final check over his gear before heading out with Zane. The plan was simple. Charge through the south gate, and breach the compound interior. Once inside, they would meet up with Kal, who was clearing the top, and then they would face off against Delkis and whatever security measures he had in place. Ada and Sarah would be secure away from all the action, and he sensed Sarah was nervous. For him, this was another opportunity to get in and let loose. He cherished moments like this.

"You ready?" asked Zane.

"Let's roll!" said Blake as he aimed his striker forward.

Zane charged out into the street.

They took the back streets until they were close to the compound.

Pausing in an alleyway, Blake could see Selva Tong getting gunned down by the south-gate turrets.

"Ada, you sure those turrets won't hit us?" asked Blake over the group communication channel.

"Yes. They have our profiles."

Blake slapped Zane on the arm. "Time to test it, big man."

"Gladly," said Zane. He activated his forearm energy shield while lowering his hellthrower and pointing it forward.

Blake tensed as he watched Zane wade out. If the turrets were not friendly, he would know shortly.

After a moment, Zane said, "We're good."

Blake exited the alley and walked a bit behind Zane. The corpses of Selva Tong members littered the streets. Some were firing from behind cover and facing toward the turrets. Unfortunately for the members, they found themselves exposed to Zane's firing arc. Blake picked off the stragglers trying to flee or taking potshots at Zane.

When they reached the door, it slid open.

"Ada, I love you," said Zane.

"It's appreciated," said Ada.

Blake surveyed the compound's inner courtyard. Dead bodies were everywhere. His attention turned toward one of the turrets taking fire. "Ada, what the hell's hitting that?"

"Reinforcements are beginning to arrive. I suspect the commotion and lack of communication has caused them to investigate."

"Shit," said Blake. "A little early then, but we got time. Let's get inside."

They hustled up to the front door.

"Clear the ground floor. I'll meet up with Kal on the upper levels. Then we'll all head down," said Blake.

"My pleasure," said Zane as he stomped off.

Blake activated his camouflage shielding and crept up the nearest stairwell. It was harder for him to smell and hear with his helmet on, but his helmet could take hits. As he reached the second floor, he paused. He could hear sporadic firing coming from a bit down the hallway. Probably some confused Selva Tong members.

He shouldered his striker and pulled out his dual blades. As he crept along the hallway, he peeked into each room he passed. It was obvious the Selva Tong spared no expense for luxury. When he reached the room where he suspected the members were, he peeked in. Two members were taking turns popping in and out of a window and shooting at a turret.

"What the hell is going on!" said the left member. "We have to get out of here!"

The right member grabbed the left member. "Get a grip. It's probably just a malfunction. Hold position!"

The left member sat back against the wall.

Blake cracked his neck and then charged into the room. With a swift motion, he decapitated the left member, while slicing off the raised arm of the right member.

The member screamed as Blake tossed him out the window.

Blake figured there were probably pockets of these throughout the compound. He decided to check in. "Kal, where you at?"

"Just grappled to the sixth floor. I've secured the room I'm at, but more are coming. Talk later."

"All right, I'll meet you on the fourth in a bit," said Blake. With Kal causing a commotion up top and Zane below, Blake's plan of chaos throughout the compound seemed to be working. He knew the turrets would not keep the rest of the Selva Tong at bay for long. They had to clear the compound before their sweep of the underground levels. The sound of footsteps approaching the stairwell caught his attention. He crept up to the door of the room he was in.

Three Selva Tong members rushed by.

Blake's camouflage shielding dissipated as he rushed out and stabbed one through the side and impaled him against the wall. He then sliced the back of the neck of another.

The remaining member stopped to wheel around.

Blake pulled his blade out from the wall and grabbed the member whose neck he had slashed. With a push, he sent him flying into the one trying to bring his weapon up. They tumbled to the ground, and Blake was on them, shredding them to pieces. Painting the hallways with blood triggered his bloodlust. He closed his eyes for a moment and took deep breaths. Losing his cool was not something he wanted to do at the moment. After calming down, he focused and continued his sweep of the second floor with his camouflage shielding reactivated.

One of the rooms he entered looked like a command center of some type.

Workstations lined the walls, and various screens showed video feeds of the compound. The two Selva Tong members inside were sweating profusely as they talked to someone on the screen.

Blake knew they would not see him through his camouflage shielding, so he crept up behind one of the workstations and squatted to listen in on their conversation. Before he did, he got a look at who the members were talking to. It was Daniel Greer.

"We don't know who they are," said one of the members. "One of them has heavy armor and is tearing up the ground floor. The turrets are firing on our own men, and we can't communicate outside the compound."

"Then grab a weapon and eliminate the threat!" said Daniel.

"We'll do our best."

The screen faded away.

"Shit . . . are you kidding me?" asked the other member. "I'm not going against that metal monster downstairs. Have you seen what he did to the crew down there?"

"I know, I know. Umm . . . maybe we can go out the window."

"Yeah, and then get massacred by Daniel later."

Blake popped up and aimed his striker at them. "I have an easier solution." He fired two precision shots, hitting each in the head.

The men slumped to the ground.

Blake walked up to their workstation. He examined the controls and flicked a few switches. A grin formed on his lips as Daniel appeared on the screen.

"What do you . . . Oh . . . well . . . what have we here?"

"I'm Blake Brown, or didn't you know?"

Daniel raised his eyebrows while smiling. "So . . . you're here to collect Delkis. I'm sorry, I can't allow that."

"Thankfully, that's not up to you," said Blake.

"Oh, really?"

"We know where you are, and we'll be with you shortly."

"Good. When reinforcements arrive, they'll secure the compound, but I don't think you fully understand. You'll be trapped . . . with *us*."

"Sounds like a party. I'll bring the whiskey."

Daniel laughed. "I like you. I think Delkis has chosen wisely, as always."

Blake's smile wound down. Daniel should have been scared or nervous, not giddy with anticipation. Something was off. Daniel was right that once the reinforcements arrived, they would be trapped below, but the plan was to exit from the elevators down there. It would be a race to capture Delkis before reinforcements could swarm them. "What can I say? Anyone that chooses me is wise."

Daniel winked an eye. "We'll . . . see you in a bit." He wagged a finger. "Don't kill too many now."

The screen faded.

It was obvious that Daniel did not care if his men died. That did not sound like the Daniel Greer whose passion led him to the top of the Selva Tong. Putting together what Gobe Rallz said and what Blake saw from the Emrakus video, it was clear that something had possessed Daniel. Maybe it was Delkis. Blake opened his group communication channel. "Just talked with Daniel. He's . . . not himself and is looking forward to everyone going underground to meet him."

"Say what?" asked Zane.

"He seems to have given up on the top level being secured by his men. However, he also said that reinforcements would arrive, but we're already beginning to see that."

"Has the plan changed?" asked Ada.

Blake sighed. "No. Zane, head out and escort Ada and Sarah to the compound once you've secured the ground floor. Kal and I will continue to clear things up."

"I'm on my way, ladies," said Zane.

"We're packing up and will head out," said Ada.

"All right. Stay in contact if anything changes," said Blake. He took a look around the now-silent room and then exited it.

Blake headed up to the third floor and heard footsteps in one of the nearby rooms. He put his dual blades away and pulled out his striker. The footsteps seemed to be in a random pattern. Once he was at the door, he kicked it in and stepped back, expecting gunfire. Instead he heard some women shrieking in surprise. Intrigued, he entered the room and lowered his helmet. Four scantily clad women stood before him. A quick scan revealed no weapons, and he determined they were not a threat. He grinned. "Ladies . . . there's no reason to fear me. I'm just . . . cleaning out the compound of undesirables, of which you are not."

"Please don't hurt us."

Blake nodded. "Stay in this room, and under no circumstance are you to leave it until a Selva Tong member comes. Understood?"

They all nodded in agreement.

"All right, go back to being lovely and hanging out," said Blake. He bowed slightly toward the women and exited the room, closing the door as he went.

TWENTY

Sarah looked over the roof's edge at the assembling mass of Selva Tong. They were taking up positions and trying to take out the turrets. There was only a wide street to the compound, with buildings on each side. Unfortunately, the buildings did not connect, and the space between each made it difficult to go from roof to roof. There was a big wall on the backside of the buildings, so they could not use that route either. She pointed outward. "We're going to be exposed out there."

Ada was busy packing things into her backpack, which she had pulled off and set beside her. "There are obstructions we can use to obscure ourselves. When Zane reaches us, we can just walk in front of him."

"You're so calm and steady," said Sarah.

"I try to be," said Ada.

"Anything I can to do to help you pack up?"

Ada shook her head. "I almost have everything. We can pick up the surveillance drone when we reach the compound. I don't think we'll be retrieving the remote access drone."

"We can always make a new one."

"Exactly," said Ada. She grabbed her backpack and put it on as she stood. With one final look around, she said, "I think we're ready to go."

Sarah was glad to be around Ada and felt she would become a long-lasting friend. What the Fredorian government did to androids had angered Sarah. The ones on the *Arcturus* were well liked. It bothered her that while most had escaped or fled, the ones left behind were forced into assigned roles, mostly doing manual labor similar to what mindless robots did. She bet Ada felt liberated to be where she was, and Sarah would do her best to make Ada always feel welcome.

They left the roof and headed to the ground floor.

Sarah activated her private communications channel with Ada. "So how do you like everything so far? I know we haven't had much of an opportunity to talk."

"I like it," said Ada. "Blake is a fair leader, Seth is a great person, and everyone else has been a pleasure to work with so far."

"Same thing for me. I thought my career was over, but now look at me, I'm in the field deep in Selva Tong territory."

Ada studied Sarah when they reached the ground floor. "Hopefully you will not regret it. I suspect these types of missions will be common."

"I realize that," said Sarah. "I'm ready for a challenge."

"Good. Our first one is before us," said Ada. She pointed at an angle out the door. "There is a Selva Tong member on the roof. I'll disable him. Once we head out, we need to stick to the sides of the street, using the entranceways and other objects as cover as we move. Before we go, though, we should update Zane."

Sarah nodded.

Ada paused for a moment. "Zane, we are about to leave the building."

The sounds of grunts and gunfire came over the communication channel.

After a moment, Zane said, "All right. I just left the compound. Had to waste two members who thought they could hang with me. What a laughable mistake that was." He paused for a moment. "Okay, I see where you're at on the overview map. I'll see you here shortly. Out."

Ada grabbed her pistol and stepped out the door. She aimed at the member on the roof and then fired.

The member slumped onto the roof.

"Nice shooting," said Sarah.

"I have autoaiming."

Sarah grinned. "I wish I had that."

Ada nodded as she took off toward the compound.

They had gone past two wrecked vehicles on the street when they ran into a small group of Selva Tong taking cover. The startled members jumped up and swung their weapons forward.

Sarah's heartbeat surged as she sprayed them down with her FLP-40.

They fell over and stopped moving.

Her eyes widened as her breathing went haphazard.

Ada laid a hand on Sarah's shoulder. "Are you okay?"

"I . . . I killed them."

"Yes, and if you hadn't, they would have tried to kill us."

Sarah's eyes misted as she swallowed hard.

"You can't dwell on this right now. We're still exposed."

Sarah licked her lips and nodded. She gazed at the dead men as she passed them. Killing was something she figured she would do as part of this crew, but not quite this early, and instead of one, it had been three. Did they have families? Kids?

Ada tapped Sarah's arm. "This is not the time to reflect. Let's go."

Sarah let out a measured breath as she focused on Ada weaving in and out between obstructions. There were a few members here and there, but Ada was able to kill them before they could focus on her. Sarah admired Ada's confidence and skill with a pistol. Killing was not an issue for Ada, it seemed. Maybe that could be discussed with her later.

After navigating the hazards of the street for the next fifteen minutes, they paused behind a burning armored vehicle.

"Stay where you are," said Zane. "There's a sniper some-where, and about five or six others tucked away and shooting at me."

"All right. We'll see if there's anything we can do," said Ada. She glanced at Sarah. "Check that side, I'll check this one."

Sarah gulped as she scooted over to the left edge. She peered out. All she could see was smoke and Zane's shield in the distance, lighting up from small arms fire. She jumped when she heard Ada fire. Heading over and looking out, Sarah saw that Ada had hit a sniper on the roof.

"Finally. I thought I was going to have to climb up there and beat his fucking ass," said Zane, laughing over the group communication channel.

"I see two more to your right," said Ada.

The winding-up sound and subsequent barrage of noise from Zane's hellthrower filled the air.

Sarah crept back to her side and saw that Zane had punched hundreds of holes in a makeshift shield that resembled a thin sheet of metal. Behind it laid several dead Selva Tong members in a puddle of blood. She inhaled and placed her back against the cover she was behind. It was hot from the fire consuming it on the other side. Closing her eyes for a moment and taking deep breaths helped her overcome the nausea she could feel brewing in her stomach. An intense pressure hit her kinetic shielding and slammed her to the ground.

Ada hustled over and took aim at a sniper that had tried to take Sarah out. The sniper was looking through his scope when Ada fired a precision shot that hit him in the head. She attended to Sarah. "Are you okay?"

Sarah trembled as Ada helped her up. "I . . . I didn't even see him."

"Your kinetic shielding took a pummeling. I suspect it won't take much more punishment, if any."

Sarah nodded as she wobbled for a moment.

"Are you sure you're okay?"

"Yeah . . . I . . . just a lot to take in."

Ada placed both hands on Sarah's shoulders. "I understand, and I'm here for you. Right now, we need to keep moving."

"Of course."

"I think we're clear," said Zane over the group communication channel.

Ada motioned forward. "Let's go." Her hovering discs moved to cover Sarah.

Sarah nodded and followed Ada out. Zane was easy to see in his massive suit.

When they met up, Zane stepped behind them and half turned to point at the compound. "It's a clear shot to the compound. I'll cover your rear."

The group proceeded toward the compound.

Sarah took stock of the mass death all around her. There must have been dozens. Some were sliced up, others were shredded, and some looked like they had been mauled by a wild animal. Had she not had the improved gear with Kane's and Luke's modifications, she might have joined them, something she would contemplate later. She found

Zane's reaction puzzling. He was wading through death while laughing. It did not appear to faze him, and if anything, it seemed to put him in a good mood. Maybe that was a killer mindset that she could never reach, a mindset she hoped she never had to experience.

She was glad she could not smell anything with her helmet up. There was only one functioning turret yet, and she knew that when it went down, the place would be swarmed with the Selva Tong members she saw before they moved from their original position. Despite everything looking grim, she felt comfortable in Zane's and Ada's presence. Zane waded through enemy fire to get them without a moment's hesitation, and Ada continued to be a role model in how to act in a combat situation.

"You keep stopping," said Zane, laying a beefy metallic gauntlet on Sarah's shoulder. "You all right?"

Sarah nodded. "I think so. Let's get inside."

//////////

Zane walked backward with his hellthrower pointed forward. Although he had not seen any more Selva Tong members around, his enhanced view had a zoomed in view of members in the distance. His helmet was tracking their movements, but they were still out of range for his hellthrower. A smile formed on his lips as he stepped around a burned corpse. The flamethrower was as lethal as advertised. He never had a suit with this much power, and being able to let loose with it was more exhilarating than he had expected. The main issue he ran across was which approach to use to silence the opposition.

"We're almost there," said Ada over the group communication channel.

"Good," said Blake. "The compound should be cleared . . . for now. We'll meet just inside the entrance."

Zane peeked forward to make sure Ada and Sarah were doing okay. He was not sure what had happened prior to reaching them, but Sarah seemed rattled, based on the way she trembled and looked around. Ada was cool as always. He faced forward again.

After ten minutes, they reached the compound's inner doors.

Blake opened the doors and waved everyone in. Once they had assembled, he addressed the group. "The lower level of this compound is actually a secured warehouse of some sort. I don't know what we'll be walking into, but Daniel Greer appears to want us to go down."

"A trap," said Kal.

"Most likely, but our group is tough," said Blake. "Zane, take point. Ada, you'll need to open the door. Once inside, we'll need to lock it to make sure the reinforcements that take back the compound can't come down."

Ada nodded. "I've unlocked every door already, but that one is isolated. One thing to note is that communication with the remote access drone will cease once we are inside. I suspect that the Selva Tong will find it and destroy it."

"We can always replicate another one. Once we capture Daniel and Delkis, we can then exit via the elevators at the opposite end," said Blake. "Everyone ready?"

Everyone acknowledged Blake.

"Let's go."

They headed out to the far side of the compound on the ground level. A massive door greeted them when they arrived five minutes later. A red light above the door pulsed.

Blake walked up to the door and examined it. "I guess we have to manually open it, despite it being unlocked. I'll need some help, Zane."

Zane stood alongside Blake, and together, they pushed the door to the right.

Kal shook his head. "Of all the things not to automate."

"It makes sense that even if the system is hijacked, like Ada did, a manual effort would still be needed. If the other side of this door had a lot of enemies, it would be to their advantage," said Blake.

Kal shrugged. "It makes you wonder *why* this door is so big and requires a setup like that, though."

"It has something we want, and that's all I care about," said Blake, licking his fangs. "All right, in we go."

Everyone followed Blake through to the other side.

The interior area looked like a widened portion of a tunnel that was flat for a bit before angling down. The metallic floors and ceiling were clean, and the lighting was bright. He lowered his helmet and sniffed the air. A repugnant smell assaulted his nose. He knew the smell well. It was one of decaying corpses. His eyes narrowed as they searched ahead. After a moment, he gestured at Blake. "Smells like dead bodies in here."

"I smelled that too," said Blake.

Zane and Blake slid the door to the left, sealing it in place.

"Do your thing, Ada," said Blake.

Ada nodded and then headed over to the wall console just inside the area they were in. After a moment, the red light above the door turned green. She pulled out a flat circle-shaped device and connected it to the console. "The door is now sealed, and this device will keep it that way."

"Good job," said Blake. He motioned at Zane, and then waved forward. "Lead on."

Zane surveyed the environment as they walked. The tunnel headed down, and the farther they went, the dimmer the lights became. The odor he had smelled earlier grew stronger. Whatever lay ahead did not seem like something anyone would want to be around, which made him wonder what exactly they were going to face.

They reached the end of the tunnel, which expanded into a wide doorway that led into a large, open area. A long ramp angled down to the floor.

Zane figured they were about fifty feet off the warehouse floor. Large metallic containers dotted the space, but the fifty white upright pods that sat in a grid formation caught his eye. Whatever they were, they were the originators of the foul odor. He pointed at the pods. "What the hell are those?"

"No idea," said Blake.

Sarah jumped as a screen on the wall near her turned on.

Zane eyed the screen. The black leatherlike outfit and ridged head left no doubt who it was.

"Delkis," said Blake.

"Ahh . . . you finally came. Nice job hacking the door. It won't last long before it's blown open."

"We only need a little time to capture you. Why don't you surrender and come peacefully?"

Delkis laughed. "I heard you had a comedic streak, but I'm more interested in your . . . uniqueness."

Blake narrowed his eyes. "There is no escape for you."

"Or for you."

"We'll see."

Delkis drew his lips to the side as he tilted his head. "Come on down. Let's play."

The screen turned off.

"Well, that guy isn't cocky at all," said Kal.

"He's overconfident, although if it's just him and Daniel down here, I'm not sure why he would be. He has something up his sleeve," said Blake.

Zane pointed his hellthrower down the ramp. "Then let's get his ass." He was looking forward to finishing their first contract and having something tangible under his belt to show his good faith in working with the team. Going back to prison was not an option at this point.

Blake nodded.

They proceeded along the ramp.

Halfway down, Blake pointed at another wide doorway on the opposite side of the warehouse. "That's where we need to go."

Zane closed up his helmet and monitored the various incoming data on his HUD. The streaming was constant, and his suit's sensors detected movement that appeared and then vanished. "Anyone picking up some weird readings on movement?"

"I am," said Blake. "I sense there are three or four people with some type of camouflage down there."

Sarah sighed. "And we're going to go right through all the pods. Figures."

"Yeah, seems like a trap. It'd be hard to fight in that confined area," said Kal.

Blake nodded. "Hmm, that brings up good point. Let's set up a defensive position here while Zane and I head to the other side of the warehouse. Kal, you can scope things out. Sarah, you can help protect him while he's scoping in case anything comes up the ramp. Ada, set up your turrets here, and you can use an assault and surveillance drone to help provide visuals and defense."

"Works for me," said Kal.

Ada nodded and pulled off her backpack. Her defensive rings hovered out in front of her.

Blake motioned at Zane. "Let's check it out."

They reached the ground floor.

As they walked up to the first row of pods, Zane paused. "Motion sensor is picking up those anomalies again. We're not alone." His shoulder-mounted turrets popped up. "I'm only sensing three or four, but these turrets can shoot five or six times before recharging. Let 'em come."

Blake shook his head. "I don't think they want me dead. I can't say that about anyone else, though."

"Well too bad for them."

"Seeing anything Kal?" asked Blake.

"Nope. If they're using camouflage, then they're also using the pods' thermal heat to obscure themselves. It's just a sea of red from my thermal scans."

Zane walked past the first set of pods with Blake behind him.

A shot rang out.

"Kal?" asked Blake.

"Something was moving fast toward you. I think I hit it. It's backtracking."

Zane could see the overhead view from the surveillance drone. He hustled over to the right. "I can't make out shit down here."

Blake licked his lips. "Probably just—" He shuddered as two shots hit him. His kinetic shielding dissipated. He moved to the right as a third shot hit his shoulder, causing him to spin and go flying backward.

Zane hustled in front of Blake and faced the direction of the shots. "Blake's hit!"

Another round of shots fired out.

"I got two of them. Snipers in the back. They were concealed until they shot at Blake," said Kal. "There was a third, but my earlier shot seems to have gotten them."

Blake grunted as he crawled behind one of the pods. "Shit, that hurts, and damn it, now my kinetic shielding is out."

"Damn, you reacted fast," said Zane.

"They weren't trying to kill me. Those were intended to disrupt any shielding and wound me."

"Still . . . damn."

Ada's assault drone hovered near Blake.

"I just need some blood," said Blake, wincing. He reached for some vials on his belt and pulled them off.

Zane had never seen a vampire drink blood in person before.

Blake downed two vials. His eyes turned a dim blue while he uttered a deep growl.

A set of hissing and whooshing sounds rang out all over the warehouse. A voice boomed over speakers. "Not bad, not bad, but now it's time to make things interesting."

The pods began to open.

TWENTY-ONE

B lake's muscles flexed as strength surged through them. His eyes turned a faint shade of blue as he used the pod to stand up. The bruising from the shot that had hit him was beginning to heal. He was thankful for his body armor. If he had not moved, the shot would have shredded his arm. Being captured alive without a functional arm seemed to be something Delkis was okay with. Blake's attention focused on the pods opening. He was not sure what to expect but gestured back to the ramp. "Let's get into a better position."

Blake and Zane hustled out of the pod area to the bottom of the ramp.

"Uhh . . . something's coming out of the pods," said Kal over the group communication channel. "Looks like . . .

humans, but they're moving unnaturally, like they're trying to figure out how to walk."

Zane pointed his hellthrower at the pods. "Unnatural or not, still flesh and blood that can get tore up."

Blake activated his camouflage shielding and then pulled out his dual blades. "Hold this position. I'm going to head to that doorway on the opposite end."

"Why not send the surveillance drone?" asked Zane.

"It needs to provide an overview for everyone."

"All right," said Zane.

Ada's assault drone hovered near Zane.

"I'm bringing the turrets down the ramp toward you Zane," said Ada.

"More firepower," said Zane, laughing.

Blake tapped Zane's arm, then took off toward the pods. He could see the humans up close at this point. They were wearing formfitting dark-gray mesh suits with no armor segments. Their eyes were pitch-black, and a foul odor emanated from their yellowish skin. "They're mutants of some type. They may have been human at some point, but they're something else now."

"Still don't matter to me, I'll waste them all," said Zane.

Blake sidestepped a few of the mutants as he hustled past. Apparently their senses were weak. Otherwise they would have either detected his smell or heard his light steps.

Zane lit into the first wave of mutants that had charged toward the ramp.

Blake took advantage of the chaos to move to the far right of the warehouse, opposite the ramp. He climbed on a pod and waited as he watched the rest of the mutants focus on Zane's gunfire. Loud single shots rang out from Kal, and the steady fire from Ada's turrets and the assault drone could be heard.

The top-down view from Ada's surveillance drone gave Blake the information needed to determine a path to get to the doorway. He hopped from pod to pod until he reached the other end of the warehouse. When he jumped down, he slid behind a pod when he noticed two large robots had positioned themselves just outside the doorway. They had four wheels and a rectangular base, with a pyramid-shaped body and turrets for arms. "Zane! They have devastators!"

"Bring 'em on!" said Zane.

Blake shook his head. He enjoyed hearing Zane get excited about fighting. It was what Blake had envisioned when he picked Zane.

The two robots rolled through the doorway and moved toward Zane.

"They're headed your way now," said Blake. He hugged the wall near the doorway as the robots went past him. Checking the overhead view, he could see that the mutants were about to swarm Zane, despite the overwhelming firepower at his disposal. He smiled when he saw jets of flame engulf the mutants. What surprised him was Sarah standing next to Zane and firing her FLP-40. The mutants were lined up due to the pods' grid formation. That allowed Zane and the others to fire in straight lines.

"We got a problem," said Kal. "The Selva Tong topside are trying to blast through to here. I think they're close."

Blake sighed. They were getting pinched. "Everyone, follow Zane. Zane, put up your shield and clear a path for the others to where I am. We'll set up a new defensive position here."

"Bulldozer time," said Zane.

Blake entered the doorway and saw that it was a large hallway. Indents on the side indicated it could be sealed off. With that in mind, he scouted down the hallway a bit. After determining that he would not need to clear anything out, he hustled back to the main area where everyone was fighting.

Leaping into battle, he sliced and diced any mutant that came close. Their unusual movement was a hindrance to them, and with his enhanced vampiric speed, he zoomed around them, chopping off body parts. It was unclear what purpose these mutants served, other than maybe a distraction.

He reached one of the devastators and sliced up the back of it, causing it to fritz, then stop moving. The other one was approaching Zane. "Zane, devastator almost on you."

"I see it," said Zane.

Blake watched as a volley of bullets shredded the devastator's kinetic shielding and then the devastator itself.

"Sarah's been infected with something," said Ada over the group communication channel.

"I'm on my way," said Blake. He continued cutting down mutants as he headed off.

When he reached Zane, he noticed Sarah on the ground, trembling with Ada over her. "How's she doing?"

"She is not doing well, and was scratched by one of those things. Their claws went right through her armor," said Ada. "It seems to have some impact on her, and there's something in her blood. I'm administering some microbots, but it doesn't appear to be helping."

Blake knelt next to Sarah.

She began to hyperventilate with her helmet off.

He could sense her irregular heartbeat, shallow breathing, and increased body heat. "Well, I know one possible solution." He lifted Sarah a bit off the ground and pulled down her neck guard. His nostrils flared at the sight of her bare skin. His vampire strain controlled blood flow through semihollow fangs, allowing him to give blood or take it. It was common to give blood when seducing or hypnotizing, and the amount given determined the effect. He sank his fangs into her neck, allowing a small dose of his blood to enter her system.

Sarah trembled for a minute, and then went limp.

"It'll take some time, but if it works, she'll be okay," said Blake.

"Your blood can heal?" asked Ada.

"It's a little-known fact, and mainly used as an aphrodisiac, but yes, it can obliterate foreign material, but only in humans."

"Interesting," said Ada.

A burst of gunfire emitted from Ada's assault drone. Two mutants had rushed over and were now twitching on the ground.

"I think that's the last of them," said Zane. "They were sorta weak."

"They were a stalling measure," said Blake. "I also suspect they knew whatever would infect you and the others would have little impact on me."

Everyone's attention turned toward the explosion near the top of the ramp.

"Let's move!" said Blake. He picked up Sarah.

Zane activated his large shield and faced the top ramp doorway. "Go! I'll cover!"

They hustled through the pods and entered other doorway.

Once Zane and the surveillance and assault drones arrived, Blake said, "Ada, seal it up."

Ada headed over to the console and interacted with it.

Zane stood in the doorway with his hellthrower and fired at the Selva Tong coming down the ramp. Although the fire was not accurate at that range, its spread was enough to encompass the entire area at the top of the ramp.

"Closing it now," said Ada.

Zane stopped firing and stepped inside as the doors closed.

"It won't hold them for long," said Ada.

Blake nodded. "That's all right. According to the layout, this hallway has some offices off to the side, and then the elevator area. Ada, send the surveillance drone forward."

Ada complied.

As the drone flew out, Blake studied the 360 view. The offices seemed empty. He drew his head back when the feed disappeared. "What happened?"

"The drone has been disabled," said Ada. "I can't communicate with it."

Blake sighed. "At least we still have the assault one. Zane, take point."

Zane pivoted and, with shield forward, advanced down the hallway.

They paused at each office.

Blake laid Sarah on the ground and took a few steps forward. He raised his hand. "I sense . . . something."

Delkis, with two forearm blades on his formfitting black leatherlike suit, stepped out at the end of the hallway. "You sense me."

Blake drew his blades.

Delkis smiled. "However . . . I think it's time to go." He took off to the right.

Blake burst forward to the end of the hallway.

As the others followed, an explosion blew out from both sides of the hallway, caving in the ceiling. Kal and Ada were blown back while Zane covered Sarah.

As the dust cleared, Blake could see through the small gaps to the other side. A human with an advanced heavy-armor suit dropped from the ceiling, obscuring Blake's view. The human lowered his helmet and peered back through the rubble. It was Daniel, and he wielded a pistol in one hand and a glowing red energy blade in the other.

"That worked well," said Daniel.

"Go! Get Delkis!" said Zane over the group communication channel. "We'll take care of Daniel and catch up."

Blake gritted his teeth. "I can't leave—"

"Go! Trust us!"

Blake narrowed his eyes and exhaled form his nose. "Kick his ass."

"You got it."

//////////

Zane shook his head as he stood up. He pulled Sarah off to the side as Kal and Ada stood next to him. Zane pointed at Daniel. "You're in our way, small man."

"Is that so, *big* man? Don't worry about Blake, since you seem so concerned. He's been . . . cut off," said Daniel.

Zane tried to contact Blake but got static. As Zane pulled out his mace, he shook his head and said, "I'ma beat that ass." He strode forward and swung at Daniel.

Daniel jumped up and landed on Zane's arm.

Zane fell forward.

Daniel leapfrogged over Zane and somersaulted through the air to deliver a kick to Ada's chest, sending her flying back. He took a shot at her, but her kinetic shielding deflected it.

Kal pulled out his dual pistols and opened fire.

Daniel's kinetic shielding lit up, but his blade that poked out of the shielding went flying out of his hand. He laughed as he pointed his pistol at Kal. "Normally . . . that might have killed someone. Unfortunately for you, I'm not just someone." He fired point-blank at Kal.

Kal's kinetic shielding lit up.

Daniel growled as he tossed his pistol down and rushed forward.

Kal took a step back and continued to fire.

Daniel reached Kal and grabbed both of his wrists.

Kal screamed and dropped his pistols.

Daniel seized Kal by the throat and lifted him off the ground. "Such a waste. You could have been . . . serviceable."

Kal hit a button on his belt, causing his shielding to pulse, pushing Daniel back.

"Forget me?" asked Zane, appearing next to Daniel. He swung forward with his mace.

Daniel jumped out of the way and ran around Zane. "Of course not, big guy." With a forceful push, Zane went flying into Ada, who had been approaching. They both tumbled to the ground. Daniel looked around. "Is this all you got?" He walked over and picked up his blade. "Time to end this charade."

Zane had landed with both arms extended to the ground, and Ada under him. He was thankful she was not hurt. Daniel was fast and strong, like Blake. Zane furrowed his eyebrows. Over the group communication channel, he said, "Ada, I'm gonna stand and spin around, then fire my boosters. I'll need a shove once I'm up. You got me?"

"Of course."

"Kal, get his back to us, then jump out of the way when I come flying."

"Got it," said Kal. He picked up his pistols and ran to the obstruction that blocked the hallway. He pointed both pistols at Daniel. "If I'm gonna go, I'm taking you with me."

Daniel sneered as he cracked his neck and charged forward with his blade raised.

Zane pushed off the ground at an angle, making him spin. When he was facing the obstruction, he activated his shield and then his boosters.

Ada jumped and planted her feet. Using both hands, she shoved as hard as she could.

Kal jumped to the side as Daniel drew near.

Daniel paused to laugh. "Sidestepping me? Really? You're—" His eyes widened when Zane's shield hit him. Daniel's kinetic shielding lit up for a moment, then dissipated. As Daniel was forced through the obstruction, parts of him began to tear off. Once through, Daniel fell to the ground, wriggling in pain.

Zane shut off his boosters and pulled out his shotgun. He aimed at Daniel's head. "Charade ended, bitch." He fired point-blank, shredding Daniel's head.

Blackish blood seeped out onto the ground around Daniel.

Kal whooped and shook two fingers at Daniel. "You got stomped!"

Ada pulled out a remote access drone and interacted with it. After a moment, it had connected to one of the consoles in a side office. "We will get as much information as we can until the Selva Tong get to it."

"Good idea," said Zane. He could see why Blake picked Ada. She was logical and efficient.

Ada picked up Sarah. "We should go, Blake may need our help."

"Yeah," said Zane.

"Kal, in my backpack, in the bottom slot, there is a vial. Get some of Daniel's blood," said Ada.

Kal complied and then put the vial back in Ada's backpack.

As they walked forward, the door they had sealed earlier blew open.

Zane pivoted and faced his shield toward the door.

Selva Tong fired as they rushed into the hallway.

"Go!" said Zane as he began to walk backward.

They reached the corner that Blake had turned down and ran along the hallway.

Zane pivoted and held his ground when they reached an elevator lobby with four elevators. He turned his head and saw that two had already gone up, but the third was on their level. The fourth had some red writing on it, but he could not make it out. Looked like Gertus's layout was accurate. "Get to the elevator!"

Kal and Ada, carrying Sarah, hustled in.

"C'mon!" said Kal.

Zane walked backward as a few Selva Tong burst into the lobby.

Kal pulled out his dual pistols and unleashed a volley over Zane's shoulder.

The Selva Tong fell.

Zane reached the elevator and backed in. His shield had adapted to the smaller space, and as the elevator doors closed, his shielding lit up from the gunfire. "What floor?"

"Topside one," said Ada. "Blake wrote it in blood on the other doors."

Zane nodded.

"Damn, that was close," said Kal.

Zane exhaled as he closed his eyes. "Yeah, but we did good."

"Teamwork," said Ada.

Kal slapped Ada's and Zane's arms. "That's what I'm talking about!"

"I hear you, man," said Zane. "Let's go help Blake, but I doubt he'll need it."

Blake rushed down the hallway until he reached the elevator area. He could sense Delkis, but not locate him. Maybe he had escaped. That idea was laid to rest when Blake saw Delkis in one of the elevators with the door open.

"You're a tough one," said Delkis. "However . . . it's time to go. You got further than the others. We're impressed."

Blake noticed that the elevator next to Delkis was on the ground floor, but the other two were topside. He sped toward the elevator. As he neared the one Delkis was in, the doors closed. He pounded the doors. Over the next minute, he watched to see what floor Delkis's elevator stopped at. Over the group communication channel, he listened as Zane talked with Daniel. Blake was confident Zane and the group could handle themselves. After a moment, the communication fritzed, and he could no longer hear them. It could be a result of the fighting, or a dampening shield going active.

Once Delkis's elevator had stopped at the highest floor, Blake rushed over to one of the elevator doors that showed it was topside. He pushed the call button so the others would have one waiting for them. He tried to contact the group, but nothing went through. He pricked his finger and wrote, using his blood, on the next elevator door over for the group to go all the way up top. Satisfied that it was readable, he rushed into the other elevator on the ground floor.

The doors slid shut.

Blake rubbed his wound as he was alone with his thoughts on the elevator. When it hit the top, he would be alone with Delkis, and whatever was waiting. Blake needed to contact Seth and have him get the *Exceltion* over, regardless of the outcome. Seeing Sarah unconscious bothered him. Although he would have preferred to give her his blood in a more intimate setting, it was necessary for the situation. He would deal with the bond formed from that experience at a later time.

Zane was as advertised. Tough, loyal to the team, and a good personality. Ada and Kal had done their parts, and Blake could see the makings of a great team. While they handled Daniel, he would take care of Delkis. It was not the way he had planned it, but he would adapt to the situation.

He pulled out his stun device and flipped it around in his hand. Getting close enough to stun Delkis should be easy, assuming he could catch him. Once stunned, then Blake would use his magnetic wrist constraints to restrain Delkis. All that would be left then was a trip back to Fredoria. He could almost taste the victory of the first successful mission.

The elevator began to slow after a minute.

Blake latched the stun device to the inner part of his gauntlet. He pulled out one of his blades, even though he knew he would not fatally wound Delkis, but Andia never said how much of Delkis needed to come back.

The elevator stopped.

As the doors began to open, Blake activated his camouflage shielding. Peering out, he did not see any sign of activity. He crept out and surveyed the environment. There were no Selva Tong to greet him, just a small area in a building. Judging by the stairway ahead, it seemed he was in a basement. The place looked like it did not have many visitors. The elevator doors blended into the wall, making it difficult to determine whether there were any doors there at all. The one he had called down earlier showed that it had reached its destination.

He lowered his helmet and sniffed the air while he focused on listening. The scent of Delkis led to the stairs, and the faint, irregular heartbeat Blake detected emanated a bit away from the stairs. He opened his forearm screen and sent a signal to the *Exceltion*. At least Seth would know where to go. Blake took off toward the stairs. Once he reached the top of the stairs, he realized the building he was in was abandoned.

"Blake Brown," said Delkis, standing in the a flat, open, circular area ringed by garbage and debris.

Blake narrowed his eyes as he crept toward the space.

"No need to camouflage with me. We can see you."

Blake turned off his camouflage shielding. "And I can see you."

Delkis put his hands behind his back as he paced. "Your friends are going to learn a harsh lesson. You don't have to. Surrender yourself to me, and come quietly."

"I don't think so," said Blake.

"Worth a shot," said Delkis with a grin. He tilted his head. "How tough are you?" He removed his forearm blades.

"Tough enough," said Blake, tossing his blades off to the side.

"And honorable, an admirable trait," said Delkis. He raised a weapon and fired.

Blake dodged out of the way. Based on the fizzing sounds of the shots as they made contact with the wall behind him, he realized they were stun rounds. He lurched forward and grabbed the weapon from Delkis's hand. With a toss, the weapon went flying off into the garbage pile.

Delkis punched Blake in the chest, sending him sliding back.

Blake came to a stop and then took a moment to catch his breath. That hit would have shattered a normal human's chest. He stood back up.

"Quite resilient. You're just what we need."

Blake clenched his jaw and charged forward. In an exchange of hits with Delkis that resembled a stop-motion animation sequence, Blake was able to distract Delkis enough to knock him to the ground.

Delkis spin kicked his legs in the air and used the momentum to pull himself upright.

Blake's eyes narrowed as he reengaged Delkis.

Delkis sidestepped Blake's strikes and grabbed him by the neck.

Blake struggled as he grabbed Delkis's wrists. With a downward push, he broke free from Delkis's grip and then kicked him in the groin. With an uppercut, he sent Delkis flying into the air. Before Delkis could land, Blake burst under Delkis and punched up into both of Delkis's upper legs.

Snap!

Delkis cried out in pain as he landed and tried to move.

"It hurts if you try to move," said Blake as he pulled out his stun device.

Delkis began to laugh. "We're impressed. You win." He coughed up some blood. "This body is no match for yours, as we suspected. It's yours. Take it to Andia. A gift."

Blake paused as he tilted his head. "I intend to . . ."

"Good. We underestimated you, but wanted to see for ourselves. You . . . are what we need."

"Who's this *we* you keep talking about?"

Delkis began to breathe harder. "Do your stun thing and restrain us."

"I said . . . who's this we?"

"Wouldn't you like to know. Sorry. You're powerful, perhaps more powerful than even we could know. We realize that's due to your Daedrould energy, and in particular, your strain. You're unique out here. You have put on quite the demonstration but . . . we'll meet again."

Blake drew his head back a bit as he approached Delkis. His eyes widened when he saw a black fluid flow out of Delkis's mouth and then slither away into the garbage. Blake used his senses to try to locate whatever it was that had crawled out, but with the powerful odor of the garbage and the heat it generated obscuring everything, it was impossible. He pulled out his striker and fired into the garbage piles. After a few rounds, he paused to see if he could detect anything. He could sense the faint presence of an Outsider, but it was scattered and the garbage was affecting it.

Delkis groaned.

Blake walked over to Delkis, who was struggling to breathe.

Zane and the others had reached the top and entered the room.

"You got him," said Zane with a big smile and open helmet.

"No . . . I don't think I did."

"Say what?" asked Kal, lowering his helmet. "He's right there."

Delkis began to whimper.

"Something . . . drained or . . . crawled . . . out of his head and went into the garbage piles. It looked like . . . oil," said Blake. He kicked Delkis in the back. "I suspect this is the real Delkis."

Delkis cried out in pain as he turned over onto his back. "Please . . . don't kill me."

"Yeah . . . that's the Delkis I've read about."

"Where . . . where am I? Who are you people?"

Blake sighed. "Apparently, whatever that thing was in Delkis didn't allow any memories to be retained. Interesting."

"What are you talking about?" asked Delkis, wincing. "I can't move!"

Blake shook his head as he approached Delkis with the stun device out. "Fortunately for you, you'll be knocked out for the rest of the trip." He applied the stun device.

Delkis stopped moving.

Blake applied the wrist constraints. "He might have a broken leg or two. Ada, he'll need something to stabilize him. After that, Zane, you can carry him."

Ada knelt next to Delkis and scanned him. She set her backpack down and rummaged through it. After a moment, she injected microbots into Delkis and then pulled out a roller-like device. With the press on one of the ends, the roller extended into a thin, solid slab. Zane and Kal helped load Delkis onto it and then Zane lifted the slab.

"What happened with Daniel?" asked Blake.

"Teamwork," said Zane, glancing at Kal and Ada. He beamed a big smile. "He just . . . couldn't keep himself together."

Kal laughed as Ada tilted her head.

"I look forward to seeing the video feeds," said Blake.

Ada raised a finger. "I took a sample of Daniel's blood for further analysis."

"Excellent," said Blake. He accessed his forearm screen. "Seth? You reading me?"

"Yep, loud and clear. I got your signal earlier," said Seth over the group communication channel.

"We're ready for pick up."

"All right," said Seth. "Whatever you did has riled up the Selva Tong. They're on high alert, but I can swing past them. Just be ready to board when I get near."

"Will do," said Blake.

Ada, with Sarah in her arms, tilted her head. "So Delkis was being controlled? Like Daniel?"

"Apparently. Whatever that thing was, it had the ability to alter the body. Even though it's left Delkis, I can sense that Delkis has been changed somewhat."

Kal tossed a hand out. "We didn't see anything come out of Daniel."

"Probably because he got a shotgun to the face," said Zane with a grin.

Kal shrugged.

Ada nodded. "While we were headed to the elevator, I used one of the drones to download some information from the offices. I got as much as I could before the Selva Tong got to the drone."

"What did you find?"

"Delkis was trying to meet with powerful people on Zakara Prime. Judging by Daniel Greer, I place a high probability that Delkis wanted to get them under his control."

"It would seem that way," said Blake. "Something bigger is going on. Delkis was just one cog. Anyways, how's Sarah doing?"

"She is stable. Your blood is quite powerful and . . . interesting."

Blake grinned, baring his fangs. "Let's get back to Fredoria. I'm sure Andia and Rakar will want to know *all* about this."

TWENTY-TWO

B lake inhaled the smell of the hangar that the *Exceltion* had initially been launched from. The trip to Fredoria had taken one day, and it was around 10:00 a.m. Earth time. While everyone had rested up on the return trip, he had spoken with Gertus and informed him of the Selva Tong situation. Blake was not sure what Gertus would do, but he understood that by informing Gertus, he was trading a favor that could be used later, maybe for information without requiring a prison breakout.

Delkis moaned as he struggled, strapped-down in the chair Blake was pushing.

To Blake's right were Luke, Kane, and Seth, and to his left were Zane, Kal, and Ada. Sarah was still on the ship in the medical bay.

"What . . . what's going on?" asked Delkis.

"You were stunned and then sedated. The stimulant is waking you up," said Blake.

Delkis swung his head around. "You didn't answer my questions last time. Who are you people? Where am I?"

Blake sighed as he glanced at the others. "All your questions will be answered soon." He focused on the group approaching them. Andia and Rakar led a team of presidential guards.

When the two groups converged, Andia scrutinized Delkis. "That's him."

"Andia Kiggs," said Delkis. "Why am I not surprised you're involved in . . . *whatever* this is?"

Andia wrinkled her eyebrows.

Blake raised a finger. "I can clear some of that up. Delkis doesn't seem to remember how he got to Zakara Prime."

"Zakara Prime?" asked Delkis with wide eyes. "I was sleeping in my cell and woke up with two broken legs and all you crazies around me."

Andia looked at Blake. "No memory from that long ago?"

Blake shrugged.

Andia focused on Delkis. "We have a lot to talk about."

Delkis spit on the ground. "I don't know what's going on here, but if you're involved, it's not good."

Andia raised her hand. "Take him to a holding cell."

Blake stepped to the side as one of the presidential guards took over his spot. The guards headed off.

Rakar stepped forward and clasped forearms with Blake. "I knew you would do it."

Blake swung his arm in an arc at the others around him. "It was truly a team effort. There were some injuries, but we made it through, and there's a lot to discuss."

"You have video feeds?" asked Rakar.

Blake nodded.

Rakar walked up to Kal. "Kal Modan, the Trickster. It's an honor."

Kal slapped his hand to his chest at a forty-five degree angle. "The honor's mine. You're legendary as a ranger."

"I may be passed by this guy one day," said Rakar, pointing at Blake.

Rakar and Kal nodded at each other.

"Where's Sarah?" asked Andia.

"She was infected by some type of mutant when we fought Daniel and Delkis," said Blake. "Whatever was in her system was messing her up. She's recovering now."

Andia's eyes narrowed. "How did you counter it?"

Blake licked his fangs. "I may have given her some of my blood."

"I thought that was for . . . pleasure."

"It can heal as well, but only humans."

"I see."

Blake cleared his throat. "What's our next step?"

Andia raised a finger. "For you and your crew, take some time off before your next mission. We can debrief tomorrow. Rakar will schedule it and contact you on time and location. Please give Rakar all data and evidence you collected before you go, though."

Rakar shook a finger at Blake. "Oh . . . and we have a small compound for your team to stay in. It has all the amenities usually afforded to ambassadors."

"An ambassadorial compound?" asked Zane with wide eyes. "Hell yeah."

Andia eyed Zane. "Please don't destroy it. You also have private transport as needed. Nonetheless, I'm *anxious* to hear what you have to say at the debriefing tomorrow."

"We'll be there," said Blake. He watched as everyone dispersed. Andia and her guard headed back the way they had come, while everyone else headed to the ship to get their things for an extended stay. Blake noticed Rakar stayed behind until it was just the two of them.

Once the area was clear, Rakar said, "You seemed disturbed."

"Well . . . it's not every day you see something able to control another person without some interaction. I read reports about someone on Earth that could do it, but I've never seen it out here. It's extremely rare. Daniel Greer and Delkis had . . . something in them that controlled them, something . . . from elsewhere."

Rakar narrowed his eyes. "I think this will be a *very* interesting debriefing. How did you capture Delkis then?"

"Fought him one-on-one and broke his legs."

A grin formed on Rakar's face. "You're tougher than you look. Reminds me of an old friend."

Blake furrowed his eyebrows. "Well . . . there's something odd about all of this. I hope you have some insight."

Rakar looked around for a moment. "I think I do. We've seen an unusual pattern developing across Fredorian territory. We can't pin anything down, but your data will be the first concrete evidence we have. Putting everything together will take time, and your missions will be related to getting the next steps as we progress."

"Damn. Did you know it was possession?"

Rakar shook his head. "We suspected something like that, maybe brainwashing or a neural implant. Nothing suggested possession by a creature, but it does raise some questions."

"Yeah, no kidding."

"You had a great first mission."

Blake sighed. "Some bumps along the way. I suspect the Selva Tong are about to have a power struggle. We may see Gertus, leader of the Kahan, step up to the plate."

"It's possible. Care to get something to eat?"

"Maybe later. I need to attend to Sarah."

Rakar grinned. "I bet you do."

"I'm just protecting her, among other things."

They shared a laugh before going their separate ways.

////////

Sarah winced as she stared at the ceiling. She was not sure what happened after she got infected, but this was not the lower levels of Delkis's compound. Looking around, she could see that she was in a luxurious room, with replicator consoles in the walls, a comfy bed, and several chairs around a couch. A bathroom sat off in the distance, as well as some other doorways. A digital clock on the wall displayed various times, one of them 11:30 a.m. She jumped a bit when she saw Blake approaching her from the side.

"You're looking rested."

Sarah tried to smile, but the pain prevented the smile she wanted. "I'm doing okay . . . I think. What happened after I passed out?"

Blake sat in a chair next to her bed. "I gave you some of my blood to counter the effects of the toxin."

"Oh . . . I hope I didn't embarrass myself."

"You were passed out. We took care of Delkis and Daniel, and now we're in an ambassadorial compound that will serve as our living arrangements while on Fredoria."

"Wow," said Sarah. "It sounds like we had a successful first mission."

"Yep, and tomorrow, I have to debrief Andia and Rakar. I'll make a copy of it so you can watch it at your leisure."

"I should be there."

Blake lightly tapped her shoulder. "Not in your state. You need to rest."

She furrowed her eyebrows. "You seem to be . . . glowing or something."

"We have a blood bond now, at least for a few days. I may seem more charming to you during that time."

She chortled, and then winced. When Blake had touched her shoulder, it was like a lightning bolt had shot through her body. "Yeah . . . just your light tap is like touching an electrical outlet."

Blake grinned. "That's the general feeling."

"Where are the others?"

"Zane, Kal, and Kane went out to get lunch. Luke said he had some personal business to attend to. As for Seth and Ada, I'm not sure what they're doing. I brought you here after we landed and have been here since."

"Ahh. Well, not much for me to do here except rest, I guess. If you have the video feeds from after I passed out, I'd like to see them."

Blake tapped her hand. "We'll watch it together."

She enjoyed being around Blake, and it dawned on her that he had given up celebrating with the guys to attend to her. Watching him configuring the screen on the wall and then getting her something to drink and eat, she noticed a softer side of him that she was sure most did not see. Although he could be kind, she knew he could also be ruthless. Her heartbeat ramped up as Blake sat next to her.

The screen began to play the video feed from Blake's chest. He sat back down and described what was on the screen.

She could get used to this.

Blake observed the briefing room as everyone began to filter in. He had spent the previous day with Sarah, and although she was still somewhat groggy and tired, she seemed enthused to have company. She was not at the debriefing today, but he promised her that he would record it and show it to her later. Zane, Kal, and Kane looked like they had hangovers, judging by the way they trudged in.

Luke and Seth looked well rested and had taken their seats. Ada, Andia, and Rakar were prompt and arrived just a bit before 1:00 p.m. The debriefing was held in the afternoon to give everyone time to get up and handle any morning issues.

As everyone got situated, he fidgeted with his forearm device, making sure it could connect to the large screen in the room. The room was large and consisted of a half-arced table that spanned the room on one side and a screen that covered the wall opposite. Several workstations sat on the side, allowing for interaction with the screen. He found it easier to connect using his forearm device.

Once everyone was seated, he strode to the center of the room and cleared this throat.

The room went silent.

"Our first debriefing, hopefully one of many," said Blake with a smile. He tapped at his forearm device. The large screen behind him showed Holryn. "Let's start from the beginning, or do you want me to start someplace else," he said, gesturing at Andia and Rakar.

"Holryn is fine," said Rakar.

"All right. We went to Holryn and met with Xenizate Cronis. He told us that Delkis was on Zakara Prime and showed us this video."

The large screen played the video of Delkis killing the Covendrin mercs.

Rakar sat forward in his seat with a hand on his chin. When the video stopped, he said, "How did they get that feed?"

"Cronis said that they have contacts everywhere. It would definitely answer some questions I had."

Rakar eased back into his seat and nodded. "Continue."

"Cronis mentioned that there was something odd about Delkis, and from the video, that was clear. Zakara Prime was where Delkis was, so we headed there," said Blake. He changed the screen to show Zakara Prime. A green outline surrounded a surface area. "That's Selva Tong territory, where Cronis said Delkis had been sighted. On level sixteen was the Kahan, led by Gertus, and the point of contact that Cronis told us to check out, so we did."

Andia narrowed her eyes. "I'm not familiar with the Kahan."

"They're a race known as the Gulltissarians, and they have an agreement with the Selva Tong. We met with Gertus, and he said he would tell us where Delkis was in exchange for freeing his prisoners form a Selva Tong prison, which we did. Seth stayed behind as insurance."

"You raided a Selva Tong prison?" asked Rakar.

"Yep. We released the prisoners, and that's also where we met Kal."

"I'm damn glad you swung by," said Kal with a big grin.

Blake nodded. "We're glad to have you." He pointed at the screen, which had changed to show an overhead view of level sixteen. "Gertus was true to his word, and he gave us Delkis's location. It was a compound in Selva Tong turf. We decided to pick up Seth and head back to the *Exceltion* and rest up, and then we would hit it. When we went back to see Gertus, Seth was gone, captured by Alcarez."

"Name sounds familiar," said Rakar.

"Seth shot him with a ship weapon on our first freelancing contract. Apparently . . . Alcarez didn't die. He issued a bounty, picked up Seth from the prison, and put him in an abandoned shack on the edge of Kahan turf. Alcarez wasn't there when we found Seth, so I sent Zane and Kal back to the *Exceltion*. I had Ada wait outside, and I stayed inside.

When Alcarez returned . . ." Blake showed the video of him slicing up Alcarez.

"Holy shit," said Kane.

Andia looked away and put a hand out. "We get the idea."

Blake grinned as he changed the screen to show the overhead view of Selva Tong territory on the topside. "Zane and Kal ran into Emrakus, a bounty hunter."

The screen changed to show the video from Zane's chest view.

Andia drew her head back a bit when it showed Emrakus talking after most of his body was gone. "That's . . . a little creepy."

"Yeah," said Blake. The screen changed to show Gobe Rallz. "Ada, Seth, and I ran into this bounty hunter. He let us know that Daniel Greer might have been compromised by Delkis. Nonetheless, we regrouped on the *Exceltion*, which had to flee to Mularin turf, a neighboring territory. Once we were rested, Zane, Ada, Sarah, Kal, and I headed out to Delkis's compound. The details of how we secured it are available to you. I'll skip to the warehouse under the compound where we grouped up after clearing everything on the above floors."

The screen showed the white pods and mutants coming out of them.

Andia scooted to the edge of her seat. "What are those?"

"Some type of mutated humans," said Blake. "We took care of them and entered another part of the facility. I got separated from the group and went after Delkis. This is what happened to Daniel." He changed the screen to show Kal's video feed.

Rakar grinned at Zane, Kal, and Ada. "You make a good team."

"Damn right," said Zane.

"Ada got some of Daniel's blood as well as information from the Selva Tong network, which you have now," said Blake. He sighed. "I sensed . . . a presence in both Daniel and Delkis, as well as the mutants, one I associate with Outsiders."

"A dimensional presence . . . ," said Rakar.

Blake nodded. He gestured at Ada. "She discovered that Delkis was planning to do what he did to Daniel Greer to all the leaders of the various criminal organizations on Zakara Prime."

Andia swallowed hard. "All of Zakara Prime, united under one influence. That would be very dangerous for Fredoria . . . and maybe even the Kreagan Star Empire."

Blake nodded. "Delkis also referred to himself as 'we,' and not 'I.' It was a little odd." He changed the screen to show the encounter with Delkis.

"Damn, man," said Kane. "You're fast as hell."

"And strong too," said Seth.

Blake tossed his hands out to the side. "Of course, I'm Blake Brown."

Seth shook his head as everyone chuckled.

Blake paused on the moment when the black fluid exited Delkis's head.

"That is . . . utterly disgusting," said Luke, rubbing his chin.

"I agree," said Blake. "Whatever that thing is, apparently it can enter and exit via the mouth, or I would assume any opening. The host has no recollection, at least based on Delkis." He nodded at Andia. "I know you have a . . . special box . . . that can detect exotic energies like this. I would suggest you use it."

"We plan to," said Andia.

Blake nodded. "What's our next step?"

Andia put her fingers together in front of her, touching at the fingertips. "This has been a . . . disturbing development. There's been some unusual activity, and now this is the leading possibility as to why. What the ultimate purpose is, we don't know, but we *will* find out. We'll need some time to go through everything, and then we'll select the next mission based on priority. Until then, just hang out, and I wanted to say to everyone . . . excellent work and congratulations. You've proven a lot of doubters wrong, and I've enjoyed showing them my faith in an Earthborn unit wasn't misplaced."

"Hell yeah," said Zane.

Blake looked around the group. "The Earthborn Unit. Just the way I like it. Here's to hoping for another successful mission."

Everyone clapped and cheered.

THE END

NOTE FROM
THE AUTHOR

I hope you enjoyed the first book of the Earthborn! This book introduces the crew that will be present throughout the series and also the growing threat that is discovered. Each installment in this six-book series is a self-contained mission but also continues the main arc of the series. The setting is the same one from the Evaran Chronicles, my other series, and takes place twenty years after The Fredorian Destiny, book 2 of the Evaran Chronicles. The Earthborn series is standalone, and reading the Evaran Chronicles is not required, although if you like this book, you might like the other!

If you enjoyed the book, and have the time and inclination, a review would go a long way in helping out this indie author. If you do submit a review, I'll put in a word to Blake and crew should you find yourself being harassed by galactic thugs! Want to be notified about new book releases? If so, you can sign up below.

WWW.ADAIRHART.COM/MAILINGLIST.ASPX

I will only send you email about new book releases, major updates, and the occasional newsletter, usually once a month. I dislike getting spammed too, so I will use this sparingly to keep you in the loop.

ABOUT THE AUTHOR

I have been dreaming about fictional worlds since I was a kid. I devoured anything related to fantasy and science fiction. I developed a setting over the last twenty years and struggled to find a medium I could express it in. Several years ago I discovered I enjoyed writing. It is a passion of mine now, and exploring my setting with it has been an awesome journey.

I work in the information technology field and have my bachelor's and master's degrees in it. It has helped me to shape some of the concepts I write about. I also enjoy keeping up on futurology and science in general.

I live in central Ohio and enjoy walking, reading, gaming, learning, listening to music, and trying to keep up on my never-ending list of TV shows and movies to watch. If you want to contact me, you can do so on my website at

WWW.ADAIRHART.COM

YOU CAN ALSO REACH ME ON

Facebook.............................fb.com/AdairHart
Goodreads.....www.goodreads.com/AdairHart
Email..............Adair.Hart.Author@gmail.com

ACKNOWLEDGMENTS

This was a great journey for me, but I wouldn't be here without the help of others. I would like to thank, in no particular order,

My amazing editor, Laura Petrella. I thoroughly enjoy working with her and am overjoyed to have her on this series! As always, she helps me to refine and polish the story so it is the best it can be. I am a better writer for having worked with her!

My cover artist, Tom Edwards (tomedwardsconcepts@gmail.com), for another fantastic cover. This is his second character-focused one for me, and I'm always blown away by his artwork.

My family and friends who helped encourage me along the way.

My proofreader, Alexa, for being responsive and professional.

My formatter and interior designer, Colleen Sheehan (www.wdrbookdesign.com/), for continuing with me into a new series and making my book interiors pop.

B O O K S

You can see all books in the Earthborn
and the Evaran Chronicles at

WWW.ADAIRHART.COM/SERIES/ALLBOOKS.ASPX